OMITTED PIECES

TRANSFORMED NEXUS #2

STEPHANIE HANSEN

OMITTED PIECES

Copyright © 2022 by Stephanie Hansen

ISBN: 978-1-955784-21-4

Fire & Ice Young Adult Books
An Imprint of Melange Books, LLC
White Bear Lake, MN 55110
www.fireandiceya.com

Published in the United States of America.

Cover Design by Caroline Andrus

For my mother, father, and siblings
You have always believed in me even when I have given you every
reason to not.

ACKNOWLEDGMENTS

The transformation this novel has been through would not have been possible without many people. There's no way I can name them all but I'd like to give it a try. They know how hard I've worked and how many years I've dedicated to books. First, I would like to thank the readers. You breathe life into books and for that I will be ever thankful.

Next, I would like to thank the professionals that helped me trudge through this thing called publishing: everyone at Fire and Ice YA, Tantor Audio, Mekisha Telfer, Nancy Schumacher, Caroline Andrus, Kim Budnick, Kelsey Skea, Jennifer Newens, Reka Simonsen, Amy Brewer, Erica Christensen, and Karen Lynch.

I would also like to thank my friends who saw me through dark times and helped me celebrate the good times too: Shana Bartlett, James Young, Miranda Nichols, Jeff Sifrit, Stacked Book Club, Sarah Smith, and Cathy Wissing.

Finally, I would like to thank my family for putting up with me: Nate, our kids, Vic Hurlbert, Debra Scarborough, Cassandra Hurlbert, Victor Hurlbert, Vondell Neill, and Peggy

Hurlbert. If I inadvertently left someone off the list, please let me know so I can add them to the next book.

1

PLANET SCEPTER

Sierra the CLONE

I AWAKE HUNGRY AND THIRSTY. IS THIS WHAT THE afterlife is like? I never expected Dr. Cromwell to follow through on his promise to put my conscience and memory in a qualified body. Hunger pains me again and I rise to find myself in a tropical forest. I'm surrounded by lush green, but the color is unlike any I've seen before. It's as if the leaves are neon shining off of their surroundings. My body knows what to look for, even though I don't. Where am I? What planet have I been transported to? Where's Mom? I look down at it, this hourglass figure. I'd never been blessed with such curves in my sixteen-year-old body. I wonder if my dad will recognize me in this new one. I wonder if Al will still love me after everything? I also try to map out how to get home, but it's all too much for this newfound body and I quickly find myself napping under a sea of green.

I'm roused by a series of clicks and identify the circular metal in front of me immediately out of place as it may be.

"Vex, how'd you get here?"

"I told 'past' you your mission was full of danger, Sierra."

"How long has it been since I lost consciousness?"

"I calculate two weeks and five days since the 'new' you left Planet Vortex."

"What? How have I been out for that long? Where's Al? Did the shuttle make it to Earth?"

There's a stream of beeps. "My universe data scan shows that the Al you're asking about still has a pulse. It's the Al 'old' you met on Planet Vortex, right?"

My heart warms, it beams. "Yes. Wait, your universe data scan, what's that?"

"The World Government equipped all clopils with new scanners and applied all Counter Friction strings when the Planet Vortex revolution hit the news. The scan also shows that everyone who had been on your scheduled shuttle made it to Earth. The processes at the medical facility ended, too, but more on that later. We need to get to your mother."

Mom, are you okay? I try to reach her telepathically, the way I had back on Vortex.

I'm fine. Just need to figure out where I am exactly.

"Sierra, there's much at stake. We must embark on our journey at once," Vex says.

Sunrays stream through openings in the canopy of leaves above us as we hike. I keep having to reassure myself it's me when I look down and see someone else's smaller feet. At least Cromwell dressed this body in proper attire. I don't know what I'd do without these boots. Vex, on the other hand, is not well equipped for this terrain at all. He was made for modern city living. He's used some of the tools he brought to lengthen his arms in order to help, but I keep assisting him, wishing he'd move faster. I think being locked up in the Vortex facility for so long gave me a sort of cabin fever. Now, being out in the open, I want to stretch my (these, no my, oh whatever) legs and cover the ground between us and Mom as quickly as possible.

Also, the weight's gone. My legs had felt like they were filled with lead because of the guilt. But now, now that Viscerous and Albina are alive and safe on Earth; now that Pixie's where no more harm can be done (well, no more harm than a painful exam in the graduate mathematics program at Stanford); now that Dad is free and no longer having to save Cromwell's subjects, my legs feel light as air.

Mom, we're headed to you. How are you doing?

I wait for what seems like an eternity, but she doesn't respond.

"Vex, are you sure this is the way to Mom?"

"Yes. While she appears to be moving constantly, she has continually returned to the location toward which we're headed."

"Why? What's there?"

"I'm not 100% sure. A new blocker is interfering with my scanner, causing inaccurate readings. I'm running diagnostics to prescribe next steps."

"That's weird. Isn't it weird?"

"There's a 3.34% possibility of it occurring. But it is 'weird,' as you say, that it's occurring now not only where your mom is but also on Earth."

"What? Where on Earth?"

"My coordinates match home base, Sierra."

No, no, no, it's as if the wind has been knocked out of me. Not again. Not them both! They need to be together so we can get my brother back. Then, I'll finally meet him.

"Your heart rate has increased. A health scan would be beneficial."

"I just need a small rest, Vex."

I sit on a log and Vex stays near me. I try to let the breeze flowing through the leaves soothe me. It's not like this means something's wrong. All it means is that I can't communicate with them. I take a deep breath in and a deep breath out while envisioning meditation circles.

That's when the idea surfaces. I begin gathering a plant that appears to be similar to tropical milkweed. Once I have a decent supply, I sit back down in order to break out the core fibers using a rock I found.

"It appears you are making something. Can I be of assistance?"

"Actually, this is to assist you."

I tenderize the core fibers and braid the best I can.

"You are taking the steps to build rope. How will that be used to assist?"

"I'm going to carry you so we can get to Mom faster. I need to confirm that at least one of my parents is okay."

"I see. I'm not 100% sure that follows all clopil safety procedures."

As soon as the rope's assembled, I tie it around Vex so that I'm able to carry him on my back. The sound of the rapids in the jungle river nearby becomes monotonous during our trek. I want to stop and rest, but we must keep going. I engage Vex in conversation to pass the time.

"You never answered, Vex. How did you get here?"

"Why, I was on the shuttle that brought your mom to Vortex and I traveled here with you both."

"But how? I don't remember seeing you at the facility. I doubt Cromwell would have allowed that."

"Quite simple. I snuck into the cargo hatch. My engineering allows me to escape many things like being seen."

4

"Bloody hell, the cargo hatch. Of course, you could avoid leaving anything behind for the particle scan, you little gomer."

Suddenly there's a stream of clicks. What's Vex up to? Then, I hear a new sound.

"Who goes there?"

The voice isn't quite human, but definitely not a robot. It feels like forever since I spoke to anyone but Vex. Dr. Cromwell's who I spoke to before that. Even Mom and I have only conversed telepathically recently. I didn't realize how much I was craving the sound of another living, intelligent being.

"Unknown, Sierra, this one isn't registered in my database," Vex says.

"Not another step. Who goes there?" the voice asks again.

I freeze. The voice is low.

"I'm Sierra. I was actually brought here against my will. I…it's a long story."

"Are you unarmed?"

"Yes. I only have my clopil and the clothes on my back here with me."

"Hi, I'm Vex. You should be the one identifying yourself."

An auburn-haired and slender female with lustrous olive skin steps out from behind the greenery. Her gold-flecked, hazel eyes stare at me, full of questions.

"I'm Marrit." She reaches out her arm while cupping her hand sideways. I'm unsure what kind of handshake greeting she's offering, and I don't know her well enough to warrant any kind of trust, but something pulls me forward.

Vex begins a string of noises, "Beep, beep, Hmm." I'm not sure what Vex is doing.

"Where are we?" I ask while reaching for her hand, but she slips her hand through mine and grabs my forearm, then brings me in for a bearhug. Perhaps she too craves the touch of another. A breath of air moves my hair as she exhales, as if holding in some great burden.

"You're on Planet Scepter. Where are you from?"

"This is one of the newest additions to counter string mapping," Vex interjects. "Ah, yes, the coordinates line up."

"I'm from Earth but I came here from Vortex."

"You didn't come alone. Nice 'friends' you have. I wish they would have stayed where you came from." The look of acceptance that had briefly crossed her face is gone.

"She must be talking about the fuzzy area on this planet's coordinates, Sierra."

"You've seen the others? Where are they? Did you see a woman with rich, brunette hair, on the short side, and in her forties?"

"Um, yeah. Your friends are, like, taking over."

"My lie detector shows she's telling the truth." Vex has lost all concept of being subtle. "Oh, and the features such as brunette hair have changed now, remember."

"What do you mean 'taking over'?"

"Like setting up shop. All these people in lab coats hired local contractors to build this...I don't know what to call it... large facility."

"Oh, no."

"That's what I thought."

"Can you show me where?"

"I'm able to show you," Vex says. "I think I register the location." We ignore him.

"Why, so you can join them in taking over Planet Scepter? Forget it. I thought you were brought here against your will. Why would you want to go there?"

Marrit storms away. Her hair moves in the breeze. She sets her shoulders back and increases her pace when I follow her. Her hips move eloquently from side to side despite her serious manner.

"Wait. Please wait. I'm sorry. Let me explain."

She turns around with a minty huff.

"I want to stop the people building, but I think they took my mom."

"You know how to stop them?" Marrit asks me.

"Well, I helped to stop the last facility."

"I'm able to confirm that what she says is true," Vex says. "Actually, I have documented video proof."

I'm afraid of how much Vex might have filmed. "Not now, Vex."

"You mean you have intel of the bastards right here?"

"Technically, they're not bastards," Vex interjects.

"And, technically, they're not all evil. My mom's there, you know. I need to save her."

"Then you will help me."

"I don't know," I say while blocking her path to Vex. "Will you help me?"

"Your mom was really taken there against her will?"

"Yeah." I sniff despite my intense desire not to and turn my head away from Marrit so she doesn't see the tears I'm holding back. I don't know where they came from.

I feel her hand on my shoulder.

"I'll help you."

My breath catches and I want to turn to her. I want another hug. I want to be back on Earth in my own gosh darn body, with both my parents alive, together, and with my brother. I want things to be the way they should be.

"Sierra, your heart rate has increased again. Do you need a full vitals scan?"

"Leave me alone, Vex." My face warms when I look away from him and see a smirk on Marrit's face. She play-punches me in the arm.

"Come on. Let's go get your mom and take those bastards down."

7

"Technically, they're not bastards."

"Yes, they are, Vex," we both say simultaneously. Then I'm smirking at her.

The journey's much better with Marrit taking turns carrying Vex.

Vines in this jungle spin and melt as if forming a stunning net, like the framing of a red velvet crown. And this is just the first thing that gives me an indication of how vastly different this planet is. Leaves curl and uncurl like ribbon pulled with scissors. It has an amazing effect that's whimsical, bringing a soothing peace over me until I remember what we're headed toward. Another facility! Another one that's imprisoned one of my parents. Another one of Crowell's mischievously evil plans.

Then there's a stream of clicks and beeps from Vex like I've never heard before. "Sierra, we're approaching our destination."

"Can you please silence your clopil?" Marrit asks.

We approach a wall of green. Marrit crouches and silently moves closer to the wall. She turns back and places her index finger to her full lips.

Once we've complied, she moves a handful of leaves to the side. I peek through and see the same chain-link and cement fences. There are also the same guard posts. It looks just as much like a prison as the last facility. The cabin fever returns, freezing me into place. My legs feel heavy as lead. It's back.

"Vex, now that you have the UDS, can you get communication out universe-wide?" I ask in a whisper.

"Why yes, Sierra. I'm capable of reaching many places." He matches my volume to the best of his ability.

"Can you reach Earth? Is just home base unreachable?" Then another thought dawns. "Wait, what about Vortex instead?"

"I'm definitely capable of reaching Vortex."

"Please call Yesha."

Da, da, bring. Vex uses a relic phone ring to connect.

"Hello?" Yesha answers.

"Yesha, it's me," I whisper.

"Sierra, is that really you? You look…different…I'm used to the tall, dorky you, but this…"

"Yesha!" I whisper. "Please be quiet. It's important."

"Who's that?"

"Hi, I'm Marrit."

"Yesha, I need your help." I turn Vex in the direction of the facility so Yesha can see.

"No! Cromwell? Where are you?"

Before I can answer I feel an eerie, creepiness. It crawls over my hand. I look down. It's a petri-dish-sized spider… on…ME! It's large enough that the hairs on its legs rub against my skin like it's laying spider eggs in my cells.

"AH!" I scream at the top of my lungs louder and louder until the volume matches my terror.

Alarms ring and laser dots head our direction. Every visible guard turns our way.

2
PLANET VORTEX

Al

I swear, if the food in the cafeteria was nasty before, it has progressively become more disgusting over the past couple of weeks. It doesn't help that I've been on edge trying to figure out how to save both Vienna's mom and Vienna's clone, Sierra.

"When are the World Government officials going to arrive again?" I ask Colsam, yelling over the noise. Now that the guards don't have to serve Cromwell, there's a constant poker game going on during meals, which seems to get longer every day. Even the scientists have joined in. It's been pretty incredible to see the relationship between the guards and scientists heal. Well, for the most part, they've healed. There are still a few scientists unable to forgive.

"Theopat said they'll arrive tomorrow. Take a chill pill, Al," he responds while calling a bet.

The guard across from him lays down a freaking royal flush

and Colsam throws his cards on the table, curses, and then rises to walk with me.

"Everyone's getting stir-crazy waiting," I tell him.

"They're fine," he says and then pats me on the shoulder as we approach another table.

"Read 'em and weep, boys. Read 'em and weep," Yesha calls out. She shows her full house, gathers her winnings, and joins us.

"Al's complaining that everyone's getting stir-crazy even though it's only going to be a couple more days until the officials are here," Colsam rats me out.

"Which one is it? Tomorrow or in a couple of days? If you're going to lie to me, at least keep the story straight," I counter. "We still have no clue where Cromwell went, only that he's set up another facility. I haven't been able to get through to Vienna recently but I don't want to tell her about the new facility. It will only worry her more."

"You're right, Colsam. He needs a chill pill," Yesha says.

I step toward her in mock attack, and she rolls her eyes at me.

"It would be nice for the officials to finally show up with the pardon documents. Everyone here is ready to move on with their lives," Colsam agrees...finally. "The scientists will be thrilled to receive renewed passes so they can return to their homes clear of all charges too."

"You haven't been able to reach Theopat today either?" Yesha asks.

"No, I'm afraid we're going to be forced to initiate alternate measures if it takes more than a few days," I respond.

I have to find out where Cromwell took Vienna's mom if I ever expect her forgiveness. The pain she suffered from losing her dad was now replaced. All these missing pieces are nothing but aggravating.

"Hey, we'll get it figured out." Yesha nudges me with her elbow.

"Yeah, there's still one more set of data we need to explore," Colsam says.

That reminds me of Cromwell's desk and how I found his plans for Vienna. Maybe he had the plans for what he was going to do afterward, hidden somewhere in his journal as well.

"Where would Cromwell take his family to be safe?" I ask.

"Well, Al, he's running from the law now too," Colsam says.

"That's it!" Yesha says.

Colsam and Yesha nod their heads at each other.

"What's it?" I ask.

"He's gone off grid," Colsam says. "Even though they've been able to apply the Counter Friction strings to all planets, it's too much for them to govern. It will take decades to regulate them all. They have to be on a planet the World Government doesn't have in their grip yet."

We've entered my old lab and Colsam rolls up a screen and roams space coordinates. Yesha points over his shoulder. They remind me of Viscerous and Albina, except Albina doesn't say things like miffed, wobbles, or keen. I miss them. We've been through so much. Viscerous' vein transplantation, Albina's pigment extraction, and my limb removal; they've been like parents to me for so long. I join Yesha and Colsam in the search.

"What about there?" Yesha points at the map on the holograph screen.

———

When I get some time alone in the halls, I remove one of the metal vent covers, crawl in, and replace it. Now I'm in the small, plastic tunnels surrounded by watermelon smell again. This is the fastest route to Cromwell's quarters, and I've kind of missed it. I remember the first time Vienna and I crawled into each other. I knew immediately that she wouldn't stand for what was happening here, but I had no idea to what extent she'd go. I miss her. We need to find her mom. That's why I'm back in the tunnels.

My first stop reinforces why we went through all of this, why it had to come down to revolt, and why Cromwell's reign had to end.

"Stem cell therapy has allowed regrowth," I hear Dr. Bargory House say. I was pretty amazed when he stuck around. I had him completely pegged as Team Cromwell, but he was so sickened by what was going on here that he's remained to mend anyone that he can.

"Do you think my arm will be exactly like it was before, Doc?"

Not only has he helped many, but he also showed me where the emergency shuttles were housed on Planet Vortex. He keeps trying to talk me into stem-cell therapy. Why can't people just get that I like my new bionic-limb self exactly as it is?

"Hey, Cromwell said not to tap into that unless it was an extreme emergency," I hear another voice say from a different room.

"Duh, this is an emergency. You saw the food in there."

Moving farther through the tunnel to the next vent, I'm surprised by what I hear.

"Fine but be careful and don't tell anyone about our stash."

"Have you gotten through to him yet today? Any new directives?"

"So far I've been able to keep the government officials away, but I won't be able to do that forever."

"He's going to be pissed if they discover where he's hiding."

"He'll be more pissed if we lose all control here."

"I know! Can you believe Bargory turned? Traitor!"

What the hell? I thought all the guards had made peace. Don't they want freedom? Don't they want pardons from those false charges? I'm glad I'm hidden in the tunnels and able to hear this.

"Yeah, but how's Cromwell going to hold up his end of the bargain if the government's after him?"

It's the same guards that I saw from the tunnels chilling with Dr. Cromwell and mugs of low-gravity beer. I need to warn Colsam and Yesha, so I crawl to the hallway access.

The mirror through the vent cover doesn't show anyone in the hallway, so I exit the tunnel and put the cover back. I keep thinking about the guards as I walk.

We're going to have to use some of Cromwell's tactics and I know Colsam will be angry. We can't allow them to help Cromwell any further. Luckily, all of the guards are now using the incubators, as Vienna used to call them, because their old quarters were in such a dark and cold place (which one would think would be coveted on this planet...I've never been able to locate it). Even Colsam won't tell me where it is. We can send sleeping gas through the ventilation system. It will allow us to finish our mission without being reported to Cromwell, but it's crossing a line we haven't crossed before.

———

I give Yesha the signal as we pass in the hall. Now's the perfect time. Everyone's busy with outdoor exercises and no one will notice all three of us missing at once. We couldn't meet at any of my and Colsam's previous spots because we need to be free to speak. Instead, we've decided to make my old lab the new meeting spot. Colsam nonchalantly nods when I give him the signal. He's been pretending to fix the drink refrigerator in the cafeteria so that he can avoid gambling and hide the fact that he's been running low on things to bet.

In my lab, I'm reminded of so much. The bucket of water pouring over Vienna and I. Viscerous and Albina laughing on the sidelines as they'd already been tagged by a glove. Working together to help non-bios. This thought reminds me of Vienna's clone, Sierra, and Vienna's mom, Dr. Perierat. Were they given donor cells? How will we continue to administer them in order to avoid atrophy and seizure? Shit, they're in more trouble than I thought. I need to get to them now.

Colsam enters first, with Yesha shortly behind. He stands in front of the wall and puts his right fist over the left side of his chest. Before, when Cromwell was here, Colsam didn't have as much freedom. He wasn't able to fully express his anger and sadness at the lost and abused. Yesha walks up to the wall and runs a finger along one of the tallies, the one that stands for the loss of her brother. I remember the shock Vienna felt when she realized each tally stood for someone harmed or killed. I walk up to Colsam and put an arm around his shoulders.

"All these tallies. They're another reason why we have to do it."

"I still don't like it," Colsam complains.

"I know, but we can't risk them telling Cromwell," I answer.

"Just cover for us while we move the shuttles, okay," Yesha says as she turns away from the wall with a tear in her eye. "We don't have to knock the gomers out until we're actually leaving."

"By the way, how are we getting back after we've moved the shuttles to a new location?" I ask.

"Um, about that," Yesha says. I can see the sadness slowly going away.

"What about that?"

Colsam slaps me on the back. He has the beginning of a grin on his face.

"We're going to ride vultures to get back." Yesha smiles.

"No-oh! Why can't we take camels?"

"Tick-Tock. You guys have to get back in time to help me search for the gas when the guards have gone to bed."

"What about a hover bike?"

"Too loud," Yesha says. "If the rails extended that far we could travel silently but they don't."

"Why can't Colsam go instead of me? He loves those birds as much as Vienna does."

"I need to stay here and keep the troops calm."

"Thanks. Thanks a lot for the help."

Since everyone's exercising on the other side of the facility, we need to exit out of the incubator side. Luckily, we've been able to locate the source of the oxygen pills to keep everyone not originally from Vortex safe outdoors. The ladder Vienna built makes it much easier to get to the shuttles, but we need to move them so they're away from the sensors. We don't need a code blue calling attention to our departure.

We've packed some of the weapons Cromwell had the guards use. I'm not a fan of them but if I'm going to be able to get cells from Vienna's clone and Mom which are now inhabited by the memory and conscience of Sorna, Cromwell's wife, and Damien, his kid, it might require weapons.

Yesha seems thrilled at the idea of possessing a weapon anywhere near Cromwell. I'm going to have to keep a close eye on her. I don't want her going away for life because she murdered him. I know she's angry. She has every right to be, but I don't think that's what her brother would want for her.

As we near the shuttles, I see movement. It's wings. I freeze.

"We're not there yet. Why are you stopping?"

"Why are they here? I thought we didn't need them until we were coming back?"

"How are they supposed to know where to meet us unless they follow?"

She closes the twenty-five feet between us and the vultures, who had been behind the shuttles. One of the vultures lowers its head next to her. She pets it like Vienna had petted the vulture that saved her life. Maybe they're not all bad. As I take one step forward, a second vulture comes out from behind a shuttle. I take another step forward, trying to breathe slowly so it can't smell my fear. Yesha snickers. Cog her. I look back at the vulture and it utters a caw in my direction, freezing me in place again.

"Shoot, the guards might have heard that. We need to go now."

3

PLANET EARTH

Vienna

SEEING A WHOLE NEW WORLD THROUGH MY CLONE'S EYES is magnificent. It's a jungle where she is instead of a desert or an Industrial Earth 2.0. That's my new name for it, Industrial Earth 2.0. It's the only way I'm able to keep old Earth and new Earth straight when I'm talking to Viscerous, Albina, and Theopat. But the jungle my clone's in is magical. The neon leaves reflect light like prisms. I wonder if it's luciferase binding with luciferin that makes them glow? I'm so glad Vex is with her. Maybe I can try hacking into his system later to see what's going on, because the phantom visions are becoming less frequent. In fact, they often only appear when I meditate.

We're growing further apart. Eventually, she'll be her own person. And we're going to have a lot of explaining to do. I can't call and explain or at least all the attempts we've made have been unsuccessful. Even hacking Vex wouldn't allow for back-and-forth communication like a call unless I broke the safety features, and only one person I know could possibly do that, Yesha. But I'm taking Theopat to my school later and we're going to try to get in touch there.

I bend my legs into the butterfly sitting position, straighten my back, and close my eyes. I breathe in, feeling my lungs expand as far as they can. I breathe out until my chest is compressed, imagining a large, dark circle. I'm interrupted by footsteps approaching.

"Vienna, I'm going to go to the Scientific Assembly. How do I lo…I'm sorry. Am I interrupting?"

Cog it all.

"Meditating here."

"I remember when your mom used to do that before I was imprisoned on Vortex."

The pain in his eyes is visible even though he's trying to hide it. He and Mom should be together at last.

"What were you asking me, Dad?"

"Oh, yeah, how do I look?"

"You look fine. Nervous about seeing everyone again?"

"Who is the parent here?"

I smile and he smiles in return. It's been great having Dad around, but I can tell Septimus is struggling to get back into the swing of things here. He was stuck on Planet Vortex for so long under Cromwell's thumb. I hope he hits it off with his old friends at the Scientific Assembly. I go up to him, straighten his tie, and then pat him on the shoulder. He gives me a hug. The hug I've missed for years.

When he leaves, I continue my meditation. Within the large, dark circle, a violet circle forms, and inside that a blue one. I inhale and exhale again before green, red, and yellow circles form. There they freeze and oxygen exchanges without thinking. Finally, the last circle swells like the sun expanding toward the Earth.

Neon leaves blur by in the vision. My clone, Sierra, is on

the run. What could she be running from? I hear a soothing mix of jungle insects and water running but it's interrupted by yelling. Someone's running with Sierra. The new person's auburn hair flows behind her. The pair suddenly stop and hide behind foliage. Vines and leaves seem to move, curling and spinning. Then glowing red dots appear from nowhere.

"Vienna, are you ready or what?"

Cog it all! It's impossible to get a moment's peace with four other people in the apartment. What was that?

"Give me five minutes, Theopat."

"Oh, I can't wait. We're still going to stop by the clothing store on the way to your school, right?"

"For the thousandth time, yes."

Theopat jumps up and down squealing. There's no way I'm going to be able to meditate anymore. Being a Vortex resident her whole life she already had a huge interest in learning Earth lifestyle, especially fashion. That interest grew exponentially when her brother deboarded the shuttle. He decided to stay at the Vortex facility instead of being free and coming to Earth with her. She's been devastated ever since, except when the topic of clothes comes up. I get it. It's her escape. We all need one of those from time to time. I swear she almost jumps through my ceiling when I put on my shoes. I'm still taken a little aback by the numerous voices we hear in the once quiet apartment as we exit.

"Wait, step back," I tell her when she reaches for the poli-magno before the solar disks have a chance to lower.

When they do lower, she is awestruck. "What is that?"

"It's how we charge our vehicles." It reminds me of how little studying I was capable of doing on Vortex given the dire circumstances. "How do they charge hovers on Vortex?"

"Is that what those things were, solar panels? The solar rechargeable cells are imbedded within the hover metal for automatic charging."

We board the poli-magno and I'm instantly reminded of my mom sitting in the seat I now occupy, hands gripping the metal steering wheel. I had to learn to drive when I arrived on Earth. No one else knew how, and it had been too long for my dad. Mom had practiced with me a few times. Honestly, I'd rather fly on a vulture than drive one of these things. During the trip I think about testing Faradays Law. That's what happens when I know I'll be back in my old lab soon.

"What's that?" Theopat points to buildings.

"Our buildings have new, colorful art each month to make up for the lack of vegetation not confined to labs and other protected areas." The current piece is 3-D bubbles that look as if they're bouncing from one building to the next. Theopat can't help but stare.

Pulling up to Magasin, she notices the advertisements. With her new identification, they now show the most recent fashion trends. For me, they're back to Science Olympiad and poli-magno repair ads. I had to convert back to my old identification instead of using the one that would have caused the floating messages to report the latest medical advancements. I needed it for Dad.

The momentum is nonstop as soon as we walk through the door. Theopat's running up to different racks. She's obviously done enough searching to warrant a visit to each one. The system moves her style and size to the front of each rack as she approaches. Long sleeves, short sleeves, clothes of every kind. The only similarity I notice is the dark colors. On Vortex, she'd been restricted to only lighter clothes due to the sheer heat of the desert planet. Here on Earth she's allowed more freedom.

I notice a guy stare at her as he walks by. She doesn't even pay attention.

"You've caught someone's attention." I nudge her in the side and tilt my head in his direction.

All she does is shrug her shoulders. I underestimated her love of clothes.

"I kind of fell for someone back home," she says.

"Oh! Anyone I know?"

"Yeah, it's, well, it's kind of complicated."

"You're so far away from there now. You can tell me."

"Okay, I thought perhaps you had it figured out, given my awkwardness when you arrived at the Stem Cell Harvesting Center...it's Colsam."

My heart stops, but why, it shouldn't matter. "The fitting rooms are over there." I point while pushing the stack of clothes she's holding.

She gives me an odd look and goes to try on her clothes. It shouldn't bother me that she likes Colsam. I love Al. And yet, my blood is boiling.

I lose track of how many outfits she's tried on. Once she has ten new outfits, I tell her we need to get to the school before it closes. A clopil arrives about that time to take the clothing and deliver it to the house. Since Vex went on an excursion of his own, we've had to hire clopils. None of them could ever replace him. At least I can see him through meditation...for now. I know he's just a mechanical being, but he's like the only brother I've ever had or at least would be if I didn't have a brother...a brother I've never met.

———

Walking into the school reminds me of the facility. I remember the first time I met Al. It was in the cafeteria. His northern-lights-green eyes captured me with that first look when he saved me from falling. I had tripped at the sight of Viscerous. We're close now but seeing someone for the first time with all of their veins on the outside of their epidermis shocked me.

Once we're in the lab, I'm able to breathe a little more smoothly.

"To make a smoke bomb, all you need is potassium nitrate, sugar, water, and a fuse. Programming holograph messaging to be 'smoke screen projection only' is much more difficult. It's a digital version of invisible ink and completely security cam resistant."

Theopat looks at me like I'm speaking gibberish.

"What is that smell?" It's a voice that brings back the past. Danver, the voltball captain.

"Yeah, it's worse than the sweaty locker room after a game." Another voice I recognize. This one I despise, though now, after being on Vortex, I recognize that the level of hate I feel for Milcah is nowhere close to the loathing I reserve for Dr. Cromwell.

"Why can't you two ever give me any freedom?" I complain as they enter the lab. "Don't you hate experiments?"

"What can we say…school was cogging boring without your shenanigans," Milcah says.

I walk toward her. "What, being the visual arts queen doesn't keep you occupied?"

She rolls her eyes at me. I reach for her tranquilizer gun, having learned a lesson from the last time we had an encounter.

Then I turn and whisper something to Theopat that will make her hate Milcah just as much as I do. "Her mom's part of the Government."

Danver catches Theopat's fist before it hits Milcah in the face.

"All right, all right, I can see when we're not welcome," Milcah says.

"Maybe we should call Principal Skidmore," Danver adds.

Uh…this pair. Can I really get in any more trouble, though? It's not worth it.

"Whatever. Hang around if you want. Just don't be upset if we say anything against your corrupt mom, Milcah."

"You have no idea," Milcah says, and a dark gloom settles over her as Danver puts his arm around her shoulders. Maybe there's more depth there than I gave her credit for…

"You sure?" Theopat asks.

"Yes," I say.

"We're calling an off-the-grid planet," Theopat tells the pair, who instantly show interest.

Given Yesha's reports, the phantom visions, meditation, and logical reasoning, I think I've pinpointed my clone's location. Making the call to Scepter is risky, but I want to know more. Is my clone okay? She did save me involuntarily. Is my mom there? But there's only one connection we can try and I don't know to whom it belongs.

"Do you think we'll get through?"

"It's worth a shot."

The ringing seems to go on forever, but then a voice answers.

"Cromwell Scepter Facility, how may I help you?"

The hair on my arms raises and I freeze. Not another one. This cannot be happening.

———

Luckily, I don't have the same issues calling Planet Vortex as I do when trying to call my clone. From home, I can call Al without the need of a smoke bomb or to delete history. Vex can't even tell on me as he's left the planet. And the facility on Vortex is no longer evil!

"He's at it again," I say.

"Um, I miss you too. Who's at what again?" Al asks.

"Cromwell, another facility."

"That's not good."

"I know. What are we going to do?"

"We'll work on it. You don't need to worry. We have it under control. I'll let you know as soon as we figure something out. I did find something else, though."

"You don't seem surprised, and it almost seems as if you've been planning how to deal with the facility. Why didn't you tell me?"

"We didn't want to worry you."

"We?"

"Vienna, I'm sorry. Please, can we discuss the thing I found?"

"What's that?"

"Your brother."

I have to take a seat.

"And?"

"Well, I don't know his exact location but I found him in the academy system."

"That's great. We can work from that at least."

"Vienna—it's kind of weird calling you that again, but I get how it will keep things less confusing with the clone—I have to tell you that it's not good he's there."

4

PLANET SCEPTER

Sierra

I SHAKE THE SPIDER OFF OF ME AND THEN KICK IT AWAY. The alarms are still wailing. A small laser lands on Vex and I move him out of automatic reflex. Marrit puts her hands on my cheeks, causing my skin to tingle where she touches, moving my head so that I'm looking her directly in the eyes.

"Follow me."

She grabs my hand, the one the spider left alone. Her grip is firm and warm. I'm glad to find the spider hand still works, and that I wasn't contaminated with a numbing poison or anything, so when Marrit pulls me, I'm able to grab Vex's rope and bring him with us. We sprint away from the facility as fast as we can. I keep watching for more red dots to appear. The sun glints off of Marrit's gorgeous auburn hair, making me think it might be a laser circle. We abruptly stop when a tangle of glowing vegetation trips me. Marrit tries to pull me free, but a large leaf keeps grabbing my leg, momentarily releasing, and then grabbing again. Each time, it grabs me with a stronger grip.

"Go, take Vex," I tell Marrit.

But she doesn't go. She gives the leaf another yank while removing a retractable machete tied to a small leather satchel strap I hadn't noticed before. Marrit has weapons. She's much more prepared than I am, but I don't think a machete will be capable of contending with the weapons giving off the laser dots. Where did Cromwell get ahold of banned firearms, and how are we going to take over a facility with that kind of ammunition?

We run for a bit in a new direction. Traveling territory I don't know is a little disorienting. Then I hear footsteps in pursuit…of us. I don't want to be caught. Why did I have to let the spider freak me out so much? Mom is at the facility… maybe we should get caught so we can free her…like Cromwell would allow that. Before I can think another thought, Marrit pulls me again. Next, Vex and I are sliding down a mudslide completely out of control. I reach for vines and leaves, trying to grasp anything to slow us down.

"Waterproof shields up," Vex says.

"Why do you…" We hit the water before I'm able to finish. We're both beneath the surface of the jungle river in a heartbeat. When I make it to the top and sputter for breath, Marrit grabs me again, but this time she puts a finger in front of her mouth, shushing me. I try to be quiet, but it's not easy. She pulls us over to the side where we're able to swim a bit beneath the foliage and not be exposed in the center of the river.

Marrit and I keep a lookout, waiting for someone to appear in pursuit, but after a few minutes I slow down my breathing. Did we somehow escape them? I gamble and take a deep breath, relaxing ever so slightly. I notice bright, neon fish swimming all around us. Then I see what looks like a piranha dart after another fish. Close to Marrit's feet, I spot an electric eel. The water is clearer than I would have ever imagined. When I take a step, instead of a dirt cloud floating up, the water becomes clearer in the vicinity of my foot. What is this stuff?

"Be still," Marrit turns to me and says.

"Why? Did they find us?"

She holds her finger in front of her lips again, and that's when I spot it. Slowly and stealthily, an alligator swims near us. I freeze and feel goosebumps despite the warmth of the jungle. It swims back by, lifting its spikes above the water. Sparks fly from the spikes as soon as they meet the air. This planet is definitely different from Earth. Wait, I don't see it. Where did it go?

There's a noise behind us. It's just land back there. Did the little gomer somehow sneak around without being seen? An attack from behind? But then I see a silver cylinder contraption over my shoulder. It's held by a gloved hand, attached to an arm in a jacket sleeve. Before I can turn around to see who it is, there's movement in the water. First, I see alligator nostrils and then white, pointy teeth. The cylinder over my shoulder fires a mist of some sort and where it hits, the water turns to ice. It's close to the alligator, who does not like the change in temp one bit. The reptile lifts itself out of the water, causing bubbles when it comes back down. Then it gurgle-growls and I kind of back pedal/crawl, whatever I can do to get away. The cylinder fires again and the alligator swims off.

"Barren," Marrit says as she stands and gives the glove-jacket guy the same hug greeting she gave me when we first met. He has dark hair instead of auburn and his eyes are charcoal instead of hazel, but you can tell the two belong to the same tribe. Their garments both have a jungle, ready-for-adventure feel. Even Marrit's clothes look amazing, as if they shed the water the moment she steps out of it. My clothes, on the other hand, are drenched. I'm sure I look like a kitten just rescued from drowning. I try to swipe the water off of me and out of my hair.

"Thank you for that," I stretch my hand out for a shake, forgetting that isn't their tradition and before I know it, I'm hugging another person within seconds of meeting them.

"Ah, it was nothing. You have no idea how many times I've had to save Mar. Always getting herself into trouble."

"Well, you arrived in the nick of time."

"We better get you dried off before nightfall."

Barren and Marrit look at one another, speaking in a silent code of some sort.

"I think we should introduce Sierra and her clopil to everyone. She's seen a facility like the one they're building before and was able to dismantle it."

My clopil! Where's Vex? Why isn't he bothering us with annoying data collection? I spot him a few feet away, lying on the ground, not moving. My heart drops. He's the only thing I have from home with me right now. I need him. I go over to him to assess the situation. Water droplets fall from his crevices.

"I need a rarefaction device. Do you have one? I need to vacuum the water out of Vex."

"I think we have one. It's old, but I think it could work. Follow me." Barren walks. Marrit grabs the rope so she can carry Vex and I follow numbly.

We walk for a bit, surrounded by some of the same moving-leaf greenery, but quickly come to a veil of moss vines. There's so much vegetation here it overwhelms all taste and smell. As Barren moves the veil aside, I'm mesmerized by the sight of a cavern passage long enough to remind me of the poli-magno tunnels back home. A turquoise color shines in from the jungle on the other side, bouncing off of the water on the ground. It's spectacular. As we walk through, light beams off crystals within the walls and ceiling. Partway through, there's a hole above. With the sunlight and the moss vines hanging from the hole, it looks like crepuscular rays, something my mom called angel fingers back on Earth.

"How much longer? I need to work on Vex as soon as possible."

"Just outside, see," Marrit says.

As we step outside, I'm taken aback by what I see. It's a city suspended above the ground as if floating. It's almost like a structure or tower with a round aqua wall circling the perimeter and a soft yellow, upside-down cone in the center. It's as if the whole thing is lit up. Not like the neon leaves or the electric alligator spikes, but like a lantern. It's amazing.

"What's that?" I ask.

"That's our Capital," Barren says.

"Is it always floating? How do you get up there?"

"You fly on my back," a voice says from behind us. Marrit turns around, approaching a giant parrot who appears to be the only possible source of the voice we just heard. What is it with me and giant birds? Marrit pets the parrot and I instantly miss my Aviator. I wonder what she's doing now. I hope Al has managed to keep the vultures safe.

"You can speak?" I ask the parrot.

"Why, yes, why wouldn't I be able to speak? Have you never seen a talking parrot?"

"Well, yeah, but it's more like just repeating things where I'm from."

"How dull."

"May I pet you too?"

"Of course but be sure your hands are clean first. I had a recent grooming with Nobilia."

I pet the parrot as delicately as I can. I think Theopat would love to meet this Nobilia.

"You can't possibly carry us all?"

"No, we'll take turns. Barren, why don't you go first?" Marrit interjects.

Barren jumps on the parrot's back without any assistance. Marrit and I step away to give the wings space and he's off in the blink of an eye. He lands on the lawn surrounding the aqua fence. That's when I notice the dirt and roots below the city. It's as if the place lifted off from where it belonged and flew to this location.

"Is this your home planet?" I ask Marrit as we wait for the parrot to return.

"You ready? You're next," she responds, ignoring my question.

She'd been so worried about people showing up here and the facility, but part of the Capital doesn't seem to belong, so I'm confused. But then the parrot lands. Marrit clasps her hands together to form a step for me. I mount and before I know it we're flying. All worries and questions evade me. I feel free, just like when I'm on Aviator. For a few brief moments, I'm able to forget. I don't need to consider how to save Mom, or escape, or somehow miraculously find my brother. I can just be a teenager, let the wind rush through my hair, and be cogging carefree, the only drama being the increasing crush I seem to be developing on Marrit. I care for Al so much, but something about Marrit draws me in even more. And then we land and I'm back to worrying of things beyond my years.

"Here she is," Barren says to a group of people in front of him. "Mar says she can help."

"Um, Hi, I'm Sierra." Nervousness fills me. It's one thing to help a group of people behind the scenes, but to have them expecting you to make a difference is an entirely different beast. What have I volunteered for?

"What's Marrit carrying on her back?" someone in the crowd asks.

"It's too much weight is what it is," says another person in the crowd. "Look at how it's affecting Tango."

"Is Tango the parrot?" I ask Barren, watching with concern.

"Yes."

Tango falters to the left and then to the right, not making the same straight flight he had with both Barren and I. He looks about the way I would if I were to try to cartwheel on a balance beam. Marrit holds on to the ropes with the same hand that holds Tango while using the other hand to steady Vex, a new form of juggling. I hold my breath, unable to do a thing except watch them both in danger.

5

PLANET VORTEX

Al

I DUCK AND ROLL IN ORDER TO GET BY THE VULTURE, BUT also to be out of beak plunge range. When I first saw a Planet Vortex vulture, I mistook it for a dragon due to its sheer size. With further investigation, I noticed that the neck wasn't as long as a dragon's neck, but the fear of fire breath and doom has never left me. I'm a lot more comfortable on shuttles. The ones that land on Vortex remind me of some of the vintage cars on Funen. It's been a long time since I've been in a shuttle liftoff, but of course we don't get to do that now. No, we'll drive it on land to the secret location. The location that will allow a takeoff from the facility to go undetected. Still, it's exciting leaving the facility property.

Yesha takes off as if driving a shuttle is something she does every day. It takes me a little longer to get started and then I'm catching up to her.

In order to remain as unseen as possible by the outside

population, we have to navigate through the high rocky hills and dense trails. We have to slow a bit to be sure the shuttles are protected. Once we're in open expanse, we can speed back up and before I know it, Yesha and I are racing. We quickly go by the stem cell harvesting center. Its height still intrigues me, and how much it looks like a metal tree. I remember Vienna's face when they released the rainbow fireflies during our time there.

As we approach a populated area, there's a wall in the distance. Yesha veers left and before us is a sight I thought I'd never see on this desert planet. A beautiful patch of Parkinsonia trees. Their brilliant color stands out against the sand. Each tree is pretty wide, and the group together will do a decent job of hiding the shuttles. Yesha seems to be more familiar with the area than I am. How is that? She and Vienna arrived on Vortex at the same time. Parking the shuttles is a relief, but I fear the return to the facility. The shadow from the vulture landing appears to have swords sticking out of its wings, taking me back to the medieval fear of a fire-breathing monster, impossible for even the best knight to fight. I don't want to ride on one of those vultures.

"You sure this is the best way back?" I ask Yesha over the radio as I see the vultures landing next to us.

"Come on, it will be fun. Trust me."

"Uh, fine."

I exit the shuttle, take a deep breath, and slowly approach the vulture I assume I will be riding as Yesha's petting the other one. I try to mimic her moves. I approach slowly and with my hand down below the beak. The vulture makes a subtle noise and then moves a step away. The bird looks like it's trying to begin the game Colsam had played on our way to the stem cell facility. Figuring I might have more luck making a friend of the bird if I participate, I make to grab one of the vulture's legs, and it jumps back and then approaches again. I think it's working so I make a move for the other leg and the vulture spins. I smile despite myself.

"Will you mount already!" Yesha almost shouts.

"I'm trying to establish a relationship here before my life is put in danger. Lay off, will ya!"

I attempt to start the game back up, but the word "mount" had its effect on the vulture, who has lowered to the ground, making the task easier for me. I guess this is it. I put a hand on the vulture's back, steadying myself. My heart's about to pound through my chest. I put one leg over and hold onto the bird's neck. Yesha's vulture takes off, they're up in the air, and before I know it my vulture's moving too. I hold on tight and squeeze my eyes shut.

"You're missing a spectacular view, you little gomer."

"You're not helping," I scream back at Yesha.

Slowly, I lift my lids. She's right. Everything looks miniature. It's freeing. I straighten up a little to see better and feel the rush of wind. I make sure to look far ahead and not directly beneath us.

"Want to race again?" Yesha asks.

"No, I'm good. This is actually peaceful."

"What was that? I think you said yes."

And with that, Yesha's vulture dives a bit while picking up speed. And, to my utter dismay, so does mine. I'm gripping onto the vulture for my life now with my eyes shut again. I feel the bird lean this way and that. We must be near the high, rocky hills. Good, we're getting close. Then it slows down and lands, but I'm not ready to open my eyes. Though I know we have come to a stop, I still feel the rush and my muscles have not untensed.

"Will you get down already?" Colsam asks. "The guards aren't working out anymore. Everyone's gathered in the cafeteria. We can enter on the training side where the sleeping gas is stored. Let's check on it to be sure everything's ready to go."

"You've finally come around on that?" I say.

"That doesn't mean I'm happy about it."

We make our way to the other side of the facility. Colsam shows us passageways that had gone undetected by security. Rounding the final corner, I realize this is my first time here. There's a garage, a shed, and what appears to be a sacred garden for training. I've never seen one in real life before. Colsam and Yesha head to the garage. They can take care of what we need. They don't really need me so I head to the garden, jumping on the first rock. A taste of freedom feels so close.

"What are you doing?" Colsam asks.

Cog it, I thought I'd gotten away with it.

"You better not move a single grain of sand out of place," Colsam says.

"Strict much?" Maybe Yesha is on my side.

Nope. She looks at me with disgust.

I jump out of the garden and join them in the garage. As I approach, I see that they're standing in front of cylinders taller than any of us. There's a system of pipelines connecting to the cylinders. Next to the cylinders is a holograph screen.

"How will we be sure not too much is administered?" Colsam asks. "I don't think that had been a concern of Cromwell's, but it is one of mine."

"Too bad we don't have Vienna here to hack into the database," I say.

"Ahem, where do you think she learned those mad skills?" Yesha asks and then works at the holograph screen. She navigates through the system like a pro. Maybe she did teach Vienna a thing or two. "Actually, Cromwell may have been more interested in the mechanics than you think...just not in the same way you are, Colsam."

"What do you mean?" he asks.

"Well, he pretty much had a kill switch on all of us, ready to be activated by the mere push of a button," Yesha says.

"Gives a whole new meaning to sweet dreams…what a creep," I say.

"It's not funny," Colsam says. "That means he could have killed any of you any evening he wanted."

"Glad he's gone now," Yesha says.

"Yeah, we're going to use the very same technology," Colsam says.

"But that's the thing," Yesha says. "He had the system so controlled that you can ensure safety."

"So, we're good?" I ask.

"Fine," Colsam says.

Yesha moves the switch to a portable device so she can administer the anesthesia gas from anywhere.

———

When the time comes, I'm actually looking forward to flying on the vultures again. Everyone else has gone to sleep. Yesha and I go back to using the ladder because it's the easiest route. My vulture jumps up when they spot us. He's ready to begin the game again. This turn, Yesha allows us a little more freedom and it's great.

"No racing, okay."

"Okay, party pooper."

We mount and take off. Flying in the dark is even more fun. While I'm able to see miniature things way below in the moonlight, now the height does not seem quite so daunting. The wind rushes through my clothes and I feel a coolness unlike anything I've experienced in years. I think the vulture must know that I'm not a fan of sudden dips and turns. He glides with a smoothness that I appreciate, as if ice skating.

When we land near the shuttles and the trees, my vulture lowers his head and I pet him. That was awesome, but it stinks that I have to leave Vortex when I just found something new to enjoy here. I should be thrilled that I'm finally escaping this place full of tortured memories and heading to get Vienna's mom, but this place still oddly feels something like home. Hopefully, when I help Vienna get her family together and when I'm finally back with Viscerous and Albina, I'll have a new place to call home.

"What if I did use the kill switch?"

"What are you talking about, Yesha?"

"The guards don't really deserve forgiveness after everything they did. They could have revolted or not listened to Cromwell. They cared more about their precious records than saving lives."

"Yesha," I calmly say as I approach her. "Hand me the portable device."

"No, they killed my brother. They deserve to die."

She begins opening up the system that controls the anesthesia. I step forward and swat the device from her hands.

"Hey, give it back."

"No! They didn't have a choice. Remember Rigled?"

She's circling the tree after me as I walk with the device.

"Think about it. Theopat's brother is there. He could still be saved and made to see the light. He was never detailed on any of those experiments. You want to tell Theopat that you killed her brother?"

That stops her in her tracks.

"You'd kill Colsam too…remember, the guy played a key role in the revolt and is helping us now," I continue.

"Fine."

I administer the small dose that will only have them out long enough to be sure our departure goes undetected. She rolls her eyes at me like she didn't just threaten to kill dozens. I take a deep breath, hoping that was the only hiccup we were going to have. We board our shuttles. I'm glad we have two. If Cromwell's new facility is anything like his last, we'll need the room to take people to safety. As I sit, I notice the hexagonal shapes of the internal walls. They remind me of when I first came here. It had been strange seeing those walls and then seeing the facility. It had been like a blip in my memory erased. Vienna informed me of what occurred during that time, the invisible ink tattoos marking those for experiment. And now, we're causing a blip in guard memories. Perhaps we are crossing a line we shouldn't.

"You ready?" Yesha asks via headset.

"Yes." I begin the sequence of actions to initiate takeoff, checking the monitors to be sure everything is reading clearly.

When we lift off it feels like the elevator at the stem cell factory, except ten times stronger. I have to take a deep breath to stay focused and not be frightened. I close my eyes but have to open them when the shuttle shakes. It seems like it could fall apart, and even though I'm scared, I'm compelled to assure myself that isn't happening. Clouds zoom by, but when I notice the ship isn't facing the moons as I had expected, worry takes over me.

"Yesha, why aren't we facing the moons?"

"Correction, you are not facing the moons. I am."

"Yesha! What did you do?"

"I have to kill him, Al. I can't risk you stopping me again."

"Cog it, Yesha. So where am I going then?"

"Earth, silly. Tell Vienna hello for me."

"Wait, Yesha. Vienna's mom and her clone will need donor cells so their non-bodies can avoid atrophy."

She doesn't answer me and then I'm at superluminal speed.

6

PLANET EARTH

Vienna

AL SAID IT'S BAD THAT MY BROTHER IS IN THE ACADEMY system, but we weren't able to talk longer so I don't have much to go on. Why would it be negative? The academy system can't be as horrible as one of Cromwell's facilities, can it?

"No, I do not want turnips and kale," I hear Viscerous say loudly as I walk down the hall. He's really struggled with Kitchen, our home bot that looks like cooled, melted steel except with the fluidity of a slithering snake. Viscerous fumes as Kitchen's metal arms assemble dinner.

"You need the ingredients. You all have been under a lot of stress lately. Right, Vienna?"

Kitchen always knows the second I walk into the room. Viscerous puts his hands together in a pleading way.

"Can you add steak to the turnips and kale?"

"Of course, as you wish, Vienna."

Viscerous mouths a thank you. It seems the more limited

vegetation becomes on Earth, the more Kitchen is drawn to it.

"What about dessert?" Albina asks as she enters the room.

I zone out while Kitchen lists every possible dessert available for Albina. Kitchen might be a robot, but I think she's enjoying all the company. I've pulled up the holograph screen at the side desk hutch. I'm researching academies the best I can. They all look reputable and seem to provide the kind of education that would allow a kid to attend a college of my parents' dreams. Nothing flags me that they're any different from other boarding schools. I review faculty to see if I notice anything suspicious, but it all seems to be checking out.

The door opens and more sounds fill the apartment.

"Closet is going to be happy that I'm adding so much couvrir to the inventory list!" Theopat says to Harper, Danver, and Milcah. (She can't seem to stop saying the word couvrir since I taught her about French fashion history and how Closet lapses into the language from time to time.) What in the actual world is going on? First, Milcah and Danver are the last two I would ever expect to be in my home. They almost kept me from saving the koalas before my journey to Planet Vortex. Second, I haven't seen Harper in so long. She hates Milcah even more than I do. Do they stop to say hello to me? No. They walk right on by, heading to my room, all with garments in their hands.

"Hey, guys," I say. "Where do you think you're going?"

"Oh, they're just helping me with all of this stuff," says Theopat. "Isn't it great?"

"I can take that. Viscerous, Danver might have better luck convincing Kitchen to alter menus." I grab the garments Danver's holding and he gives me a scared look. It's kind of funny seeing the voltball captain anything but cocky. I guess the sight of Viscerous spooked him. In fact, the entire group is gawking.

"Everyone, this is Viscerous and Albina," I say while also

signing to Harper, putting the garments over my shoulder. "They came here from Planet Vortex with my dad and me. They were crucial to our escape and they're brilliant in a lab."

Albina puts her hand out for Harper to shake. Harper doesn't miss a beat. She shakes Albina and then Viscerous' hands without hesitation. Milcah's face is to die for when Albina extends her hand, but, to Milcah's credit, she collects herself and shakes both of their hands too. Danver is the most freaked out by the pair, but he's also had the most time to collect himself. He clears his throat and steps forward, offering his hand to shake.

"Viscerous and Albina, this is Harper." I point to Harper while saying this and she waves because she was able to read my lips and knows what I'm doing. "This is Milcah and Danver." I point to each as I had with Harper, and they both also wave.

Theopat, Harper, Milcah, and I take the garments back to my room. I never before would have thought this possible. I mean, I've always considered myself extinct in social circles.

"What are you doing?" I ask Milcah.

"She was in the middle of the street looking at the artwork on the building. I couldn't just leave her to fend for herself like someone I know did." She gives me the "you are always trouble" look and I stick my tongue out at her.

"Theopat, I thought you weren't a fan of this one," I say.

I catch Harper up. Signing what transpired the last time Theopat and I ran into Milcah. *Theopat about punched Milcah's head off when she found out her mom was with the World Government.*

"Hey, we all have family members that do things we don't agree with…I mean, my brother decided to stay at the Vortex facility," Theopat says. "Plus, she has a Magasin discount!"

Theopat places the new "couvrir" in Closet.

"Thank you, Theopat," Closet says. "Maintaining a log of

one's wardrobe is important so that the best possible outfit may be produced. I wish you could teach Vienna the value of it."

I roll my eyes.

I'll never understand the fashion craze Harper signs.

Me either, I sign back. *Did Vitamin D work in the photosynthesis study?*

You remember that? You're not about to ask me to cover for you again, are you?

No, I am sorry.

I understand. You had to get your dad, but where's your mom? We have so much to discuss, Harper.

"I'm starving after all of that shopping," Theopat says.

"I better ask Kitchen to make three extra servings. I assume you all want to stay. Or do you need to get back home?"

"I'd rather never go back to that place," Milcah says, and the gloom I saw before returned.

"Yes, let's have a sleepover," Theopat says. "Isn't that what it's called on Earth?"

Well, that would be something I had never planned on… Danver, Milcah, Harper, and I having a sleepover together. This day just seems to be getting weirder and weirder by the second. If this were a scientific experiment, I would check to see if protocol had been followed.

We all head back to the kitchen.

"Kitchen, please add three more place settings."

Kitchen actually beeps a few times. Another thing I've never encountered before.

"Ah, Vienna, that might be quite a tight squeeze," says Kitchen.

"No, we can take our meals to the living room," responds Viscerous.

"Yeah, I don't want to miss the voltball game," Albina says.

"I'll join you," Danver adds.

I return to the holograph screen to continue my academy search while everyone gets situated. I had to have missed something before.

"What are you doing?" Milcah asks.

"Not that it's any of your business, but I'm searching for a student at one of the academies."

"Then why are you searching the faculty?"

"Isn't that where corruption begins...the leadership?"

"You really have no clue, do you?"

"Harsh."

She nudges me aside with her shoulder and navigates on the holograph.

"You need to look at the board."

Looking at the screen, I realize how she's so well informed in this area. The president of the board for all academies is her mom. Thinking of the sullen way Milcah has looked recently whenever her mom is mentioned, finding out that's who runs the academies, and knowing my brother is being held at one does not ease the tension that's been building in me. But maybe with Milcah's help, I'll be able to find out where my brother is now.

"Does your mom ever work from home, Milcah?" I ask.

"Well, yeah. Why?"

"Do you think we could access her computer so I can find my brother?"

"Even if her remote holograph interface was available, we wouldn't be able to hack into it."

Harper gives Milcah and I an evil grin. I thought she'd been reading our lips. I nod my head and grin myself because I know between the two of us we'd have a good chance of getting in.

"You don't understand. Even if you could hack it, you'd be tracked. It's government territory." She covers her mouth with her hand, realizing she's said too much.

"The government is linked to the academy board. I assumed your mom was president only to show goodwill."

"No, it's part of why I'm so mad at her."

What? Harper signs. *What is it?*

Milcah takes a step closer and whispers, "They've developed a—"

We're interrupted by a loud, red flashing alert that scrolls across the screen. What was Milcah going to say? My heart rate quickens.

"WANTED: Viscerous and Albina Hoag are two fugitives on the run after stealing property from a scientific lab on Planet Vortex. They are both in their late thirties and have easily identifiable traits. Viscerous' veins and arteries are on the outside of his epidermis and Albina's pigmentation has been extracted. They originated from Planet Arcane and held lab positions on Planet Vortex but are believed to now be on Planet Earth. Please contact us if you believe you have sighted one or both of these two."

Cog it all, what now? This day really is all sorts of messed up. It's not as if just a theory was incorrect. It's like doing an experiment using equipment that hasn't been properly calibrated. I really, really don't want to have another person I care for in danger.

I hadn't realized Viscerous, Albina, and Danver had reentered the room to get seconds.

"What in the world?" Albina asks.

Viscerous squeezes the bridge of his nose with a thumb and forefinger. "Why is he still targeting us if he has his family back?"

"Who's targeting you?" Danver asks.

"A man who goes by the name of Cromwell."

"Yeah, and why does he have another facility?" Theopat asks.

Viscerous' eyes get huge. He looks at me and tightens his

jaw muscles. "When were you going to tell us? I thought you learned your lesson about keeping stuff from us on Vortex."

"I wanted to be sure first, plus there hasn't even really been time."

"Vienna, this is not something that should be kept from us. What are we going to do now that we're wanted? We could have been more help had we known before."

"I'm fine with staying in and watching voltball," Albina says.

"Good thing we're using Rigled's ID and Cora allowed us to use hers," Viscerous says with a smirk. "I had a feeling it would be necessary but had hoped it wouldn't be."

"You'll have to be sure not to answer the door to bots. Oh, and Kitchen, run a continual erase of data pertaining to Viscerous and Albina," I say.

"That is not protocol, Vienna."

"As the only owner present right now, I'm overriding."

"Duly noted."

"Please share the new directive with Closet."

Despite the panic rising in me, it seems Albina and Viscerous move on from the development just fine, which allows everyone else to remain calm. I guess the couple has been through far worse.

Viscerous and Danver get seconds while the rest of us finish our meal. It's all so strange. My whole life I've lived as an only child, most of it with a single parent, too. But now, that warm feeling I'd experienced at the facility when sitting with my new friends in the cafeteria returns. There are additional problems when you add people to your life (drama, noise, constant activity, and worrying about them, to name a few), but it's so nice no longer being lonely. It makes it worth it, even if some of the people I'm surrounded by used to be my sworn enemies. I kind of like them being here, too.

The door opens and Dad walks in. He's been going to

more and more Science Assembly events. Now, his button-down shirt is half untucked. He stumbles a little but rights himself. Is he drunk? I don't remember ever seeing him that way.

"You all right, Septimus?" Viscerous asks. "Why don't you take a seat and try to eat some of the food Kitchen prepared?"

"Is everything okay?" I ask.

"Fine, just fine. No one sat by me. They're taking Cromwell's side. I don't know what's happening."

"Well, that's ironic timing considering there's a bounty on our heads." Albina points to Viscerous and herself.

"I thought you said Cromwell doesn't have ties with the World Government," Milcah says to me and I'm taken aback by her interest.

"I knew he had ties with the Planet Vortex government, but I didn't think he did with the World Government. Why?" I ask.

"There's another level to the level of irony," Milcah says.

"What is it? Do I want to know?"

"The World Government just enacted academy drafts."

"No! But they don't affect minors, right?"

"I'm so sorry, Vienna."

What is she talking about? Harper signs. *What's wrong?*
It means Cromwell's found my brother.

Dad gets my attention and quickly signs. *Vienna, did you find your brother?*

Tears well in my eyes. We don't know where he is, only that he's in the academy system. "What does a draft entail?" I ask Milcah.

"It's a draft into the new World Government Military branch."

This day has officially become one of the worst three days in the universe. The others occurred on Planet Vortex. I want to go to the rooftop and scream.

7

PLANET SCEPTER

Sierra

MARRIT, VEX, AND TANGO STRAIGHTEN OUT AND THEN tilt precariously to the other side. It's nerve-wracking watching Marrit hold onto Vex while they ride the parrot. My wrist muscles are weak and I know that if I were to hold my hand out right now, it would be shaking. It's like watching someone walk a tightrope, that's how wobbly they seem up in the air. When they finally land, I breathe in a huge gulp of oxygen.

Barren and I help them off of Tango. Marrit hands me Vex and then turns back to Tango to be sure the bird wasn't hurt during the flight. Next, Barren turns to me, looking at Vex like he's already a lost cause.

"Well then, the rarefication device is in the warehouse just over here," he says. "Please follow me."

I'm glad Vex still has the rope I made from jungle milk-weed attached. It makes carrying him much easier. As we walk, I notice an abundance of grass and vegetation. I had wondered if it would be possible, seeing the floating Capital from below. A lot of it almost looks like algae. That causes me to hypothesize so many things. Was it heat that allowed this city to float? I'm surprised by the tower. I would have expected the city to be in the shape of a sphere. It must have taken years to build, as they probably had to watch weight distribution with each new level. Unless it was built on the ground, but it would still require great alterations in order to sustain levitation on a long-term basis.

"Here it is. There's a table inside that you can set your clopil on while I get the rarefication device ready."

"Thank you, Barren." I'm so relieved to be able to work on Vex, but worried for him at the same time. While he can be annoying when spouting off what's protocol or not, he's always been a presence in my life, and that means a lot to me right now. Part of me feels lost in a body that's not my own, on a planet I've never been to before, without my parents, and with a missing brother out there whom I've never met.

I set Vex down, using a cloth I find on the table to wipe away any liquid I see. I continually rotate him to find more. Luckily, the flight on the parrot stripped some of the moisture out, but he's still not responding. Barren rolls up the device. It's a bit different from any I've seen before.

"Where do you get your power supply?" I ask Barren.

"We run mostly on solar and wind energy here."

That makes sense. I review the best points of entry for suction tube application and begin the first step in rarefication. It will pull the air and moisture out in a tiered process. I connect the diagnosis machine to Vex' hard drive, but there's still system failure. I initiate the second suction, allowing it to reach deeper. Diagnosis notification beeps ring out, but we're not in the clear yet. I run a third process and the green that appears on the machine causes me to smile.

"Vienna, I must increase the rate at which my waterproof shields raise."

"Vex, buddy, what you need to do is rest for a bit. I'm so glad you're okay."

"I told 'you' there were many dangers on your path."

"Yes, yes, you did." Same old Vex. I smile, glad that he seems to be okay, but continue full diagnostics to be sure I haven't missed anything.

"Hey, you're pretty good at that," Barren says to me.

"Thank you." *I think.*

"We're a self-sustained city. Perhaps you can work in the warehouse as well as help take down the facility while you're here in the Capital."

"Can Vex help me?"

"Sure, I don't see why that would be an issue."

"What's Marrit's job at the Capital?"

"I thought you had figured that out. She's our spy." Barren smiles.

"For real? Should you be telling me that?"

"Never been good at secret keeping."

"What do you do here?"

"I'm search and rescue, but I also double as a farmer."

"Do you recirculate water for irrigation?"

"That and, another reason we chose Planet Scepter, we can gather water after a rainstorm by drifting near the jungle tree-tops to collect."

So this isn't Marrit's home planet.

"What protection do you have from storms?"

"We store air to use as resistance."

"What about the temperature changes?"

"You sure have a lot of questions for a newcomer."

"Sorry. So what do we do now?"

Barren walks to the door and peeks outside, looking at the

sky. Then he looks me up and down. "You need to make a visit to Nobilia so you can get cleaned up before dinner."

My jaw drops. Great. It was one thing to have Theopat braid my hair on Vortex, but I'm not really the kind of person who visits beauticians.

"You'll love it. Nobilia makes everyone's hair look wonderful and there's a whole inventory of everything you need there, cosmetology and fashion-wise."

He's gently nudging me out the door. I look back at Vex.

"Don't worry. I'll watch over your clopil while you're gone."

"That's not what I'm worried about. Do I really have to see Nobilia?"

He looks me up and down again. "Yes, it's non-negotiable. It's not just for looks, silly. Didn't you notice that Marrit's clothes were impermeable to the elements?"

"Well, if that's part of the trip, I guess I can go."

"Great. Now, follow this path. It's the third door on the right."

And with that, I'm outside of the warehouse and Barren closes the door.

I look behind me and see the aqua wall that I believe extends around the entire perimeter of the Capital. I turn back to the path and see that it leads to the soft yellow, glowing tower. I take one last look at the warehouse, noticing that it's made of what appears to be bioplastic. There's a bed of algae in front. I take a few steps down the path, soaking in my surroundings.

I've been to an alien planet. Even Earth has progressed and is reasonably advanced. But the next sight makes me realize how limited my universal travel really has been. A couple of green, teardrop-shaped structures float just beyond a fence like rain-drops suspended in the air. Surrounding them on the ground appear to be robotic arms similar to Kitchen and Closet but not as fluid. There are rows and lines of them with what appear to be hydrogen tanks. It's a manufacturing assembly line. I place my hand on the gate to open it and investigate, but an alarm beeps.

"Restricted area. Please show your credentials."

I guess I won't be venturing that way.

The next building appears to be a school. Kids are running around a playground screaming and full of smiles. Maybe I could just hang out with them instead of going to Nobilia's. I reach for the gate but again hear an alarm beep.

"Please place your teacher, student, or parent identification tattoo under the scanner."

Uh, the mention of tattoo reminds me of landing on Vortex and the disappearing ink tattoos given to the selected without their permission or even knowledge. I walk to the third door. The building's walls are silver curves structured like waves. I reach my hand for the gate, but it opens automatically. The path leading to the front door feels more like a glass tunnel. The walkway itself is like soft rubber. It's red and curves its way to the building.

The entryway is quite grand. Faux stone steps lead to the entrance. They're lined with shaped potted shrubs. The door opens when I'm halfway up the stairs and I'm greeted by who I imagine to be Nobilia. Brilliantly colored feathers are before me, perfectly set with a spike of feather at the back of Nobilia's head.

"Welcome to The Salon of Nobilia. I'm Nobilia." The parrot extends a wing for me to shake.

"Hi, I'm Sierra." I shake the wing gently, careful not to ruffle any feathers.

"What do we have here?" Nobilia walks around me, assessing today's victim.

Then the parrot's clapping wings together and giving

demands. Humanoid assistants materialize with utensils, garments, and things I've never seen before.

"We need a hairbrush. Get better boots for day-to-day but for tonight let's have heels."

I lift my hand. "Um, I've never worn heels."

"We're going to need a miracle."

My face warms.

"Where did you get these clothes? They do nothing for you and are not in the least flattering. They make you look like a box."

My face warms even more. Um, the mad scientist who implanted my conscience and memory into this non-bio body is the one who chose this outfit.

"They were the clothes I was wearing when I woke up on this planet."

Nobilia's eyes get huge.

"I'm not against new clothes."

The parrot smiles, and it seems kind. Maybe this won't be so bad. But then I turn around and see sequins, bright colors, dresses, and heels.

"I think I forgot something outside."

"Oh, no, you don't!"

Some of the assistants block my path to the door. I take a deep breath and turn back around with my eyes shut.

"Tell me when it's over."

The sounds of scissors, zippers, and other devices of torture are all around me. They hand me outfits and I try them on without looking in the mirrors until they've decided on one.

"I love what the peplum hem does to her figure," I hear Nobilia say and instantly wonder what peplum means.

"Can you handle a long train?" Nobilia asks but I hear feathers rustle in response to the horrible pucker that develops in my facial muscles.

"Get the strappy heels," I hear Nobilia tell a helper. I hope this is almost over.

I tell them to decide, otherwise I'm going to wear what I came here in. They size my feet and put shoes on them, but I don't dare look. Then there's hustling and bustling throughout the place until it goes silent and I open my eyes.

One of my shoulders is exposed, accentuating a diamond necklace. I barely recognize my new self. I look like one of the models in holograph ads. I touch my face to be sure it's still the new me, then notice my leg muscles. The dress has a cut on the side that exposes my leg. I've never seen my new legs look this muscular, not even hiking through the jungle. It must be the heels. Looking at the straps, I wonder how long it will be before I break them.

"Oh…My…Goodness…we did it. It's a miracle."

"I…uh…ahem…Can my old things be delivered to wherever I'm staying tonight?"

"Oh, I burned those…sorry, not sorry." Nobilia says. "Trust me, you'll want the new hiking gear. It's tougher."

"I do not believe your definition of trust matches mine." But looking in the pack of gear I notice the same impermeable clothes Marrit and Barren wore, waterproof boots, and useful gadgets filling every pocket. I find myself smiling at Nobilia despite everything.

"Just wait until everyone gets a look at you tonight. You'll see."

"Everyone?"

"Why yes. The whole town's coming to meet the guest of honor who is also going to get rid of the horrible facility."

"That's it. I'm out."

I march or try to march…not sure how to do that in heels to the door. One of the assistants moves to stop me, but the look I give him is enough to make him halt. I have to slow down for the steps but pick the speed back up once I'm on the path. The gate must have a sensor because it opens automatically as I approach. I head to the warehouse so I can chew out Barren or Marrit for deceiving me, but a group of the Capital citizens stop me.

"The dining hall's this way. Follow us."

Not until I've had a chance to yell at someone.

"I need to go make sure my clopil is all right."

"Your clopil will be just fine. You don't want to be late."

We walk down the path faster than I walked to the salon. I'm unable to view the properties we pass because I'm looking at my feet, trying not to fall in these stupid heels. It doesn't matter, because as we near the tower it takes all of my attention. It's hard not to stare at the tall structure. Before I know it we've arrived. The group heads in the front door and I follow them.

"Oh no, VIPs enter up there." They point to stairs that lead to a door one floor up.

"Really?"

They shake their heads up and down in unison.

Walking upstairs in a dress and heels has got to be one of the most not-bright things to do. I open the door but I'm too blinded by light to see beyond it. As my eyes adjust, I notice that the stairs merely gave access to another set of stairs. They wind down to the dining hall to allow for VIP grand entrances. I'm so afraid I'll trip. Then I look across the way to the other side of the dining hall and my breath catches. Marrit's hair is curled and half of it is pulled back. She smiles, and it's as if her hair is a frame. Her dress is knockout gorgeous, a sleeveless black thing with a pattern that looks as if a beautiful, gold crown was turned upside down and imprinted on the material. Then she looks at me, raises her eyebrows, and nods in approval. For the fourth time today, my face warms.

8
PLANET EARTH

Al

Proxima Centauri B quickly whips by almost faster than the naked eye can catch, and I know I'm getting close. More planets follow while I continue at superluminal speed. Then I see the Heliosphere's radiant light and the Oort Cloud's milky mist. I've heard some people experience adverse effects traveling via the Fifth Dimension Friction Inhibitors and the warp drive, but it's a rush for me. Outside is a beautiful darkness pierced by streams of light while I drive through contracting space-time. That being said, I do appreciate when the shuttle slows down and I'm able to see Earth, even though this wasn't my intended destination. I've missed Vienna, Albina, and Viscerous. It'll be cogging nice to see them again.

"Please state your full name," Ground Control barks over the connection.

"Name's Al Dandrige."

"We don't have a landing scheduled for a shuttle your size,

Al. You'll have to park it at The World Government Space Station."

"Should I take a taxi from there to the elevator?"

"Unfortunately, the elevator's full. We're going to need you to make a Spacedive."

I've conquered my fear of being near Vortex vultures, but falling that far isn't exactly on my bucket list.

"Are you there, Al? We need to confirm your plans."

How can I get out of this?

"Hello?"

I clear my throat.

"Are you sure the dive is the only option?"

"It's that or stay at the Station until clearance is granted."

"When would that be?"

"I'd expect in three days."

"That's too long. May I have a minute to consider?"

Cog it all, Al. You can do this. Quit being a scaredy-cat.

"Al?"

"Yes, I'll do it."

We're interrupted by a moment of static. Instead of the normal sounds I'm accustomed to hearing over these kinds of connections, I hear clicks and unusual noises. Have I lost connection? A short, high-pitched sound squeals through and then I hear the voice of Ground Control again.

"Wait, I've just gotten word that a spot has opened up on the elevator."

Hey, a turn in the right direction!

"That's good. You're a lifesaver, man."

Aligning the shuttle to the World Docking Adapter goes smoothly. Perhaps I should have stuck to the engineering industry like my dad and not sought a medical career. Maybe I could have been navigating different space routes and traveling to different jobs instead of being held at Planet Vortex. I give my head a shake to clear my thoughts. As I lock into the space station, I get a sudden pang of homesickness for Planet Vortex. Instead of just shaking my head, I slap it with my hand. Who would miss Vortex?

Waiting for the taxi takes an eternity. I've heard Earth had originally planned on connecting the elevator to the station, but that proved dangerous. The thought of it makes me consider the safety of the elevator itself. But hell, anything has got to be better than a Spacedive! Finally, I've made it to the elevator.

"Phoenix Station, correct?" the attendant asks. "That's what the coordinates imported from your shuttle indicated."

"That's right," I respond. What else did they see?

I take in Earth's layout as we descend. When there's reprieve from the blinding sun, I'm able to see clouds with land and water below. The clouds remind me of the fog that rolled over the pond near my childhood home on Funen. Where normally there would be the green of vegetation, I see unnatural colors. I've heard and viewed footage of Industrial Earth 2.0 as Vienna refers to it, but this is the first time I've seen a planet stripped of its organic colors, all of them replaced with artificial ones. Something about it doesn't feel right.

Once my journey is complete and I'm on Earth, I realize that I don't know my exact destination.

"Ahem, hey, man, can you tell me where the nearest directory is?" I ask the attendant.

"Directory?"

He gives me a confused look.

"You know, how you find out where someone lives, or a business is located," I say.

"Oh, you need a clopil guide."

He points to a covered parking lot full of clopils. This planet just keeps getting weirder and weirder. As I approach the lot, a dozen of them turn in my direction. I look one directly in its eyepiece and ask, "Could you please take me to Dr. Marie Perierat's residence?"

"I can provide enough details here. No need to escort. Is this for business? Do you require a session? The office would be better than her residence."

"Do I look like I need a session?"

I swear the dang thing manages to roll its eyepiece while making a sound like an exasperated breath.

"You won't need me to guide you. It's almost an hour public transit gliding pod ride away, near downtown. Here's the apartment building."

The clopil projects a photo of the building Vienna lives in and I memorize its features and address.

"Where's the public transport gliding pod station?"

"Just over that way." The clopil pivots to the right before continuing. "The next one leaves in five minutes. I'd skedaddle if I were you."

Did that clopil just say skedaddle? I run to the station.

I board and take the first window seat available in order to people-watch and study this new planet as we go. When we move, I'm able to see why they refer to the vehicle as a glider because it's as smooth as a voltball pass made perfectly over the heads of the defense and right into the arms of the receiver. Mechanical advertisements suspend in the air in more engineered colors. When I make direct eye contact with an advertisement, though, it says "recalibrating." That's odd. Robot helpers different from the clopils seem to be everywhere along the streets and I also see the poli-magnos Vienna had mentioned. They're like a cross between the loud Vortex railcars and hover bikes, except they're shaped more like boxes. It's all so strange.

I wish we could be on Funen instead of here. I'll have to take Vienna there after we save her mom and find her brother. It's so much more natural. A person is one with the environment there. I wonder if it's safe from government officials yet. Is anywhere safe?

A buzz vibrates through my bionic limbs as if they can sense my excitement and nervousness as I step onto the street in front of her home. A man in a business suit trips and falls in front of me. Then a woman offers her hand in assistance. Perhaps Earth's not as bad as it originally seemed.

Before I'm able to enter the apartment building, Vienna exits and the look she gives me has me feeling like fireflies are swarming in my belly. She runs up to me and gives me a hug, not just a regular embrace, but one with her arms fully wrapped around my neck. I put my arms around her waist, holding back my urge to lift her up entirely and carry her. Before I can give in to it, she pulls her head back to take a look at me.

"What are you doing here, Al?"

She peck-kisses me on the cheek, but concern clouds her face.

"You should be on your way to go help my mom."

She peck-kisses my other cheek.

"Where's Yesha?"

She looks around.

"It's a long story. Can we go inside and talk?"

Before stepping back, she places a hand on the side of my face where the burn is still healing from the flame-throwing club during the revolt. She softly rubs her finger next to the burn. I wish I could take the look of pity out of her eyes. It's not that big of a deal.

I grab her hand and she leads me inside. When we enter the apartment, I'm surprised by the number of voices I hear. I had expected her dad, Viscerous, Albina, and Theopat, but there are three more people that I had not foreseen. Being with Viscerous and Albina again causes tears to brim my eyes. Their eyes mirror mine as they approach and give me a hug. Septimus' handshake is strong, and he pats my arm, giving me an awkward hug. Vienna uses sign language while speaking to introduce me to a small teenage girl named Harper. Then she introduces me to a girl who could probably be on a multidimensional prism magazine cover. Her name's Milcah and when I look a second too long, Vienna's eyebrows scrunch together. Then a stocky guy pats me on the arm like Septimus did except he almost knocks the wind out of me. Vienna tells me his name is Danver. Theopat approaches next.

"How's Colsam?" she asks.

Vienna's jaw clenches. She's probably wondering why Theopat isn't asking about her brother like I am.

"Colsam's got everything under control on Planet Vortex," I say, but doubt enters my mind as I envision the guards waking from their induced sleep.

Albina seems to pick up on my concern.

"You'll never guess what's new with me and Viscerous," she says to me.

"Oh, what's that?"

"We're outlaws," he answers before she can.

"You're what?"

Albina's upset by my concern.

"No worries, kid. We'll lie low. It's not that big of a deal. We're working to get it all cleared up."

I fume, but Vienna gently grabs my arm and nudges me out of the kitchen.

"Remember that long story you owe me."

"Yeah, but…"

"No buts!"

The second we're in her room and the door's closed, she wraps her arms around me and smooches me all over my face. Where did this come from? I don't care. I remember the way she blushed in our lab on Vortex. I'm lifting her like I've always wanted to do and walking to her bed before I even know what I'm doing. I finally kiss her the way I've dreamed about for so long. I let all my worries fade away.

I try setting her on the bed as softly as I can. She kisses me back, more deeply and with more passion. I grip her long, wavy, dark copper hair the way I've imagined night after night while stuck in lockdown at the facility. She wraps her legs around my waist and I lose all sense of composure. Then she puts her hands up my shirt and runs her fingers down my back. Next, she's pulling my body closer to hers with one hand while the other's at the nape of my neck. She stops kissing me to take in a breath of air, so I run my lips over her ear.

But we're interrupted by a knock on the door, which luckily is securely closed. It draws me out of the blissful state and puts me in one of worry. Is Colsam okay? He handled himself just fine over the years at Vortex. I'm sure he's fine. Albina and Viscerous are outlaws. They've been in worse positions than they are in now, a million times over. Vienna and I are finally somewhere private. There are no guards. We're not in imminent danger.

"Vienna?" It's Septimus, Vienna's dad. Perhaps we're not as free as I'd thought.

9

PLANET EARTH

Vienna

THAT'S IT. I'M GETTING MY OWN APARTMENT.

So many times I had longed for my dad to knock on my door instead of being gone. Much of that time, I had craved any interaction with him at all, or to perform an experiment together just once more. But right now, I really wish he weren't knocking on my door.

I remember Al's hand brushing my forehead when he moved the hair out of my eyes at the stem cell harvesting center. I recall the feeling of pure bliss when we finally kissed. His strong, bionic hand on the back of my neck had sent tingles throughout my entire body. We've finally been able to reunite, but now we're interrupted.

"Yes, Dad?"

"I'm going to have lunch with Dave. He went to the Mojave Desert with us, remember?"

"Oh, yeah, have a good lunch."

"I'll try."

I hear the resignation in his voice. Ever since Cromwell's rumors regarding my dad spread throughout the medical community, people have been turning against Septimus. It's not fair. My dad was not behind the evil on Planet Vortex. He was the one fighting against it, and Cromwell knew that. He's also managed to bring false charges against all of the witnesses of Septimus' bravery. The thought of it brings me back to when we discovered the news of Albina and Viscerous. We learned about the academy drafts at the same time.

Al kisses me again once we're certain my dad's walked far enough down the hall, but against every particle of my body's will, I push away.

"They've enacted an academy draft, Al. I think Cromwell's behind it too. We need to find out why he's still coming after us. We need to get my brother."

He gently lowers his hand to my shoulder and rubs.

"We'll figure something out," he says.

"I'm so glad you're here."

I've pulled him into a hug, but then extend my arms to look at him again.

"You still owe me that long story."

"So, about that…Yesha programmed my ship to come here instead of going to Planet Scepter…she plans to kill Cromwell."

Shock hits me first and then I think of my badass friend Yesha attacking Cromwell and can't hold back a smile.

"Oh no, Vienna, you don't understand. She almost pushed the kill switch on all the guards. I think she's lost it. The rage over losing her brother has taken control. I don't even think she heard me when I told her that your mom and clone need donor cells."

I stand up and pace. We're up against so much. But I remember what I learned on Vortex…never go it alone. Here

I've been annoyed by all the people crammed into the apartment, but maybe they've been the answer all along.

"We need to make a plan," I say.

"And you're telling me from step one?"

Al slaps the back of his hand to his forehead and play-faints, falling back onto the bed.

"We need to figure out what Cromwell's purpose is," I say.

"I did find something in his desk on Vortex that may be of use."

"Did he leave anything behind?"

"Well, he did have to exit in a hurry."

"Because someone insisted on revolting." I fold my arms in front of my chest and give him "the look."

He puts both hands up, palms facing me in surrender.

"It's okay. I understand…kind of," I say.

I put a hand on his shoulder.

"It doesn't include everything but I think I may have found something."

"What did he leave out?"

"Your mom."

"Oh."

"But I did find backup plans."

"Backup." I raise my voice, unable to contain myself. "I'm pretty sure he got his way. He believes he removed part of my brain and implanted it into a non-bio so his son's brain parts could be put in my body. Luckily for me, you thought of cloning. But he got my mom, Al! What could he possibly need a cogging backup plan for?"

"Every action he's taken seems to support his backup plan."

I huff.

"Think about it—another facility, damaging your dad's career, discrediting Viscerous and Albina…" Al says.

"And the academy drafts…into the World Government Military Branch," I add.

"We also know now that Cromwell's reach is well beyond the Planet Vortex government."

"Let's gather everyone together."

I open the door. I know Dad's gone, but we need to get a plan in place. I can't sit around doing nothing with this knowledge. Al follows me. Albina's in the room best suited to fit us all, the living room.

"Can you bring Viscerous and Danver to the living room? I think they're in the kitchen."

"Sure, no problem," Al says.

I head to my mom's…well now my dad's…whatever, room. Anger consumes me. It should be *their* room because they should be together.

Theopat filled my closet and now she's working on Mom's. She saved a foot-wide spot for Dad's clothes. The rest he has to keep in the dresser instead. Currently, she's yelling from Mom's closet.

"No, no, no. I do not want clothes organized by seasons. I want them organized by color. I want all the blues together in one spot."

My eyes are drawn to Milcah and Harper when I step into the room. They're sitting on my mom's bed so close there isn't much space between them. Milcah tucks some hair behind Harper's ear.

"Ahem."

"Oh, Vienna." Milcah flashes a crooked smile.

She's been growing on me, but I'm not ready to trust her with my best friend since childhood.

"Vienna, this closet is broken," Theopat chimes in.

"We can work on that later. Al and I need you all in the living room."

"Fine," Theopat grumbles.

Theopat exits the bedroom.

"What's up now?" Milcah asks on her way out.

I put my hand on Harper's arm so she slows her pace.

Be careful, I sign to Harper.

Everything's fine, she signs back.

This is Milcah we're talking about!

Our conversation ends as we enter the living room.

"Please turn off the game, Albina," Al asks, and she complies after seeing the serious look on his face.

"Ah, how cute, are you two announcing your engagement or something?" Theopat asks, clasping her hands together.

"Um, we're kind of in the middle of a crisis right now if you haven't noticed," is the only way I'm able to respond, but I'm unable to hide my blush.

"We need to put a plan together because Cromwell's up to his old tricks again. We're not sure why he is, but we do know we're going to need your help."

"Are you sure it's this Cromwell guy?" Danver asks. "Could it just be a coincidence?"

Al and I look at each other and then in unison say, "No, it's definitely him."

"Al saw some of his backup plans and they match the current activity pretty closely."

"Sounds like voltball game planning. I'm in. Let me know how I can help."

"Good. Thanks, Danver." The surprise in my voice is hard to conceal.

"Viscerous, did we bring any documented evidence from the Vortex facility?" Al asks.

"We were a little preoccupied with getting people off Vortex safely."

"We might be able to hack into the system," Albina counters.

"That would be good. If we have evidence, we can clear your names and salvage what's left of my dad's reputation."

"We also need to study Cromwell's past endeavors to try to get a better understanding of his possible future ones," Al adds.

"Um, you said you need everyone here. What do you need Danver, Harper, and me for? We weren't on Vortex," Milcah says.

"Glad you mentioned that. I need you to help me find my brother. Your mom's on the academy board and probably involved in the draft."

What about me? Harper asks.

I need you to get Dr. McPike on our side to support my dad. I sign in response.

"And me?" Danver asks.

"You're our decoy. We need to keep those after us on the wrong path."

I'm so relieved Yesha's on Scepter to save Mom.

———

I'm appeased that the meeting took place without a hitch, but I can't help thinking we're two steps behind. Meditation is what I need. And instead of trying to see what my clone, Sierra, is doing, I need to communicate with my mom. She must be warned that her non-bio body needs donor cells.

`Mom, can you hear me?`

I wait for what seems like forever.

`Who is this?` a confused voice responds. The voice sounds like my clone's non-bio, I realize.

Oh, shit!

`This can't be right…Damien?` My clone's non-bio voice continues.

I panic and mentally cut off the connection. What she heard must have sounded like her old body. The only thing fathomable to her would be Damien reaching out. What a mess!

Even if I'd tried to tell her about the need for donor cells, she'd think it was Damien playing a trick on her, trying to get her to enter the facility…that's what *I'd* think.

After that, I definitely have to meditate. I bend my legs into the butterfly sitting position, straighten my back, and close my eyes. This time, instead of moving vines and leaves, it seems like my clone's at a higher elevation. Clouds appear at eye level. It's almost magical. When my clone looks down, instead of a mesmerizing landscape, I see that Sierra's now in some gaudy dress. Crisis, people, crisis! We're in the middle of an absolute emergency and my clone's playing dress-up. My anger abruptly ends my meditation. I need to calm down.

I attempt to meditate the way I used to back before any of this. Back when the worst trouble I was ever in was detention. I breathe in, feeling my lungs expand as far as they can. I breathe out until my chest is compressed (back to the dream of a hundred plus years ago). The vision's different this time. It's still Al before bionic limbs, Viscerous before arterial relocation, Albina before pigment extraction, and me. We all look so beautiful, young, and naïve. Why do I keep having visions of us so far in the past?

We're all sitting at an old, wooden table (the like hasn't existed in years) drinking coffee. Something seems familiar. Maybe it reminds me of a time when we were sitting at the cafeteria tables on Vortex. Why would that be? Then, in the vision, Al from the past takes a sip of coffee and looks at past Viscerous and Albina. Then instead of looking at me, he looks at the table for so long it's as if a whole book is written on it. That's when it clicks. His face had looked like that once. It was when he was planning to clone me behind my back. Perhaps the meeting in the living room went too well. I'm going to need to keep tabs on him. I do not need another clone!

Now that the vision has ended, I move to close meditation, bringing my focus to the present. Then I'm jolted from that by a new vision that is quite blurry. What I'm able to capture is nothing like what existed a hundred years ago. It's not even in digital textbooks, it's ancient.

The girl in front of me is close to a mirror image except for short, tightly cropped, and curled hair. She's wearing a dress with fringe at knee level. A woman looking like Albina is wearing the same style. The guys are sporting something between a tux and a suit. Their hair's slicked back. We're at a loud and flashy party. It's as if these people are celebrating like it might be their last chance to do so. There's a precious innocence residing within the bright lights and fast music. It brings a warmth that causes me to smile.

Then the sea of people parts, allowing a figure to walk through. A sudden weight seems to settle on the group. I recognize who the man resembles immediately…Cromwell. Instead of a lab coat, he's wearing a tidy straw hat, a suit, and using a cane. What can this mean?

PLANET SCEPTER

Sierra

I HOLD THE RAILING AS I DESCEND THE STAIRS, NOT caring whether it's the proper thing to do. Falling and putting myself out of commission is not something I'd like to deal with right now. My ankle wobbles in the strappy heels without the support of sturdy boots or even plain flat shoes. The glint of the subtly lit chandeliers grabs my attention and my foot slips on the next stair, causing my heart to pound in my chest and my grip on the railing to become as strong as lockjaw. After slowing to a snaillike pace, I finally reach the bottom and I'm able to look at the beauty who descended the other set of stairs, Marrit. She's waited at the bottom of her steps while I finished trying not to trip down mine. Embarrassment floods me like a broken dam, but I manage to keep from blushing.

She and I turn to approach one another, but as I'm walking, I hear my old voice in my head. How can that be? The only thing that can make sense is for it to be coming from the person who has their memory and conscience implanted into my body. It must be Damien, but how did he figure out this communication style? How will I speak to Mom in secret now? I almost stumble on my own feet at the thought and fall to the ground, but a sumptuous, sleeveless arm catches me. Memories flash through my mind. Thoughts of green, northern-light-eyes distract me for a second, but then I correct myself so I can focus on the hazel eyes right in front of me.

"Easy there," Marrit says.

"Thanks," is all I manage to squeak back.

"Are you up for talking to the citizens?" she asks.

I clear my throat and look around. A sea of expectant eyes stares back at me.

"Just because I have some knowledge of the last facility doesn't mean I'll be able to help you much with this one."

"You offer more than what we have available without you."

"Yeah, I'm such an expert that you had to save me last time we were near the premises."

"You helped us learn something then too."

"You're preposterous."

I hear a stream of clicks. Vex rolls up with Barren walking beside him.

"Well, you healed fast," I say to Vex.

"I couldn't keep him in the warehouse. He kept insisting he had to be with you. Something about dangers in your path," Barren says.

"Protocol clearly states that I should be with you, Sierra," Vex says.

"Okay, Vex. You can be with me."

"Great, are you ready?" Marrit asks me.

"For what?" I ask.

Instead of responding, she winks at me and then turns to speak to the many citizens before us through a floating drone microphone in front of her.

"Capital Citizens, I'm tired of the facility taking up space here on Planet Scepter. They steal vital resources and kidnap our loved ones."

The crowd yells things I don't understand, but Barren lifts his hands in the air and silence replaces the noise.

"This is Sierra. She survived and helped to end the last facility."

All eyes turn in my direction and my mouth goes dry. I hear a hollow sound and my vision narrows. Then there's warmth on my shoulders. A glass of water is placed in my hand. Taking a sip brings me back to normal breathing and vision. Marrit places her arm over my shoulders again and tingles of confidence spread through my body.

"Hi! What Marrit says is true but too kind," I say to the group. "We did bring an end to the facility, but at a great cost. And all it did was force the leaders to move to a different location."

I hear a couple of beeps and then see illumination beside me. Vex is projecting Planet Vortex documentation and the calm and settled feeling has abandoned me.

Seeing Viscerous and Albina in the lab, Rigled in the arena, and Al in the cafeteria has so many familiar emotions rushing through my body—joy, fear, and love. It's been so long it seems like forever.

Marrit gently taps me on the arm and points to a table with five people seated at it. We join Barren in sitting with them.

"These are the head council members," Barren whispers.

We remain silent as Vex continues. Seeing the first non-bio that I ever met, Charlie, puts me right back on Vortex, at least I feel like I'm there. I find myself taking a deep breath just as I did back then. Marrit holds my hand. Instead of tingles, I sense grounding, which I desperately need. Then Vex shows the stem cell harvesting center. I still remember being awestruck at the sight of the metal tree with a web for a crown. Next, Vex shows my Aviator and the pain in my chest forces me to turn away. I spot Nobilia waving at me ever so slightly. A tear rolls down my cheek as I wave back. I'm filled with gratitude as soon as Vex is done. How did he get all of this footage?

"If Cromwell regained his family, why has he constructed a facility here?" a council member asks me.

"Yes, why go through all the trouble?" another council member asks. "Why not enjoy his family now that he finally has them back?"

"Unfortunately, I think this means it hasn't worked out the way he intended for his family so he's searching for answers," I say as I fidget with my ridiculous dress.

"Oh dear, and after what you all sacrificed," a third council member says. Her hand flies to her mouth as she gasps.

Marrit slams her glass down on the table, not hard enough to break it, but loud enough to get the attention of everyone at the table.

"We need to put together a team to stop this madman," Marrit proclaims.

She lifts herself inches from her chair, but Barren pulls her back down.

"Not so fast," the third council member says.

They discuss strategy and who is best fit for what.

"You look pale," a council member says to me. "Please get her some more water."

It's all so quick and so much that it becomes a blur, and before I know it I'm out of the dress, and in weatherproof hiking gear and boots, thank goodness.

"What are we supposed to be doing?" I ask.

I find myself with Vex and a group of people similarly dressed.

"We're going to stop the facility." Barren gives me an odd look.

Wow, that was strange. It was almost like I lost some time there. Cromwell said robotic bloodstream inhibitors for adaptation would be injected into this non-bio. Not just that. He said he'd also be incorporating healing adaptation. So why am I showing signs of Transient Epileptic Amnesia?

"You sure you're up for this?" Marrit asks.

"She has to be," Barren says. "All of the Capital is relying on her. Rest up, everyone. We'll fly the parrots down to Scepter at dawn."

No pressure!

———

In the morning, we walk to the parrot landing site, or at least this is where we landed when we arrived here.

"Royce, Jordan, this is Sierra and Vex," Barren says. "While she has knowledge of the facility, she is just a novice in tactical matters." Marrit slaps him on the arm. "The clopil has documented footage of another facility."

"What Barren's trying to say is that during our trek it would be nice if we could exchange information and train each other," Marrit says.

A beautifully fierce woman with a shaved head steps forward and offers her hand to shake. "Name's Jordan. Hi, Vex." She waves with her other hand.

I extend my hand and am surprised, though I should be used to it by now when she pulls me in for a bearhug.

Next, the man I assume is named Royce steps forward and extends his hand. I'm prepared for the bearhug this time. Both of them are quite muscular. I bet their tactical training level is expert. I hope I'm able to learn something from them, but I don't remember the trek taking that long.

"Um, Marrit, how long do we need to travel?"

"Well, the Capital had moved closer so I could perform surveillance on the facility but with the guards chasing us and being too close to the perimeter, the Capital moved farther away," Marrit says.

"How far?" I ask.

"Two hundred miles or so," Marrit says.

"Two hundred what? How? I didn't even feel us move!" I'm shocked.

"My calculations confirm this measurement," Vex interjects.

"Why didn't you tell me, Vex?" I ask.

Five parrots land next to us. None of them are Nobilia. I get it. It's not exactly Nobilia's thing, taxiing citizens to Scepter, but I miss the parrot anyhow.

Marrit and Royce pet a couple of the parrots. Barren jumps on another parrot's back.

"Mount up," Barren says. "I fitted your saddle with an extra seat."

Marrit clasps her hands together to form a step for me and I board. Next, she helps Vex mount behind me.

Everyone else appears to be ready to go and in the next moment, we're flying again. I'm glad when we don't land right away. It would be so much easier traveling two hundred miles by air instead of by foot. But I don't want to get too close. I remember when a guard heard Aviator flying me and it put her in danger.

As my parrot glides to the left, all worry leaves me. I feel free for just a second. Once again, I'm mesmerized by the greenery below. It seems to move and breathe with the planet itself. Vines sway in the wind and leaves move of their own accord, almost following jungle animals as if whispering rumors to each other. Thinking of jungle animals reminds me of the alligator. What else lies below?

Royce signals to Jordan and then points down. They descend. Barren and Marrit follow with my own parrot not far behind.

"My data scanners show we still have one hundred and sixty miles to go," Vex says once we've all landed.

And I'm back to making rope out of tropical milkweed. As I'm tying it around Vex, Barren stops me. He hands me what looks like a baby carrier of sorts.

"I thought we could all take turns carrying Vex on our backs," Barren says.

Marrit, Royce, and Jordan nod in approval and something about this small gesture makes me feel at home. I'm not at home though, and neither is my mom. Why did Cromwell keep her and let me go? How am I going to get her out? How am I going to help these people get rid of another facility?

And so our hike begins. The calming sound of river rapids provides a background music for our walk.

"I think the best place to cross the river is a quarter of a mile west of here," Royce says.

"The foliage is pretty thick on the way there," Jordan adds.

"Brought the machete," Marrit says with a coy smile in my direction.

I can't help but smile back.

"Let me have a turn with Vex," Barren says.

It's nice to have a team to share the weight.

"Watch out for snakes. They're larger on Planet Scepter than anywhere else I've ever been," says Jordan.

"Yeah, but at least they glow here, so you should be able to spot them," adds Royce.

"Are they electric like the gators?" I ask.

"You've seen a gator?" Jordan asks.

"Um, yeah, sparks flew from its spikes every time it rose out of the water," I say.

"That was when we escaped the deranged guards," Marrit adds.

"And I saved you," Barren adds with a grin.

We cut our way through the moving plants. Actually, we only have to hack ten feet. After that they part all on their own, ribbons floating away from us in the wind. Marrit's ahead of me and once again I'm able to see the sun glinting off her auburn hair. The river sounds closer, but there's another noise interfering. It sounds like a paper stuck in a fan but louder, almost like a jackhammer. Royce stops and taps on Jordan's shoulder. They look at each other, but I can only see them for a second. The light becomes too much. The leaves turn more and more neon, brighter and brighter. The sun's rays beam through the jungle canopy stronger and stronger. A breeze rolls in and with it, the light grows almost like the meditation circles. And then, wham, there's nothing but darkness and I fall.

Marrit's gasping and I think Barren's coughing. Through blurry eyes, I see Jordan and Royce pointing to a short rock bridge of sorts. It's not really a bridge, more like a dried-up waterfall. We should be able to use it to cross, but what just happened? Was that a blackout? Finally, my vision clears.

"Are you okay?" Marrit asks. Her hands are on my cheeks.

"Yeah, are you?" I place a hand on her forearm.

Barren stands, brushing off his clothes. Royce seems to be checking the perimeter, looking in every direction.

"Found it." Jordan holds up a beetle the size of her fist. I can't help but shiver at the sight.

"Were you looking for a beetle?" I ask. "That's kind of gross."

"No, Sierra, that's what caused our blackout."

"Maybe now would be a good time to teach her and prepare her for the dangers," Barren says.

Beeps follow. "Yes, and I'm able to record in order to program alarms and alerts for precarious situations," Vex says.

Overhead, jet propulsions shake the leaves. The sound becomes louder and louder. I spot a shuttle and gasp. I've seen a shuttle like that before!

11

PLANET EARTH

Al

As Vienna meditates, I call Colsam. "How'd they take it?"

"Many bought the glitch in the system idea, but they've also noticed that you and Yesha both disappeared. Rumors are flying, man. Pretty soon they're going to connect us and ask me questions."

"Release them."

"What?"

"I've found a way to clear everyone's name." And I need to get them away from the guards still working for Cromwell. The last thing we need is for the scientists and guards to become prisoners there or at another facility.

"How?"

"One of Vienna's friends, Harper, found a way to hack the system. She's cleared the false charges and reinstated medical licenses." Watching her maneuver the legal database was impressive.

"That's cogging, great, Al. Wait, one of Vienna's friends... how'd they get to Scepter?"

"Yeah, so about that...I'm on Earth. Yesha reprogrammed my ship..."

"She's a loose cannon, that one."

"Right, so I'm making the best of it here. At least we've made some progress for things on Vortex."

"I can go see my family! It's been so long."

"I think there's also someone here who would like to see you."

"Hey, I love you too, man, but family's family."

"No gomer, Theopat's been asking about you a lot."

There's a pause.

"Anyone else?"

"Actually, there is something I could use your help with," I say, changing the subject.

"You weren't even expecting to be on Earth...I'm guessing you've already developed some kind of plan that you're needing help with..."

"Well, I am flying by the seat of my pants."

"Do you operate any other way?"

"Hey...you and I have planned a lot together in a rather painstaking way. I have to get Vienna's brother out of the academy. The government here is instilling a draft to the World Government."

"A draft will take time. I'm sure you guys can put together a complete plan. Isn't he too young for a draft?"

"You don't understand. The academy is not a good place to be, even without the draft. It's worse than the home where I lived. They put him through a process that sped up his growth."

"Worse than the facility?"

"Right up there."

"And you're not putting together a plan with the group?"

"No time."

"Are you telling the group?"

I shouldn't have even mentioned it to him. I'm going to have to leave before he has the chance to tell them.

His low chuckle breaks the silence.

"Vienna's going to kill you, you know."

"Not if I return with her brother."

"You played too much poker during our down time. I think you're addicted to gambling now."

"So, I take that as a no. You're not coming here to help me."

"Can't I just wish you the best of luck?"

I sigh and rub my forehead while slowly shaking my head from side to side.

"Fine. Stay safe, Colsam."

"I'd tell you the same, Al, if I thought you'd listen."

———

Luckily, everyone's so busy and preoccupied that sneaking out of the apartment is much easier than anticipated. I left Vienna a message with Kitchen, so eventually she'll know. I was sure to delay delivery of the message to allow me enough time to accomplish this task. I learned a trick from Harper.

What I kept from Vienna…the part she may never forgive me for…is that I know her brother's name, what he looks like, and exactly where he is. She may never forgive me. but I hope she doesn't kill me.

From pictures I've seen around the place, Vienna subtly takes after her mom: dark hair, and a warm smile. Their height definitely differs. Her brother, on the other hand, takes after Septimus. His eyebrows form a hard-ninety-degree angle, causing his smiles to look almost evil. It's the light in his eyes that gives a youthful, fun, and warm touch. I hope he's like his dad, willing to go out on a limb for others.

I'm able to view more of this planet during the public transit gliding pod ride to the academy...or as close as I can get without triggering any alarm. It's weird seeing ghosts of what once was. Painted hills of tannish red remind me of Vortex. All that's missing are the holes for prisoner quarters. Also, there's a gray that seems to be taking over not just the hills but the open flat lands in between. A couple hours later, we're passing by the skeletons of trees that once were. I doze off for a bit to conserve my energy and awake to mountains. Unlike the mountains of past Earth, tall, strong, and sturdy, I see brittle and sad remains. I need to get Vienna and her whole family off of this planet. They should be somewhere rich with healthy nature instead.

My first stop is the employment office. In my preparation, I found that the academy is currently hiring a janitor. As a new arrival to the planet, it would only be logical that I'd be in need of work.

"Good afternoon, please have a seat," the greeting bot says. "You're number thirty-two. We'll be with you as soon as possible."

I've been sitting for a long time during this trip and don't really feel like continuing that, but I don't want to get busted by the employment office staff for not following directions. I reluctantly sit next to a tall guy with oil stains on his clothes.

"I'd pull up some reading material if I were you, mate," he says to me.

I point to the programming displayed on the holograph at the front of the room and shrug my shoulders.

"Suit yourself, but you'll be asleep in five minutes."

I extend my hand for a shake. "Name's Al. Have you had any success here before?"

He shakes my bionic hand without hesitating and, as I predicted, the sensors pick up that his hands are full of calluses. "Yeah, from time to time, but only seasonal work, nothing steady. My name's Kevin."

I ask him about voltball and his family. He has family from Funen too! What a small universe. We shoot the breeze for five minutes before I cut to the chase. "Do you have a favorite employee here?"

"Well, they all try their best."

"Trying and doing are two very different things."

"True indeed. I'm one of the hardest-working candidates here. I haven't found a piece of machinery I can't fix and every customer compliments me on my efficiency and attention to detail."

"So, what's the problem?"

"Some in this office don't think I'm qualified because I didn't come from the right background. They think holding some menial job with one of the top mechanical companies is somehow much better than running a smaller one yourself."

I bet Cromwell would have been "qualified" before the facility according to their terms…great! He has the degrees and worked for Sci-Corp.

"I had to learn every facet of the process going the route I did, and I bring more to the table because of it," Kevin continues.

I glance at the employees watching to see who is the one with the most candidates walking away happy.

"That's not what you asked though, is it? Bethany's the one to go to if you want work right away. The kind of work that can put you on the trajectory for one of those top companies I mentioned. She's right over there." He points to the desk three to the right of the hologram.

Now how do I work this so that I can be helped by Bethany? I scan the room, looking at everyone's numbers.

Watching to see if any particular process is followed, but it appears to be first come, first served. Then I notice a woman tapping her foot impatiently. She checks her digital watch twice in less than a minute and...the number beside her photo on the holograph at the front is thirty-four.

When thirty flashes big at the top of the list, Kevin walks up to an employee that's not Bethany. Part way there he turns back to me, shrugs his shoulders, and then approaches the desk. If he didn't get Bethany, perhaps the odds are in my favor...jinx. When thirty-one is up, the light above Bethany turns green. Shoot, there's no way she'll be available for thirty-two. I make my way closer to the impatient woman.

"Hey, I need to use the restroom, but I'm up next. Could I swap numbers with you?"

She looks at me like I've sprouted horns. "I'm sorry, what?" she asks as she clutches her purse.

"You're after thirty-two, aren't you?"

"Um, yes." She gives me an odd look but loosens the grip on her satchel.

"I'm thirty-two and I'd like to trade numbers with you."

She looks at her watch. "Really?"

"Yeah."

"Can we?"

The number thirty-two blinks. It's my turn and Bethany's still busy with thirty-one.

"Yeah, but we have to hurry."

"How?" she asks.

"Follow me."

I walk up to the greeting bot.

"Excuse me," I say. "Could you help us? I need to use the restroom and this kind woman is willing to trade with me."

"That's not standard procedure."

"It will actually help maintain the structure and streamline it," the anxious woman says. I'm impressed and I raise my eyebrows.

She swats me on the arm with the back of her hand.

"You are positive?" the bot asks.

"Yes," we both say at once.

And just like that, we've swapped numbers. I run to the restroom to keep up the charade. When I return, number thirty-three is up and my luck continues as Bethany's light isn't green. I look around to see if there's someone else I can swap with if Bethany's not the one for number thirty-four. I doubt the greeting bot would let me get away with that twice. Then it happens. Number thirty-one gets up! It better not be Bethany's break or anything. Thirty-four blinks at the front and I wait to see which green light illuminates. I smile when it's her.

"Al Dandridge?" Bethany asks as I sit at her desk.

"Yes, that's me."

"So, you're here for a job. Can you tell me your qualifications and what kind of work you're looking for?"

"I've excelled in medical research lab studies. I also have mechanical training from my dad."

"Excellent. What positions have you held?"

"I worked at the Vortex Medical facility."

"Okay, and what are you looking for on Earth?"

"I saw an ad. It was for a janitorial position at the academy here in town. I'd like to start from scratch and work up to teaching."

"That's not how it's usually done."

"I know, but I have the knowledge. I would work hard. I've trained others in the lab."

"I see. I've pulled up your resume. You'd fit a teaching role better than janitorial. Have you ever scrubbed forty-five thousand square feet in a night? It takes a very skilled and efficient individual to do that."

My mouth drops.

"Oh, sorry, they do have multiple janitors on staff to help. No need to fret."

"Okay?" I say.

"There's actually a teaching position available too."

"I'll take it."

———

I feel like I should pinch myself because there's no way this can be cogging real. I'm in. After another public transit gliding pod ride, I can now access the grounds and find Leon Freetown (it should be Perierat). It's kind of ironic that they gave him a surname that includes the word "free" when he's really been captive his entire life. Now I just need to win his trust and let him know about his family. That should be enough to convince him to leave with me right away. Maybe I'll have to inform him of the draft. The news better not make him worry about the comrades he's made. What if he can't leave without feeling like he's let them down? I've been there. I'm sure, though, that like me, he'd give anything to see his parents. I was in more of a home, not an academy with a militaristic background. Perhaps it's different. Nah, I got this.

My palms sweat as I go through the check-in process at the front gate. The marble-lined walkway sends a shiver down my spine. Something about it makes the place feel monumental. I'd rather not be in such a rigid place. Walking to the peaked roofs of the academy building has my heart almost beating out of my chest. They have the perfect alignment of an organized military operation. The mountains in the background make my mouth go dry, reminding me of my current altitude. I'm one step closer. He better listen to me. Either way, I hope Vienna can forgive me.

12

PLANET EARTH

Vienna

THE VISION BLURS BACK TO CURRENT TIME. I'M AS relieved as if I just spent a weekend at a satellite spa using stardust for a facial and moon rocks that have been smoothed in a stream for a massage. I really can't be dealing with the past. The current goings-on are more than enough. That being said, I can't shake the feeling that it means something more. Why would Viscerous and Albina be with me in ancient times? Why are Al and I dancing the Charleston in my visions? It's as if we were reincarnated and the vision returns to me when I'm meditating. Isn't it enough that I have a clone out there? Not just that, but the clone's mind and conscience were implanted into a non-bio and Cromwell's devious son Damien's brain and conscience were implanted into my clone. I need to process this so I can concentrate.

I think I know just the place. There's an antique shop in town known for their affinity for the supernatural, or at least what people claim to be supernatural. I really don't want to go back to Magasin again, so I'm sneaking out while I have the opportunity. I like going there because they have books that hold the smell of grandparents reading to grandkids before bed after baking homemade bread. The store's magic for me has never been in the unreal, but very real. A tattered dress that had once been worn to a festive event, the seam work beautiful and definitely not artificial. The minor human errors breathe a life of its own into the piece. Stories told with each jerk of the hand as it weaves in the thread. Plus, the owner, Pat Blackstone, always shares great tales about each piece.

Since Milcah's borrowing the poli-magno, I'm left with the pod. Riding the public transit gliding pod brings back so many memories. I remember borrowing Mom's purse and pants and instantly feel the desperation of not knowing how we'll save her from Cromwell's backup plans. Having Yesha there definitely helps, but nervousness bubbles up like vinegar dropped into a cup of baking soda. Entering the store is like time traveling to another era. Furniture hand-carved from wood fills many spaces. Board games litter the area. Pat steps out from behind a grandfather clock, removing his spectacles and rubbing them clean with the end of his shirt.

"Well, if it isn't one of my favorite customers," he says to me.

I mock an offended look. "Only one of your favorite customers? I thought I was the one and only favorite."

He smiles and I smile back. In that instant, I return for a moment to being the teenager I was before all of this started.

"What can I do you for?"

"I was hoping I could ask you a few unorthodox questions."

"Okay," he says, walking to the front desk. There, next to the counter, are a couple of chairs and a small round table, big enough to have tea, but not an inch more. "Sit. Have a cookie."

Another bonus about this place, the never-ending supply of freshly baked cookies.

"Thank you." I pick up a cookie. Pat gestures to the chairs and we both have a seat.

"What did you want to ask me?" He picks up a cookie himself.

"What do you know about reincarnation?"

"Well, that's not something I'm asked every day. What's caused your sudden interest in the subject?"

"You know how Mom uses meditation in her studies…"

"Ah, yes, the practice has done me wonders over the years. Your mom is a genius."

"She sure is. But I keep having visions of the past during my meditation sessions."

"I can't be sure what the visions mean unless you tell me a little more, and then it will still be an educated guess."

"Well, I see people in my life with me in other eras."

"Is it the same people?"

I explain what I've seen to Pat. The first such vision occurred on Vortex and they've seemed to appear consistently since. Maybe it's just my brain's way of dealing with all the trauma. I've never been through stuff like this before, so it's plausible.

"I think you might be spot-on about the reincarnation, and if that is correct, I think you and your friends from the past are trying to get a message to you."

Hm, I hadn't thought of that possibility. "What message are they trying to send?"

"I would need to conduct extensive research in order to figure that out."

"How would you research my visions?"

"Has anything new and life-altering occurred recently?"

Um, how does breaking laws to travel to another planet, not stopping a revolt, being cloned, finding one parent, and losing another sound? No, I can't risk telling him details. I am currently harboring criminals.

"Thanks. I think I can figure out the messages myself now that you've shared that's what may be happening."

"Wait, before you go, this conversation made me remember something."

"What's that?"

He gets up and walks behind the front desk. He returns with a small, artfully crafted picture frame in hand. It's an antique wooden thing with an incredibly old black and white photo inside. Not a multidimensional prism photo like those we have at the apartment.

He hands me the photo and when I take a good look at it, my heart drops to my stomach.

"I always thought the girl in the photo seemed familiar."

"It's me!"

———

Back at home, trying to wrap my brain around everything, I'm interrupted by a loud commotion. I walk out to the living room…and it's Colsam. A smile blooms from ear to ear on my face.

"Look what the cat dragged in," I say.

"How are you, Vienna?"

"You know…still missing a parent and trying to stop a madman…the usual."

I've walked up to him, but I'm unsure of what to do. I place a hand on his arm, noticing the bulge of his bicep. He puts his hand on my cheek. I awkwardly pat his arm and then step a bit away, breaking eye contact.

"Colsam, you're here!" Theopat shouts as she enters the room.

Where's Al? Guess the commotion got everyone else's attention. Viscerous and Albina are here. They've been working on hacking into the system with Harper's help. She's not here because she has an appointment with Dr. McPike, our high school teacher. Danver's here, but he's slouched in a chair staring off into space. He's been busy recruiting voltball players to commit minor offenses to keep the authorities preoccupied (luckily Milcah's mom has continued to wipe their slates clean each time, so there are no career damaging records). Milcah looks bored and jittery being stuck here. And my dad's at another lunch.

"Notice something missing?" Colsam asks me.

"I don't see Al. In fact, I don't believe I've seen him all day."

Colsam gives me the look he gave in my incubator when he knew he couldn't stop me from putting myself in danger in order to stop Cromwell. "That's because he's not here."

"What do you know? Where is he?"

"I warned him that you'd kill him."

"Colsam!"

"He went to the academy to get your brother out."

"You mean I've been wasting my time helping this pipsqueak." Milcah stands and points at me.

"Hey, I still need you to help me with the draft, Milcah."

"Um, no, not if lover boy gets him out," she says.

"Newsflash, I don't want other innocent cadets drafted either." I turn to Colsam with a glare on my face.

He holds up his hands in surrender. "Don't shoot the messenger."

"I don't get it. How did he know where my brother was? How is he going to identify him and convince him to leave?"

"You got me," Colsam says.

"Cog it, that gomer knows, doesn't he, and he kept it from me!"

"I did bring the documents you asked for." Colsam changes the subject…smart.

"Can you clear our names?" Viscerous asks with his arm around Albina's shoulders. I was afraid the isolation of them being forced to stay in the apartment because of the warrants might cause them to become fed up with one another. It's done the opposite. They're like a couple of honeymooners who can't keep their hands off one another.

"I think so. Not only were we able to recover how he instigated the false charges on the guards, but we were also able to locate his research and plans for medical experimentation. Plus, we documented how doctors were forced to act against their will."

"Wow, you worked fast," Albina says.

"Yeah, that's quite the list," Viscerous adds.

"I'll believe it when I see it," Milcah puts in. "Doubt it will stand up with the authorities here."

"Sourpuss," Theopat says. "I think Colsam did great."

"Thank you, Colsam," I say. "Were you able to get Cromwell's backup plan by any chance?"

For the second time, he gives me a look like I'm a lost puppy. "No, I can't fit in the tunnels like you and Al. Plus, with Yesha and Al's departure from Vortex, many eyes have been on me…making it impossible to sneak into the man's office."

"Why don't we review what he has brought, see if it's enough to substantiate, and, if it is, share it so we can clear names," Theopat says.

She's right and so we dive in. Finding evidence to clear Viscerous and Albina is the easiest. The more difficult part is submitting it to the appellate court because someone had pushed their charges through court without their appearance, which should never happen. I give Milcah the side-eye as this is discussed.

Viscerous and Albina are patient and kind throughout the entire process. Their connection and grace are something to be admired. They took Al in without hesitation. For that matter, they did the same with me. I'm so grateful they're here.

Discovering evidence to support everyone's claims is one thing. For example, Septimus saving Viscerous and trying to save the other patient (or victim, more accurately), Yesha's brother, is easily supported with the information we have. Finding information to protect my dad is much more difficult. Locating the original source of it all is quite the task. We can't unearth anything that shows how Cromwell kidnapped Septimus from Earth and forced him to stay on Vortex. I know it's true, though. Dad would never leave Mom and me willingly, and he was locked in an incubator like the rest of us. I had to go to great lengths to access his quarters.

"Let's take a break and then regroup," I say to avoid exacerbation of the issue.

I take the elevator to the top floor, trying to get a moment's peace. Next, I take the one flight of gray and cold stairs to the roof, remembering when Aviator dropped me off on top of the facility. This roof is not covered with the same green pyramids. It's more cement and boring. Looking out, it reminds me of Eucarpo and her brothers, and I wonder what the koalas are doing now. I breathe in the air to clear my head. Maybe when Dad gets home, he can point us in the right direction.

The stairway door opens. "Thought I'd find you out here." It's Milcah.

"What do you want?" I'm not really up to dealing with her right now.

"I think we need to get ahold of Yesha as soon as possible," she says.

"Why?"

"I've been around corrupt leaders my entire life. My gut says that Cromwell's backup plan, if your clone's body didn't work for Damien, is to use your brother's body next."

"No, duh!"

"Okay, but there's more."

I roll my eyes at her.

"Cromwell would have a hard time extracting him from the military," she continues. "He'd want to get to him before the draft. The draft is just a decoy, like Danver."

"So it's a good thing Al ran off to get him. What does it have to do with Yesha?" I shrug my shoulders.

"Yesha has to stop him," she says.

"Well, I think her plan is to kill him so that should suffice."

"You still don't get it."

"Your dragging this out is rather annoying. Spill it already, won't you?"

"Who do you think he's going to use for Sorna?"

"No."

"Yes."

"No."

"Yesha's smart. Think about it. What middle-aged jerk wouldn't want to trade the ol' wife in for a younger version?"

"You're sick."

"Not me, him…them."

The door to the stairs opens again. It's Harper and the look on her face says it all; there's something she knows that she doesn't want to tell me.

"Harper." Milcah runs up to her but also notices the look. "What's wrong?"

Did you see McPike? I sign.

Yes. She signs.

And? I sign back.

She hesitates, even bites her lip, and Milcah rubs her arms. Is that a tear in her eye?

Septimus was in on it. She signs. *From the beginning, he knew.*

"No!" I yell loudly and clearly enough that anyone could read my lips.

13

PLANET SCEPTER

Sierra

I KNEW I RECOGNIZED THE SHUTTLE. I'VE SEEN ONE LIKE it before on Vortex. The shuttle's landing isn't the steadiest I've witnessed. It haphazardly descends to a grassy pad just beyond the river, probably the only flat area between here and the facility. The wheels bounce precariously before balancing out. The hyper drive digital printer spits out a parachute behind the tail, bringing the vehicle to a complete stop. Marrit, Jordan, Barren, Royce, and I race across the bridge that looks like a frozen waterfall to get over the river. It's as if water and ground solidified mid landslide to form the bridge. As soon as Marrit's on the other side, she darts to a patch of bushes at the edge of the savannah and we all follow. The jungle neon bounces off the smooth surface of the shuttle, almost making it look green instead of white. Just like the incubators on Vortex, the entire exterior of the craft appears unbroken, with no obvious points of entry or exit.

"If this is delivering more ammo for the facility, we should take it out," Royce says.

"One moment, scanning inventory now," Vex says like he's already a full member of the team. When did he get so comfortable with this new group? I'm not there yet. I'm fairly sure the shuttle is from Vortex but I know Al revolted and Vex reported him as okay. Is it Al on board? Or has something happened to him and Cromwell's brought over more guards from the old facility? Why would it land so far away?

"That's good, Vex," I say.

"I have the antimatter pressure system in my sight. It's within range," Jordan reports, holding an arrow she is poised to release. I can't hold back a sharp intake of air in response. Marrit places a hand on my forearm.

"At ease, soldier," Marrit says to Jordan. "Let's wait to find out what this thing is carrying before launching an attack."

"Any update, little buddy?" Barren asks.

Then, a rectangular opening appears on the shuttle's side. It must dissolve into the body of the ship when closed. Looks like the science is not unique to Planet Vortex like I had imagined the first time I saw it. A nervousness tickles my belly when I see a boot emerge. Next, I see an outfit that reminds me of the ones I came here in. When blonde hair emerges, I recognize Yesha right away. Marrit's hold on my forearm tightens as I rise.

"It's Yesha. She's with me," I say to the group and run toward the shuttle before anyone can object.

"Sierra, you should let me confirm before…" Vex tries to stop me.

Yesha spots me approaching, crosses her arms over her chest, and shakes her head from side to side while smiling. Why isn't she running to me, that Gomer? She should recognize me since she saw me on the video call Vex made to inform her of the facility. So, I slow to a walk to show her but then a tingling sensation burns in the arches of my feet. It spreads all the way to my calves. I stop and sit so I'm able to massage the tingles out, but then they move to my forearms. My body collapses to the ground.

"Got to put up a show to make me approach you," Yesha says, her face suddenly in front of mine. "Well, you might look different but you can still be cogging annoying."

"Sierra, are you okay?" Marrit asks as she approaches, out of breath. Barren's right behind her.

"What's all this?" Yesha asks.

"Yesha, we finally meet person to robot," Vex says as Jordan carries him to us.

"Vex? Oh, my goodness, it really is you," Yesha says while Vex projects video from one of Yesha, and I's conversations in the past on the ground.

"Ah, how sweet. You two have known each other since high school…who's that with Yesha, Vex?" Marrit says and I swipe the off switch to Vex's projection system as quickly as I can.

"Mar and I have known each other since childhood," Barren says. "Seems you and Vex have known each other a long time too."

"Are we going to the facility or what?" Royce asks as he finally approaches the group.

"Yeah, that's why I'm here," Yesha says. "When you showed me the new facility, I could smell Cromwell's evil light years away."

"Who's Cromwell?" Jordan asks.

"He's the one who ran the last facility," I say. "The one who kidnapped my dad."

"And killed my brother," Yesha adds.

"Can you help us end this one?" Barren asks.

"I brought chain whips and flame-throwing clubs so I can kill the jerk," Yesha exclaims.

Jordan reveals her bow and arrow before giving Yesha a high five. Just as Royce is about to join, Marrit steps in, "We will settle this without violence if possible."

"Yeah, that worked out so well for us we wound up with the clone here." Yesha points at me. She must be getting non-bio and clone mixed up, but it's not like her to confuse such things.

"You mean non-bio, right?" I whisper, hoping she'll keep it down to a hushed voice.

"Oh, yeah, duh, sure, non-bio." Yesha doesn't make eye contact as she responds.

"Name's Royce." He offers Yesha a hand. Before I can warn her, she's in their customary bearhug.

Once she's released, it's Jordan's turn, and it continues through the group.

"We better get back on track," Barren says. "I think we can still get to the planned campsite before dark."

"About that, I have something on board that might help us out." Yesha goes back into the shuttle, opens the cargo hatch, and emerges on a hover bike-car from Vortex.

"Thanks, but we can't all fit on that," Marrit says.

"Just wait," Yesha responds as she goes back into the shuttle. "There's more."

"It looks like three can fit on each," Jordan says.

"We've even fit four bodies on one hover before," I add.

"Well, I guess one hover will need to carry four if you include the clopil in the count," Barren says.

"The hover safety manual clearly states the maximum capacity is three," Vex interjects.

"You'll be safe in the carrier," I attempt to soothe him. Poor Vex.

Yesha drives one hover. Jordan and Royce board with her. No questions are asked, but I wonder if it's the best grouping. It seems all of those supporting violence are together.

I drive the other with Marrit behind me. Then there's Barren, who's carrying Vex.

———

Where there isn't a leaf or grass in this jungle, there's moss the same lush, neon green. The leaves are huge. The only thing on Vortex that could compare would be the giant cacti. A few hours later we're right outside the facility's perimeter, far enough not to set off alarms or have laser dots on us because of detected sound. I dismount first and while everyone else is stretching after the long flight, I approach the green wall. Even though I know what I'll see when I move the leaves aside, I'm still a bit stunned at the sight of the chain-link and cement fences.

"Royce and Jordan, we didn't have a chance to go over Planet Scepter's dangers. Were you able to share with Yesha during the drive?"

"No, we were discussing more pertinent detail," Yesha says, pointing ahead to the facility. "Don't really need to worry about jungle dangers in there."

"Don't you think they believe that too?" I point to the facility. "I bet one of those beetles could really help us out."

"Whoa, you have to be extremely careful working with the beetles here," Royce says. "It took Jordan months of training before she could whisper to them."

"Well, we need some kind of exit strategy and backup plans," I say.

As the group forms a circle to discuss this, I notice Yesha's there, but not really there. She busies herself with checking her weapons. Partway through the ride, we took a break for bathroom needs and Marrit shared some of their weather-resistant clothes with Yesha, which should come in handy. But the way Yesha's half paying attention to our plans and constantly stealing looks at the facility worries me. She's on a kill mission, no need for an escape plan. She's internally organizing a solo rampage, and I'm going to have to stop her.

"So the hovers can take us to the roof?" Jordan looks to Yesha for the answer.

"My calculations confirm this possibility," Vex responds.

"But what about the security post along the outside of the facility?" Royce asks.

"They run on simultaneous intervals," Barren says, looking through binoculars.

"Yeah, each one facing a different direction so they can cover the largest metric area possible," Marrit adds.

"So how are we going to land on the roof unseen?" I ask.

"I make a distraction," Yesha says while running away, flame-throwing club at the ready. Shit!

I take a step after her, but Marrit grabs my ankle. "No, you don't. She's making a distraction so we can get in."

"She's going to get caught all alone," I say, exasperated, while struggling to free myself.

"It will all be a waste if we don't get in," Jordan says.

"Yeah, we can save her better from the inside," Royce adds.

"I think this has been her plan all along," Barren says. "From what I've seen, she can handle herself."

I stare after her one second longer, the older sister I never had. She helped me get into the Vortex facility and now she's making it possible to get into another. She's been supporting me this entire time and all I've done is take her for granted, a woman with a heart of gold and no fear. Damnit, why didn't she tell me? I could have gone with her. I wish one of the jungle vines would grab her and stop her so I could be the distraction instead. Marrit snaps her fingers in front of my face to wake me up so we can reboard the hovers.

"Hey, she left a multidimensional prism note for you," Barren says, handing me it.

Opening it flashes me back to the first time I met Yesha IRL because just like then, she's gifted me facility blueprints. How in the world did she get ahold of these? I wonder...no... could she have a spy within Cromwell's ranks? She's cogging good even if I am pissed at her right now.

"What is it?" Marrit asks.

"Blueprints to the facility. There's access to hidden tunnels from the top. We'll be able to get to them through the roof."

"You have one brilliant friend," Jordan says, nudging me with her elbow.

"Yeah, she's a piece of work."

Then an explosion sounds on the opposite side of the facility, sending vibrations through my body and making my ears ring. Sure enough, it's caught all the guards' attention. There's a mix of fears brewing inside me—running into something versus being seen. We fly over the perimeter as a plume of smoke rises to the sky. It's large enough to envelope the building as we're flying up and completely conceal the top. We had somewhat mastered a formation during our flight previously, but now it's a scramble. Plus, Yesha had been flying the other hover here, but now she's...busy so Royce has taken her spot and I can tell he's no pro.

The smoke is good for hiding us but not for navigation, and it won't help us find the tunnel entrance either. Plus, what are we going to do with the hovers? We can't exactly hide them. They're eye level with the guards, so we should be able to stash them behind the temperature regulation system unit at least that's my plan. The guard lookouts won't be able to see them unless they actually go to the roof. We'll just have to hope that doesn't happen, or at least not too soon.

Then Vex projects a pathway for us, not one of material but with enough wind to clear our view yet not reveal us. It greatly improves our ability to fly without crashing into something. I breathe a sigh of relief, but then I spot something else that's able to cut through the smoke…a bunch of red dots. The laser beams are pointing in our vicinity. The ringing has left my ears, only to be filled with whizzing sounds. What are they shooting at us?

It should only take minutes for us to get to the facility, but it seems like hours. I'm dipping, diving, and lifting the hover the best I can. I took the lead in front of Royce so he could follow me. What if one of those whizzing things hits a hover and takes it out? I should have planned better. I thought we'd have more time in the jungle to plan. Here I am in danger yet again, but this time I've put an entire team of people in danger too.

Then the beams go away and the whizzing sounds stop.

"I tripped the system so their infrared sensors believed to see us leaving the premise," Vex says.

Wow, I really should have brought him with me to Planet Vortex. Maybe I could have overtaken Cromwell on day one. Beating great odds, we make it to the building. I navigate to the temperature regulation system units and Royce follows. I take a deep breath once we've landed, though I know the danger has only begun.

"According to the blueprints and our current coordinates, the entrance should be twenty feet that way," Vex says. "Please set me down so I can show you."

Royce removes Vex from the pack Barren's wearing and places him on the roof. Luckily, Vex is short enough to be sure to remain out of sight. The rest of us have to duck and crawl to follow him. Jordan and Marrit make the process look organized and flawless while Royce and Barren seem to struggle with it. Not that I can say much. Pretty sure I look like a mix between an earthworm and a roly poly. As Vex rolls to the entrance, the feeling of approaching a shuttle airlock room to open a wheel handle returns. It's the same as right before we went on the Vortex water excursion, fear with a splash of possibility. I see a clear glass rectangle on hinges. Where's the handle? Luckily, no guard is visible on the ladder below.

"What's this?" Jordan points to a holograph screen on the ground next to the glass.

"It looks similar to the locking and opening mechanisms at the last facility," I say, approaching it to see just how alike it is. The symbol on it looks familiar.

Barren bends over to take a closer look, too.

"Recognize something?" Marrit asks.

"The card that was with the note had the same symbol," Barren says holding up a card. Why didn't he give me that with the note?

"Let me see that," I say.

I grab the card and hold it up to the holograph and the glass rectangle opens, sliding onto the roof and out of view. How did Yesha know? Royce had ventured to the edge as lookout while we were investigating the entrance. He sprints back when he hears that we've made headway.

Royce nods at Marrit with a solemn look on his face.

"What? What is it?" I ask.

Marrit hesitates. Her inquisitive forehead scrunches in concern. "They captured Yesha."

"Well, let's go in and get her back," Jordan says.

And with that, Barren, Vex, Royce, and Jordan descend the tunnel ladder, but my feet are frozen in place. The memory of the sound of a drill entering my skull floods my ears, holding me back from going after my best friend. My body feels like it could convulse. I want to take a step forward with every ounce of my heart but remembering the pain after the bone marrow biopsy locks me in place as if a piece of my hip was missing now.

Marrit grabs my hand. I look at her, but she's blurry because my eyes are filled with tears. She locks her fingers with mine. I wipe away the tears with my other hand and, together, we step forward.

14

PLANET EARTH

Al

LUNCH AT THE ACADEMY BEATS THE HELL OUT OF FOOD on Vortex, but the regimen involved is far from chummy. We have to file through the cafeteria in specific lines and sit in assigned seats. You even have to follow this same kind of convention when asking for ketchup to be passed from the opposite side of the table. I'd rather have people tossing condiments around like a voltball. It's too strict for my affinity here and it's made locating Leon a damn mess, despite the fact that faculty sit with the cadets.

"Have you decided what service work you'll participate in?" Brandon, the voltball coach asks me.

"I'm pretty busy with my research and courses as it is." I pick up the juiciest burger I've seen in years and my mouth waters in anticipation.

"Man, most of those without service work are being sent on tour," Chris the debate coach interjects.

107

"Fine," I say. "I'll sign up. Chill."

First, it was the drafts, but the tours weren't too far behind. Luckily, this has been confined to the faculty thus far, but that doesn't mean I'm out of the woods. Either I could be assigned a tour or they could move to cadets, putting Leon at risk any day now.

I pick specimen collection for my service work. The specimens will be for the research and teaching I'm already doing, so why not? This way, I can be sure no schmuck collects anything polluted with foreign material. But in order to take it one step further, to ensure that Leon and I don't receive tour summonses before I can get him out, I sign up for leadership administrative work as an alternate. Thinking of administration reminds me of all the ways Cora protected us, placing the calmer lab techs under Rigled's watch in an attempt to avoid abusive reprimand. She would even sneak us treats and time free from guards on our birthdays. As deranged as things were, I kind of miss Vortex.

I'm surrounded by students in tan uniforms as I walk the academy hallways. I adjust the long sleeves of my professor uniform. Opening the door to my first service assignment, I'm taken aback. Sure enough, Leon's in leadership detail.

Act cool, Al.

"Al Dandridge reporting to duty," I say to Leon, who's logging everyone in on behalf of administration leadership. He nods, eyes never leaving the rollable tablet in his hands. Then he points to a row of chairs, many already occupied, indicating for me to be seated.

"Hey, any way you can move me up in the line?" I ask him.

His eyes leave the screen and meet mine and then…they roll.

"Seriously? Just take a seat and we'll get to you when we

can," he replies, but as he's doing so a hint of recognition crosses his face.

I take a seat so as to not raise any suspicion but watch him closely. His gaze is back on the screen. There are instructors and cadets around me all awaiting assignments—the draft must have increased their popularity. There's a tension in the air that can almost be felt like a vibration. After a decent chunk of time, the feeling around the room turns to boredom. I give up trying to learn more about Leon because his attention has stayed riveted to the tablet. I pivot in my chair, stretching my back muscles.

"Al," Leon says, announcing my turn. He points to the office door last exited by a faculty member. Before I can give him a thumbs-up to confirm, he's staring at the tablet again. What's on there?

The office is well kept, as the woman behind the desk inside it. She's sorting through files on her holograph screen. As soon as she's found the one she's looking for, she turns her attention to me. Her posture improving suit doesn't have the slightest wrinkle and I don't see a single speck of lint or dirt. Posture improving suits can detect when muscles are in distress and a new position would improve their state. The material automatically moves to pull its inhabitant to the new position.

"So you're interested in wilderness specimen collection," she says.

"Yes, it will help my studies and teaching," I respond.

"And you know of our local dangers," she continues. "A moose might seem friendly but they won't be if they believe you threaten their young."

If Vienna were here, she'd need this warning. I, on the other hand, am perfectly fine keeping my distance from animals. I nod my head in agreement and to fill the silence.

"There's also coyotes, bears, and snakes."

I nod again. But how did they survive when so much of the nature on this planet has been annihilated?

"And you're familiar with the storage and collection methods required to maintain the fragile molecules of biospecimens?"

She must have a background in these studies.

"Do you have robotic retrieval tractionation, storage, and continued quality control?" I ask, and she nods.

"Please sign here and then you'll be ready to go," she says as she pivots her holograph screen my way.

I place my thumb on the screen for digital signature. Then she buzzes the front desk.

"Leon," she says.

"Yes," he responds.

"Since your shift is ending, please escort Al to the transportation pod for specimen collection."

Leon approaches the doorway and I reach to shake his hand, but he turns around.

"Follow me," he says.

He no longer has his tablet in front of him, but he's still distracted. What the crap?

We walk through the hallways with floor-to-ceiling windows on either side. Next we stroll along outdoor paths of light-maroon-colored squares outlined in white. He doesn't talk to me. How can this silent, distracted teen be Vienna's brother? Maybe the sped-up growth caused differences. Finally, we approach gates and Leon waves to the attendant, who waves back.

"Al here needs a transportation pod for specimen collection," Leon says.

"Has he been trained in navigation for local terrain?" the attendant asks. He and Leon look at me.

"Navigation's not a problem for me," I say. "Nothing here can be as bad as Planet Vortex."

"Sorry, standard procedure," the attendant says.

"Let's sign him up for training, then," Leon says.

"Can't, no one available," the attendant says. "Unless you could do it."

"Fine," Leon says. "Would you suggest the rover or the tank today?"

Leon's asking the attendant for advice. That's it, there's no way he's Vienna's brother.

"The tank is already out, so it's the rover today, my friend," the attendant says and then waves as Leon walks away.

I feel like a schmuck following this guy, but realize it takes some people time to warm up.

Once we're in the rover speeding across open land, I see what Leon and Vienna have in common. With the speed he's going, he'd probably enjoy a ride on one of the Vortex vultures. We veer around a boulder so quickly the left two tires leave the ground for a few seconds. The siblings share the same daredevil transportation habits. Of all her characteristics, this is the last I'd choose for Leon to share right now.

Even at the pace we're going, I'm able to spot plants which I hadn't seen on the way here. They're not photosynthetic but parasitic and look almost like the sad remnants of wood in the failing forests of the area. Their stems look more like red branches, their small blooms like clusters of bells. I have to turn to catch sight of an agave plant. The agave leaves reach out in all directions. How does it survive? I know the plant can handle many temperatures, but I'm still surprised by its presence. There is natural vegetation on Earth even though it may be quite sparse and only the most resilient species.

"Hey, slow down," I say to Leon. "I'd like to see..."

He speeds up.

Eventually, we come to a stop, and I release my grip from the door. I had expected puny mountains or at least sparse coniferous trees barely hanging on. But instead we're in front of a gray cement building.

"What's this?" I ask Leon. "Where are we?"

He looks at me and raises an eyebrow. "You've heard of preservation warehouses, right?"

So that's how the animals survived. Doesn't exactly seem like wilderness anymore though.

Leon parks the vehicle and we exit. As we're walking to the building, I notice a shimmer at the corner. First, I think it's a glint from the sun, but it unfolds and grows, a screen covering the entire front of the warehouse. The picture is of the same scene but different. Instead of cement there's a brick wall, and the vehicles parked in front are older than the relics on Funen. Then a woman walks around the corner. She's wearing an archaic dress—I think it was called flapper back in the day. My heart skips a beat when she makes eye contact with me. It's Vienna, but that can't be, it's impossible.

A slap on the arm pulls me out of my state of shock. "Come on," Leon says. "Why'd you stop?"

The picture disappears, leaving me with an ache for her. I move my feet and keep up with Leon. He opens the door to a green environment this planet seems devoid of. Bird sounds surround us as we walk to the right. Cabinets line part of the wall, one of the less natural things in this place. It holds collection equipment. I walk up and prepare what I need without instruction from Leon. He seems to pick up silent communication and goes to a holograph screen above the counter. He enters in my name and the inventory I'm using, then heads to the door.

"See you in a bit," I say.

"Yeah, sure."

I step through the lush green and toward the trees. It's a shiny, white beyond the trees! I haven't seen snow in ages. Planet Funen had snow from time to time, but I only remember playing in it once as a child. I kneel down to touch the cold, liquidy substance. As I enter the tree line and take a few steps in snow, the warehouse door opens. Leon's not quite to it. Someone else enters. A sense of déjà vu overwhelms me as I recognize the guard. It's one of the guards I spied having low-gravity beer with Cromwell back on Vortex. What's he doing here? He walks up to Leon and they give each other a handshake, half hug greeting.

"Hey, man," Leon says.

Their discussion continues in a hushed tone. I guess the kid *can* hold a conversation—he's infuriating. No wonder he's chums with one of Cromwell's cronies, makes sense.

I have to go farther into the forest so I won't run up and deck him. What in the crap is going on? It's not luck or mistake that he hasn't been sent on tour. He has a direct link to the source of those activities.

I spot an ash tree in the midst of pines and decide to climb it so I can keep an eye on the pair. They move to the cabinets, continuing whatever they'd been discussing. Perhaps this is just another one of Cromwell's tactics and the kid doesn't have a clue. He could be in more danger than I originally thought if that's the case, not of tour assignment, but Cromwell recruitment.

Some snow dumps on my head from above and I open the pack full of collection equipment I'd grabbed at the cabinets. I find a jacket, hat, and gloves and put them on, glad I won't have to freeze my butt off the entire time. Now warm, I turn my attention back to Leon. The guard has a rollable tablet display in front of them. I reach back into the pack for a pair of binoculars. It's a list. I notice Brandon, the voltball coach's name on the list. I move my gaze to the top so I can try to see what the list is for. It's not a shocker when I see the Planet Scepter Facility written there. That's just great. Cromwell's not recruiting people into the World Government military for a war. He truly is developing another freaking facility. Maybe Yesha killing the jerk wouldn't be all bad.

Or maybe I can get to Brandon and tell him what's happening. He could help get treatment for Vienna's clone and her mom. He could possibly help overthrow Cromwell...again.

The pair exit the warehouse and I climb down the tree. I head deeper into the forest so they don't spot me leaving right after them. I'll collect some specimens so as to not raise any alarm. That way I can avoid being sent on tour, though it looks like it would be to Scepter, where I should be right now, anyway. The thought of not coming to Earth stops me in my tracks. Remembering the way Vienna jumped into my arms brings a smile to my face. Then I shake my head, recollecting that coming to the academy was somewhat of a betrayal and now I know it was all for nothing. Leon won't listen to me even if I tell him Cromwell's not to be trusted.

As I'm bent down opening a tube, I hear rustling behind me. I turn my head to the side and see sudden movement. There's a large animal. Is it an elk? No, the cinnamon fur is too thick. With closer inspection, I see it's a big, horrifically beautiful bear! There's a low growl and air rushes through the bear's nostrils. It looks at me and chomps its jaws. Shit! My heart pounds in my chest.

15

PLANET EARTH

Vienna

MILCAH, HARPER, AND I MUST LOOK AMUSING WALKING down the street together. Milcah, the visual arts queen, has the latest style, not a hair out of place, and gobs of makeup on, though I don't think she needs it. Harper, a nutty professor nerd, always looks a bit askew, with strands of hair falling out of her bun, glasses tilted, but I have to give it to her, she pulls it off. It's like Harper matured more while I was away. The once sweet and innocent girl now has a bit of edge and sexiness. Then, there's me, half scientist, half mechanic, just put some oil stains on my clothes and latex gloves on my hands to complete my look.

As we near the building Milcah's mom works in, I notice meeting agendas and minutes on the floating holograph between the metal columns. Walking between the pillars gives the feeling of entering a structured place dripping in tradition. Retina scans shoot out from the doorway, heading in our direction. Harper's eyes get huge as she looks at me. Holographs pop up warning that Harper and I do not have clearance for entry. I hold my breath and wait. Milcah overrides the system with her scan and vocally states we're visitors. When the holograph replaces the clearance warning with a visitor badge, I take a deep breath. I'm still shocked when we somehow make it into Milcah's mom's office without being stopped by physical security guards. The bonus of hanging with Milcah is that we can pretty much get away with anything we want. We would have gone to her house as originally planned, but her mom is there packing for a trip and we can't wait.

"Here," Milcah says. "These are the court records." She points to the holograph screen above her mom's desk.

Harper, having read Milcah's lips, walks over to take a closer look. Milcah's trying to learn sign language, but it's taking some time. *We need to locate evidence of the charges being pushed through without Viscerous and Albina's appearance,* Harper signs.

"The appellate court will need that in order to allow the evidence we have in, right?" I sigh.

"You two are so sweet," Milcah says, her voice drowning with syrupy sarcasm.

Harper backhand slaps Milcah's arm and Milcah locks her into a hold. As much as I hate to think it, they are kind of cute. I'm still going to keep an eye on Milcah. A girl has got to have her bestie's back and all that.

"What do you mean we're so sweet?" I toss an Intuos Pen softly her way so she gets the point.

"I mean, we can simply send a message from my mom's account and they'll remove the charges," Milcah says. "No evidence necessary."

"Why didn't you say this before?" My voice rises at first, but then I remember the staff right outside the office door.

"What do you know, I still enjoy messing with you."

Now Harper's upset. She slowly backs away from Milcah and stands next to me.

Let's go, Harper signs, rolls her eyes at Milcah, and stomps out of the office.

"Vienna," Milcah pleads. "I was going to tell you, eventually. I had just been hoping you guys would somehow find a way without needing my mom's help."

I can see the mix of sadness and guilt plaguing her.

"It's okay," I say. "I'll talk to Harper."

"Thank you."

"Can you please send that message though?" I ask.

"Of course," Milcah says as I leave the office to catch up with Harper. That girl is faster than I thought. She's already through the hallway. I see her enter an elevator there's no way I'll catch. I have to run through the main level entryway.

Don't be mad. I sign. *You don't have to stand up for me. It's okay.*

That's not all though, she signs back. *She has an unhealthy habit of avoiding things, lying, and deflecting.*

Oh, I sign. *I guess I can see that…you still like her?*

Harper blushes and nods.

So it's serious, a done deal. I can support her. I've failed her in so many ways but I can make up for it now.

Want to go hang out with a bunch of scientists? I ask, cocking an eyebrow.

Is there time? she asks. *With everything going on?*

Yeah, we need to recruit, I say. *I want to contact as many scientists as we can before they're applying to another one of Cromwell's high-paying facilities.*

Okay, she says. *I'm game.*

Entering the university with Harper reminds me of the Science Olympiad days. Activity surrounds us. 3-D printed test tubes with bubbling liquid, floating artificial intelligence pieces that were meant to be fully integrated (via lifelong bodily inserted microchips) but had never passed regulation, and lab coats, these are safe here, they're the things of home.

When I spot Dave, I instantly remember family vacations to the Mojave Desert. I feel a bit of closeness with him. Sensing our approach, he turns in our direction.

"Hi, girls," he says aloud while simultaneously signing for Harper. We've worked with him on a science project before.

"Hi, Dave," I say.

How's your study on carbon nanotube alteration and integration going? Harper asks.

We've successfully created an auto weave for initiated skin coverage, he answers.

And the membrane pores were successful as a shield? she asks.

Um, more of a filtration, still but we're working on it, he answers.

It hits me just how much I've missed this while being away and preoccupied. I feel a sudden pang for the old days when my focus was on these types of studies. They're on the brink of creating a protective skin we could activate in space travel. They've moved well beyond oxygen pills.

Harper must see that I'm distracted.

Actually, we came here to discuss something else, she says.

"Oh, yeah?"

She nudges me in the side.

"We came to discuss the Scepter Facility," I say.

"How do you know about that?" he asks. "It's classified,"

And so I tell Dave about the corruption of Cromwell's previous facility. How scientists were brought there under a guise to only be imprisoned. How guards were forced to work against their will and participate in abusive tactics or face death. And, finally, about the unethical experiments that took place.

But it hits me part way through that Dave's known both

my dad and Cromwell for years. Could he be in on the whole thing, too? I've been staving off the heartbreak that could consume me if my dad really were involved in Cromwell's activities the entire time. If I open that door to my soul, if I allow myself to feel that, it will crush me. I wouldn't be able to help my friends because I'd be worthless, squashed to nothing.

So, even though his face is full of concern, when I notice people leaving the building for lunch I sign, *Sorry, we have to go* and grab Harper's hand.

Here I wanted to make up for the time I've missed with Harper, but instead I may have put her in danger, broadening the target circle to include her.

Halfway out of the university she pulls her hand out of mine and signs, *What's going on, Vienna?*

Dave, my dad, and Cromwell have been linked for decades, I say. *I don't think we can trust him.*

Right, because people never run off and do things without telling their friends about it, she says and rolls her eyes.

We don't communicate anymore for a bit. I don't argue with what she said. There is no evidence. There are no witnesses who will testify otherwise. As we ride down the university stair glider, I know that I'm guilty as charged. I'm grateful when she breaks the silence as we walk on the sidewalk.

That's the most you've ever said about your experience on Vortex, she signs. *I knew it was awful, but I didn't realize it was that bad.*

Yeah, I say, and she holds my hand again, providing the silent comfort I need. Harper's known me since we were kids, and she knows how much I missed my dad. She knows the hole in my life that would drive me to such extreme measures. With that single move, holding my hand, she communicates understanding and love even though she's upset with me. And that's how it should be. Or at least this feels right to me...that is, until it doesn't. We come to a stop and Harper lets go...so she can hug Milcah.

"You made it for lunch after all." Milcah smiles at Harper.

We did have tentative plans to eat at Zainy's but I had hoped it wouldn't happen. I wanted time with Harper away from Milcah and responsibility. I was so preoccupied I didn't even notice we were headed in this direction.

"Minor dilemma," Milcah says. "My mom's joining us."

Great, simply great, that's brilliant. This is going to be the worst lunch ever. I consider making up an excuse to get out of the whole thing, but change my mind. We might be able to extract important information from Milcah's mom.

Milcah's mom approaches us and stops, if that's what it can be called. Her arms move, animating her words and she talks miles a minute. She's discussing some bill as if we all have read the thousands of words and know them by heart. It's kind of impressive, her deep investment, but all I feel is overwhelmed. I wonder how Harper reads her lips.

The place is reasonably busy, but the floating hostess bot finds us a secluded table. A good chunk of me is willing to bet that happened only because Milcah's mom is with us.

Making conversation with someone I'm not fond of proves difficult. That's okay since most of the conversation is Milcah's mom giving her a hard time.

"I just don't understand how you could quit the squad after so many years," Milcah's mom says. "All of that work down the tubes. What will be pulled from the databases for your college applications now?"

Milcah rolls her eyes. Perhaps we do have something in common.

"I mean take Harper, for example, she has the science club and a spectacular GPA," Milcah's mom continues.

Harper's cheeks flush. She must feel awkward now that she and Milcah are a thing.

"I bet you have colleges lined up to accept you," Milcah's mom says to Harper, but this time Harper's looking at her food and doesn't read Milcah's mom's lips.

"Mom, how many times do I have to tell you?" Milcah asks. "Harper can't hear you."

Milcah's mom turns to Harper, and I cringe in anticipation of what will follow. She repeats what she said very slowly and loudly. It's so exaggerated, it's insulting. I slam my fork on the table and Harper looks at me. Then she looks back at Milcah's mom, who's repeating herself again. Now her cheeks turn red for a different reason, but instead of standing up for herself, she rests her hand lightly on mine to calm me down.

"Mom, enough about school already," Milcah intervenes, thankfully changing the subject. "Weren't you going on a trip or something?"

Why did you let her do that? I sign to Harper.

She didn't mean to, Harper signs back. *Hearing people sometimes think it's helpful. They don't realize it can be demeaning. Plus, it makes their faces look really funny when they do it. It's like when a multidimensional prism photo captures someone mid-sentence with the most embarrassing facial expression. Just watch.*

I smile with her. *And you say she's good at deflection.* I pick up Milcah's conversation as I slyly point at her behind the table, where only Harper can see.

"Septimus can't meet me there," Milcah's mom says. "Even though it is our anniversary."

Milcah's jaw drops as she realizes that I just heard her mom.

"Your *what?*" I ask, almost shouting. Harper looks wide-eyed at Milcah, who's signing about what just happened. Then they both look at me, pleading with their eyes. I…just…can't. I stand up and leave the restaurant. If Milcah calls after me, I don't hear her over the pounding in my ears.

So many thoughts rush through my head as I walk down

the street, not giving a darn where I'm going. Is that why Milcah always hated me? Because my dad took her mom away from time to time? But he was gone for years. How do they have an anniversary to celebrate? Did Milcah know where my dad was while my mom and I were in the dark? Or was only I in the dark? I'm such an idiot. I really wish Al was here right now.

I feel a rush of air and my hair blows sideways. Looking around, I now realize I've left the sidewalk. Poli-magnos are zooming by me so fast. They're floating at eye level. How am I going to get back? If one hit me now, I would probably be decapitated. I could crawl under them, but if they come to a stop, I'll be squashed like a bug. My adrenaline spikes and I begin to shake. Maybe I can flag one down. I lift up an arm to wave and swear I feel something rub against it. I pull it back down, inspecting it for scratches. A horn blares and I cover my ears. I hear another horn through my hands and see a poli-magno approaching with the hazard lights on. It comes to a stop beside me, lowers, and the door opens.

"Will you get in already?" Danver says to me after I've stared at the door for a few seconds. "Fine, suit yourself." He reaches to close the door, waking me from my trance. I enter his poli-magno and he flips the magnets so it's floating again. Then we're moving and so is the traffic around us. The horns have stopped.

"What were you doing?" Danver asks.

"I wasn't paying attention," I say.

"Obviously," he says.

"You wouldn't understand."

"Try me."

"I just found out that my dad's been dating Milcah's mom," I huff.

"Oh." That's all he can muster up. Wait a minute. He's not surprised. He's known all along, too.

"Will you just take me home, please?" I fold my arms over my chest.

"Sure thing."

We get to the apartment, but I feel like a zombie walking in.

"What's wrong with her?" Theopat asks Danver.

"Not much," he says. "Her dad may or may not be involved in the corruption we're fighting. And he's cheating on her mom."

"Oh, no," Theopat gasps.

"Come sit down," Theopat says as she softly puts her hands on my shoulders, directing me to the kitchen table.

I do as she says.

"I'll give you two some privacy," Danver says as he goes to the living room.

"Want to talk about it?" Theopat asks me.

I shake my head "no."

"You know, it's actually quite rare for true love to last forever," she says, and I give her a cold look. "Or maybe it's all a misunderstanding."

"Theopat, can I have a minute alone?"

She too retreats from the kitchen. In the silence, I'm able to consider her last statement. Could this all be how my parents were planning on getting my brother back?

"Ice cream can make you feel a good deal better," Kitchen chimes in, actually bringing a smile to my face.

"What flavors do we have?" I allow myself to relax a little even though I know this is Kitchen's comforting tactic.

"Let me double-check inventory in the database," Kitchen says, as if she's the parent in the room of absent parents.

"That's it," I say.

"We have vanilla bean, mint chocolate chip, and cookie dough," Kitchen says. "Would you like the usual, bowl, not a cone?"

"Of course, Kitchen, and can you bring the side desk holograph?"

"Certainly. Is there something you're looking for in particular?"

"Yes, Kitchen, but I can manage." Kitchen would not approve of the hackers I plan to recruit but Yesha will be ecstatic.

PLANET SCEPTER

Sierra

ONCE WE'RE IN THE FACILITY, I'M GLAD MARRIT KEEPS her fingers locked with mine. Smoke follows us through the closing door as we descend the ladder behind everyone else. It's as if Marrit's a shield keeping my fear at bay. Moving forward, it's clear that these tunnels are bigger than the ones on Vortex, otherwise I don't think Royce would be able to crawl. Regretfully, Marrit has to let go in order to continue moving forward. I miss the comfort but it's more efficient. As I notice a watermelon smell, memories overwhelm my senses. I remember Quintus and Lucretia being whipped and burned. That was the moment when I'd realized just how corrupt the last facility had been. And here we are entering another place of torture, not only imprisoning one of my parents but also my best friend and original body.

After a while, we come to a three-pronged fork in the tunnel. While I had seen this in the blueprints, the implication had not really struck me. Royce and Jordan begin making military-like signals to one another. The gestures appear to be indicating that they will take the tunnel to the left, Barren and Vex will go straight, and Marrit and I will go to the right. I learned my lesson at the last facility; to not go it alone.

We aren't going it alone per se with this separation, but something still feels off about it. It's not like I can argue, though. We need to be silent. At least I'm paired with Marrit. I try to mimic Royce and Jordan's communication, wishing they knew sign language. I pull out the multidimensional prism notes containing the blueprints so each group can download and access them. Why I didn't do this before, I'm not sure. Had I somehow thought it would keep us together. Jordan taps on my shoulder, points to her watch, and then gives a rendezvous time. She also projects the blueprints with Vex' help so we can all look at them at once and points to the tunnels above the cafeteria. There's a larger section of the tunnels there where we'll be able to sit up. That will be nice after a whole hour of crawling.

Marrit and I slither to the right. Approaching a vent and running into her boot feels like déjà vu. The kind you don't want to have. Marrit moves to the side so I can be next to her as we peer through the vent. The feeling of pins and needles has returned, but stronger. I'm not sure why I've been experiencing all of these new symptoms lately. Marrit taps me on the arm and then points through the vent to the room below. Puffs of purple appear as a scientist operates a machine.

"Nitrogen dioxide will turn purple," the scientist announces to someone else in the room not currently visible to us.

Then the scientist presses another button. "Ozone turns orange."

"Take a deep inhalation and hold it. When I remove your

mask, breathe out." I know the voice. It's Cromwell. I fist my hand.

The puffs disappear with the subject's exhalation. Marrit gasps and I quickly but softly place my hand over her mouth.

"It works," the scientist says.

"Of course it does," Cromwell answers.

"And the virus really is benign in my system." This must be the subject speaking.

"Yes, it's been manipulated to attack and feed off carbon dioxide, ozone, sulphur dioxide, nitrogen dioxide, and even particulate matter," Cromwell says.

At least he's not removing limbs.

"The virus is successfully recycling the atmosphere and turning it into clean, breathable oxygen," the scientist states, holding a measuring device.

But I don't fully trust Cromwell to be concerned with the subject's well-being. Viruses evolve. What would one this powerful evolve to?

After they exit the room we're above I motion to Marrit for us to continue farther down the tunnel. We need to find and free Yesha. Crawling like this feels as if we're slow as slugs. I wish I had an invisibility serum. It would make locating Yesha and Mom so much easier. We could probably bring an end to the facility and escape without a problem too. But that's an advancement yet to be discovered by scientists.

Light appears up ahead, indicating another room. As we get closer the temperature lowers. I recognize the cryogenic freezer beds immediately. I pause and Marrit must sense my apprehension because she stops too.

"What is it?" she asks in a whisper.

"They're cryogenic freezer beds and they hold nothing but bad memories for me," I whisper back.

"Well, I don't see anyone working inside the room. Let's just move on. We need to check out the hub."

Now I wish I could hit fast forward and speed up our crawl. I can't help it. I look down when we're directly over the beds. A woman and a boy are in the beds next to one another. Smile lines remain on the woman's cheeks and one of the boy's eyebrows is arched like it froze mid-smirk. Seeing Sorna and Damien's faces somehow perfectly preserved is a shot straight to the gut.

The next thing I know, Marrit's rubbing a finger across my cheek, wiping a fallen tear away. I crawl forward away from the bodies that remind me of my final experience on Vortex. I just keep going, not stopping at the next vent or the next. Panic surges through me and I silently chastise myself for allowing this to happen.

"Hey, slow down," Marrit whispers, catching up to me.

I look at her as if she's just spoken the impossible. Voices float through the tunnel from the next vent. Including one we heard recently discussing the pollution-eating virus. It's the voice of the man with the stiff, militaristic stance, Cromwell. It's the other voice I recognize, though, that takes me by surprise. I can imagine her twirling a lock of her rich, dark brown hair as if she were right in front of me in the tunnel. Is my mom talking with Cromwell? I crawl forward to find out.

"So you said that the feelings have become overwhelming." I hear my mom say.

"Yes, I think since I had thought my goal was so close to being achieved, I put everything I had into it," Cromwell replies.

"But when things didn't take, it all came crashing down."

"Yes," Cromwell weeps.

Marrit and I approach the vent and what I see stuns me. My mom is hugging Cromwell. Eew!

But it is my mom. She's in her body. I know it's her. Well, at least her memory and conscience appear to be back in her body. I wonder if mine can be returned too?

"I don't understand why it didn't take. Everything was scientifically worked out," Cromwell says.

"Henry, Sorna and I were friends before. Did you ever stop to think how it would affect her psychologically to wake up in my body? Or what it would be like for Damien to wake up in Sierra's?"

"Both of your bodies were functioning perfectly, medically and intellectually tested. I don't see what the problem was."

"Oh, Henry."

Mom?

I know it's risky trying to communicate with her this way. But if Damien's memory and conscience are no longer in my old body, he shouldn't be able to interfere. So who was that before? Was his implantation successful at first and then something went wrong?

Sierra?

Yeah, it's me.

We can't talk now. Give me some time. Where are you?

Right above you, but don't look up.

To keep herself from looking up, she of all things turns to focusing on twirling a lock of hair. It really is her.

"Will you help me with the Plan B research?" Cromwell asks. "We can meet tomorrow. I have a few more responsibilities to handle today."

"Of course, Henry."

And with that, he leaves. Marrit motions for us to move on too, but I allow myself a few seconds longer to look at my mom, wishing we were back in the apartment, safe and sound.

I'm silent as we make our way to the rendezvous point, but I can tell Marrit knows something's amiss. She keeps trying to steal glances my way, but I catch her every time. I don't even know if I could explain to Marrit everything that's wrong with this situation.

As we near the meeting spot, Royce's large form startles me. I almost think it's Colsam at the end of the tunnel above the cafeteria. He and Jordan are whispering to Barren, more than likely sharing what they discovered during their trek. As Marrit and I approach, Vex begins projecting everything that he and Barren discovered. When the projection depicts multiple rooms that look alike, my breath catches. They're more incubators. Well, I don't see the same bubble window as on Vortex, but it's the same layout. There's a dresser and commode in each but not a chair or bed for sleeping. Luckily, the projection also shows the exact coordinates of these rooms on the blueprints. It should be easy enough to locate them.

Before Marrit and I can share what we saw, a gas enters the tunnels. Royce drops first. Seeing him paralyzed brings a flashback of Rigled's lifeless form being dragged away by other guards. Barren's next, his kind and humorous personality drained from his eyes. Flashlight beams appear down the tunnel, but they're around at least one corner. Jordan readies her bow and arrow in the direction of the flashlights. Marrit tries to wake Barren but begins fading herself. As Jordan drops, I hear Vex. The gas must still not affect me.

"Sierra, come here."

"I need to help them," I say.

"The guards are twenty feet from the turn," Vex reports. "You will be unable to assist the others if you too are captured."

I look at the flashlight beams, their circles of light gradually growing larger. Then I look at Marrit, calculating how quickly I can drag her away.

"Five seconds, Sierra."

"Fine."

I move next to Vex, who instantly projects a screen image, causing the tunnel to appear empty behind Royce, Jordan, Barren, and Marrit's still bodies, concealing Vex and me. I have to hold in a scream as I watch the guards collect them. As Vex and I roll and crawl as quietly as possible away, my fear for them grows. What experiment will Cromwell come up with for them? Will he test limb, artery, or pigment transplantation? Will he find their bodies to be the new perfect hosts for his family? The leaden feeling in my body doesn't just weigh my feet down, it travels to every extremity. But I must keep going so they don't get Vex.

"What are we going to do, Vex,?"

"I have the coordinates for Yesha's quarters."

"Really?"

"Yes. We're heading that way now."

"Thank you, Vex."

Vex knows what I need without being told. I need my friend. I recognize when we've reached the quarters section because each vent shows the same thing. Most of the rooms are empty, which is good, but who knows how quickly Cromwell will fill them up.

Seeing Yesha's blonde head is so comforting, I almost forget where I am…almost. Vex pulls a tool from his cartridge and opens the vent.

"Well, look who it cogging is," Yesha says. "How much did you have to help her, Vex? It took forever for you to locate me."

"The team was a bit busy mapping out this place," I say.

"I gave you blueprints," she replies. "I must rank pretty low on the totem pole. You know how that is, right, Vex?"

He responds before I can stop him.

"Well, I was not the one tasked with diversion."

Yesha begins to fume for a second. Then asks, "Where is everyone else?"

"They've been taken."

"Sheesh," she says. "Well, they're probably in cells like this one."

"You're right."

"We should get some rest so we can free them tomorrow."

"Want me to build you a hammock?" I ask her.

"Darn right, you pipsqueak," she says. "You should consider yourself lucky to be able to do so."

"Ha, ha!"

But she's right. Isn't it lucky that I escaped? Cromwell might not associate me with Marrit, Barren, Royce, and Jordan, but he has to know that eventually I'd come for my mom. Yesha's arrival should have been a red flag.

"No, you're right," I say to Yesha. "I am lucky to be here. I would have thought I'd be more of a target to Cromwell."

Yesha rubs her forehead. "Well, I thought I'd let the cat out of the bag already when I almost slipped."

"What are you talking about, Yesha?"

"The truth about you. The one they're keeping hidden from you."

PLANET EARTH

Al

I MOVE TO PLACE A TREE BETWEEN ME AND THE BEAR AS protection. It feels as if my stomach is being twisted in knots. The bear lets out another big snort but seems to have untensed a bit, maybe deciding I'm not really a threat. It shakes its shoulders in a relaxed way. That's good because I know I would not survive a fight with this massive animal. Trying hard not to further alarm the beast, I slowly back away. The sound of my heart hammering fades as I approach the warehouse door. I breathe a sigh of relief as soon as I exit, but then I realize that I no longer have a cogging mode of transportation to get back to the main academy campus. That little gomer, Leon, must really hate me even though we haven't even had a conversation. Given that I just saw him with one of Cromwell's loyal guards, he probably knows more about me than I realize. Come to think of it, I remember the hint of recognition that came over him when he first saw me. Could he know he has a sister…and that I'm dating her? That would give him plenty of reason to hate me. I'd hate me, too.

Luckily, there are other vehicles in the lot and I know how to start them without a digital thumbprint key. I know exactly which one I'll choose the second I see the tank. Nothing can stop me from getting to Coach Brandon before they ship the poor guy to Scepter now. I bump my head getting into the tank, but don't let it slow me down.

I run over the maroon squares with white outlines instead of walking this time. There's no trouble finding the coach; he's on the voltball field as usual.

"Hey, Al," he says as I walk onto the nutrient-enriched, self-growing artificial grass field. "What are you doing here?"

"Brandon, I need to talk to you."

"Kinda in the middle of practice," he says, waving toward the players on the field.

"It's important," I respond. "You're being sent on tour."

"What?" he asks. "How do you know that?"

"I saw your name on a list," I continue. "Listen, there's more."

One of the players approaches us. "Can we hit the showers now?" he asks Brandon.

"No, one more drill," Brandon says. "Repeat the up/down circuit."

The player groans and jogs off, back to his teammates who all scowl but then join him in the assigned exercise.

"What more?" Brandon asks, nudging me.

"You're going to a facility on Planet Scepter," I say. "My knowledge of this kind of facility is extensive, but of the planet, limited."

"Why am I going there?"

"Good question. Can we go somewhere private to discuss this?"

"All right," Brandon yells. "Practice over."

There's cheering and then footsteps as they run to the locker room. Good thing faculty housing isn't too far from the field. We head to Brandon's home. He sends side-eye glances my way the entire time, trying to figure it out, trying to guess what I'm going to say. The plateau behind the housing looks frail, as if it could blow away in the wind. His place looks like an attempt to replicate what we call log cabins on Funen. The metal even has faux wood grain.

As soon as we're inside and the door is closed, he speaks, "What's going on, Al?"

"Okay, the facility you're going to is run by the same guy that ran the Vortex facility."

"Your last job?"

"Yeah."

"Wasn't that like corrupt…there was a revolution, right?"

"Yes, and there are two people I care about at this new one."

"Cog it freaking all."

Brandon sits down with a huff, bringing his fists up to his chin. He breathes out noisily, reminding me of the bear.

"I need your help, man."

"I'm the one being sent on tour, putting myself at risk, and you're asking for favors?"

"Come on, I'd do it for you if your loved ones were in danger."

"Okay, okay." He concedes. "What do you need?"

"Their memory and conscience have been implanted into non-bios," I say. "They need treatment to keep from atrophying."

"What the…?" He's confused, but moves on. "Whatever, I can take them what they need. Tell me about the facility."

I'm glad he's moving forward. Yesha should have what they need there, but I know she'd benefit from an extra set of hands, especially the hands of a guard.

"The facility will be set up with maximum security," I say. "But you'll be assigned as a guard."

"You sure?"

"Trust me."

"I'm trying."

I take a seat too so I can run through all the details of the Planet Vortex facility. He also needs to know what to expect from Cromwell and the government. Then I tell him what I can about Scepter. At first he takes big gulps of air, trying to adjust to his new role, but eventually he's nodding his head in synch with my suggestions. He's ready.

A loud knock sounds on his door.

"Tour recruiting," the voice on the other side of the door says. "Please open the door to report for duty."

As he stands, I stand too. I head to the hallway closet to be out of sight.

Brandon opens the door.

"You have your tour supplies packed?"

"Yes, just need to change out of my practice clothes."

"No time. You're to come with us now."

I wait until I hear the door slam shut behind them to exit the closet. I go to the front window and peer out. Sure enough, it's the low-gravity-beer-drinking guard. But I'm surprised...no shocked...no aghast at who else I see in the vehicle. Septimus is here at the academy, in a vehicle with one of Cromwell's cronies, taking Brandon to Scepter! I pace around Brandon's living room. Septimus knows about Leon. But he didn't tell Vienna. Lately she's said he's been away from the apartment a lot. We thought he'd been trying to earn back his reputation with scientists. But, no, he's been a double agent the whole time! Wait, no. He saved Viscerous and Albina. So that can't be right. Perhaps he and Vienna figured out Leon's location and this is how they plan to get him. But why's the guard with him? And why is Leon no longer with him?

As soon as they're far enough away, I sprint to the cadet dorms. Walking by room after room with bunks and other hints of shared living spaces reminds me of my childhood.

"Where's Leon's room?" I ask a cadet.

"Second floor, Room Twelve," he says. "Wait, what are you doing here?"

I walk away without answering. Skipping every other step, I race to the second floor and knock on the door that says "12."

"Go away," Leon says, approachable as ever.

"I need to talk to you," I say.

"You?" he asks. "What do you want?"

"You left me at the warehouse."

"Looks like you made it back."

"Will you open the door already?"

He opens the door. "I'm kind of in the middle of something."

"It will only be a sec."

"Fine."

I walk in and close the door behind me. "Who was that you left the warehouse with?"

He moves about his room, grabbing things and stuffing them into a bag.

"It was no one," he says.

"You know I used to live in a place like this."

"You said you needed a second, not a chance to tell your life story."

"I lost my parents so I couldn't live at home," I say. "I know what it's like to not have parents."

"Look, man, I'm sorry about your parents, but what does it have to do with me?" he zips up the digital, dissolving zipper on his bag.

"The guy you left the warehouse with…I just saw him with

137

your dad," I say, watching for signs of surprise to appear on his face, but they never do.

"Look, I know you were on Planet Vortex with my dad," he says. He picks up his bag as if ready to leave.

"Do you know your dad's here?" I push.

He lifts his bag higher. "Duh!"

Well, that's cogging great!

"Where are you going?" I ask.

"Planet Scepter, of course," he says. "Now get out of my way already."

"Your sister risked her life to get your dad out of the last facility," I say. "And now you're just going to take him back into another?"

"Didn't she know Cromwell was just going to set up a new one?"

"But now the authorities are on to him."

He gives me an exasperated look, as if I'm the biggest sap.

"You really don't have a clue, do you?" he asks as he steps toward the door.

"Wait, Vienna wants to meet you."

"In due time," he responds. "Until then, will you thank her for being an awesome decoy?" He slaps me on the shoulder hard and enters the hallway.

"She is not a cogging decoy," I yell. Other cadets stare at me from the hall as Leon continues his departure. I've never wanted so badly to punch someone before in my life.

I have to get back to Vienna. I need to tell her everything I just learned. We need to rethink the game plan and re-strategize with the group.

———

As much as I hate flying, I find myself in search of a small supersonic jet. A public transit gliding pod ride would take too long. I need to be there for her when she learns of this newest development. I have to be sure she doesn't go after them, that Vienna doesn't become the decoy Leon claims her to be. She's anything but a decoy. She's an unstoppable force.

I bet Septimus wants to get back to his wife. They must miss each other a lot. Vienna was able to have a few years with them together in her early childhood. Perhaps Leon is bitter about that. I thought family supported one another no matter what. Maybe siblings are different.

The nearest city has a few charters, but there's no way I could afford a flight with them. Instead, I find a retired pilot in the database who runs shorter duration flights to supplement her pension. Her fees are within my budget. The fact that the reason for her leaving the Air Force is sealed doesn't help to decrease my fear of flying.

Takeoff is so bumpy my teeth chatter even as I try to grit them. There are flurries outside—not the clouds I'd imagined. I'm seeing snow fall, not on the ground where I can enjoy it, but in the sky where it blocks part of the pilot's vision. Great!

The jet makes a sudden dip and my stomach's in my chest. I'm relieved when it doesn't last long. But winds of the winter storm continue to sway the aircraft this way and that. I'm never flying again. I have no complaints or questions when the pilot announces that we'll be descending soon.

I'm able to navigate back to Vienna's home without a problem now that I've been there before. The mechanical advertisements suspended in the air remind me of how engineered and unnatural everything feels on this planet. I quietly sneak into the apartment to see if I can get a read on the situation. Will Vienna be pissed when she sees me? I hope not. I'd rather pick up where we left off in her room. The kitchen appears empty, so I pause there to listen. I hear Colsam in the living room. It sounds like he is having a one-sided conversation.

"I can't believe you went to Scepter alone and sent Al here," he says. It must be Yesha on the other line. "Now Al's disappeared too."

There's a bit of silence as Yesha responds. I guess she hasn't killed Cromwell, or at least, if she did, she wasn't caught. I wonder what she's saying.

"What do you mean?" he asks. "How did you--"

She must have interrupted him because he's silent again.

"I don't need the entire story," he responds. "Just tell me what you saw."

I can hear him pacing in the living room like I'd been pacing in Brandon's. Could Leon and Septimus have made it to Scepter already? No, that can't be it.

"Are you sure?" he asks. "You really saw it?"

The pacing has stopped and I hear him take a seat on the couch.

"Dr. Marie Perierat was embracing Cromwell," he says. "Not Sorna implanted into her body because that didn't take."

What in the crap?

I sit down. How can I comfort Vienna with that news? The door from the kitchen opens.

"Al, you're back." It's Vienna.

I stand and nod my head.

"It's really you." She gives me the most magnificent hug, her warmth making me dread the bitter pain she's about to feel.

18

PLANET EARTH

Vienna

REACHING OUT TO YESHA'S FRIENDS IS LIKE ENTERING A world I've never been to before. Even though full-body integrated digital systems were banned, some of Yesha's friends have them. I thought they would only be able to carry out the user's conscious commands. Being able to pull forward all the pertinent information in the universe with a simple thought is pretty freaking awesome. But they do so much more. When the systems-initiated scans to research for any needed health repair, that not 100% of the brain was active all the time triggered alerts. Some of Yesha's hacker friends use their brains at full capacity twenty-four hours a day and seven days a week now, genius times ten. Which is why I'm so hopeful they'll be able to help us with our missions.

"Hey, Mantis," I say.

"Hey, yourself," he responds. "Hear you dragged our friend into some pretty bad crap."

"It wasn't actually that hard to convince her," I say.

"Yeah, I know. So what's up?"

"I need your help."

"Go figure!"

Mantis helps me locate the potential guards for the Scepter facility. Luckily, Milcah was able to grant him access to her mom's system. I had been inspired to ask her to do so after having another one of those visions from the past. Thankfully, I thought of it and spoke to her before the visit as that didn't all go as planned. The visions seem to be occurring more and more often these days. In this particular vision, I was on the attack. I literally tackled two bad guys, and in a fit of rage, somehow transported them to another world. A world so different it was as if everything were connected. It was beautiful and overwhelming simultaneously.

This time, instead of attacking like with the tackle, we're going to turn the direction of the aggression back, boomeranging their own actions. So Mantis isn't removing false charges from the records of those targeted to be guards, but merely correcting the suspects to be individuals on their side instead of ours. Now Cromwell himself will have charges to fight. Hopefully, that will keep him too busy to do more harm.

Another thing we've uncovered from Milcah's mom's records are false diagnoses. Guess Cromwell decided it would be more practical to have those kinds of patients, the ones given false diagnoses, participate in experimental treatments rather than tapping the doctor and medical staff for that. He could probably keep things more peaceful at the new facility by treating those working there better. How he imagines that telling someone they have a terminal illness when they in fact do not is ethical is beyond me. But I shouldn't be surprised. Once again, he's breaking the Oath to Preserve Life.

"Can you believe they convinced this guy that poli-magnos

were causing magnetophosphenes in his vision," Mantis says. "What a doofus!"

"Why would he believe that?" I ask, more like think aloud. "Is his vision being disrupted?"

"Well, yeah, but the dude's been suffering migraines lately."

"Oh," is all I manage as fear creeps in. If this man goes to Scepter to have magnetophosphenes treated, what experiment does Cromwell have planned for him? I cringe at the thought. "How can we stop this?"

"Hmm, why don't I just initiate second opinions for everyone!"

"Mantis, you're the best. No wonder Yesha likes you."

"Well, duh…wait…Yesha likes me? Like LIKES me?"

"Oh…well."

"I knew it."

Oh, sheesh! I didn't mean to insinuate that. How can I backtrack without derailing our progress here? You know what, no! Yesha sent Al here without his consent. She can deal with Mantis when this is all over.

———

The next day I work with Infosec. That has to be a nickname. I wonder if Mantis is an alias too. Wait a minute. Is Yesha really my best cyber friend's name?

"Hey, kid," Infosec greets me. I don't know why she refers to me as kid. I'm fairly sure we're the same age.

"Did Mantis share this access with you?"

"Of course."

"Were you able to find anything useful?"

"Are you sitting down?"

At this, all of a sudden, Kitchen starts moving around like she's preparing a holiday feast.

"What is it, Kitchen?" I ask.

"Your home bot knows what I'm about to tell you," Infosec says. "Actually, she helped me locate some of the data."

"You've been helping, Kitchen?"

"Perhaps you would like some homemade bread when you hear about the discovery," Kitchen says, talking faster than normal. "I have dough prepared."

Wow, this really has her nervous. What in the world is going on?

"Sure, bread sounds lovely," I say to appease Kitchen.

Deep down, the heartache of everything I've seen stirs awake. The betrayals I've felt break out of the thick-walled container in which I've been storing them, saving them to deal with another day. I don't know if I have the strength to hear what I'm about to hear.

I sit down and Kitchen places a warm bread roll in front of me. This triggers another memory, or what feels like a memory, but is actually another vision from the past. A grandma, not my grandma but one I've never met, in a home that feels like my home but is one I've never been to before, sets fresh, home-baked cookies in front of me. My vision blurs back to the present and Kitchen glides away from me to her next task.

"I'm glad you're sitting down," Infosec says to me.

"Yes, get on with it already."

"Your brother wasn't the only baby removed from a mother's womb and taken by the government."

"What? Well, yeah, they did that to all they claimed to be unfit."

"No."

"What do you mean, no?"

"Kitchen, you want to help out?"

"Vienna, your brother was scheduled to be taken before your dad left. The government scheduled all non-firstborn

144

children of certain families to be taken. It's why your parents have had to take the measures and make the connections they have."

I don't know what to say. I can't move an inch. My family is not the only that has had to suffer this. How many have? And my parents in the plural. So not just Dad, but Mom has known all along too. Have I been too oblivious or self-absorbed this entire time not to have noticed?

"How can they do that?" I ask.

"It's something the government has been planning for decades. Actually, I think the idea was first formulated a century or two ago," Infosec says.

"But why?"

"Think about the control you can have if an entire generation looks to you as a caregiver."

"Are they still doing it?"

"Yes, and they plan to for years to come."

"It's just awful," Kitchen says.

"How do you know about this, Kitchen?" I ask.

"Your mother hired a private investigator who was able to help connect me to the nurse bot who cared for your brother. I was able to project the images from the bot."

My jaw drops, remembering all the hours my mom spent working and locked away with holographs. I wonder now how many times she watched her son from afar. I see the dark disks below her eyes and picture her standing, rocking side to side with an imaginary baby in her arms as the nurse bot cared for my baby brother. A tear rolls down my cheek, leaving a hot trail. She really has known all along. She's been heartbroken over more than Dad throughout the years.

"We have to stop them," I choke out to both Infosec and Kitchen.

"Yes, we do," Kitchen says in a determined voice I've never heard before. "I'm reaching out to friendly bots now."

"I will fully support," Closet's elevated volume can be heard from down the hall.

Wow, how have we never considered working with the bots before? That was stupid. They're brilliant, useful, and, as I recollect how many times Kitchen's been there for me, caring.

"My friends are working on it too," Infosec adds. "We moved it up to a current priority."

I hear someone clear their throat and turn to see Colsam leaning against cabinets. "This is worse than what they did on Vortex," he says. "Babies should be off limits."

I remember the pain of the Vortex guards being forced into the facility with false charges, clasping their right hands in a fist on the left side of their chests. And here even Colsam, one of those guards, is saying how awful this all is. It's been surprisingly nice seeing him and Theopat heal recently. I hope they can move forward after the facility and mend, be happy back with their families on Vortex.

"Remember what I said about keeping your enemies close?" he asks me.

"Of course, Colsam."

"Do you have any ties to the government here?"

"There's Milcah's mom," I say.

"You've been connected to her your whole life," Infosec interjects. "If she was going to help, she already would have."

I look over and see Colsam nodding his head.

"There was this one senator who wanted to write me a letter of recommendation to a top military academy," I say.

"Imagine that!" Colsam says. Given all the negative talk about academies and my brother, I can see why he'd have reservations.

"No, it's not like that," I argue.

"Are you sure?" Infosec asks.

"Yes."

"Give me the name so I can put a meeting on the senator's calendar."

"Really?" I ask Infosec, and she nods her head affirmatively on the holograph screen.

"Her name is Kelley Cinema," I say.

"Okay, you're all set. You'll meet with her tomorrow at 11:00 a.m."

That doesn't give me a lot of time to prepare, so Colsam and I meet with Albina to discuss tactics and argument points. After a few hours, I believe we have a strong case in our hands to present.

————

Above the Capital building is a beautiful, winged statue that makes me think of flying on Aviator. The tan stone of the building reminds me of the Vortex desert and the curlicue rock pattern on the front center of the roof peak gives it a delicate, antique feel. None of these details helps to calm my nerves as I enter the front door.

I walk up to the welcoming desk in the center of the main floor.

"Name and reason for your visit," the man behind the desk says.

"Vienna Perierat," I begin, glad that I've changed the name on my identification to match (my clone really deserves the name Sierra). "I'm here to see Senator Cinema."

He flips through the holograph and touches the screen. A rectangle on it turns green at his touch and I'm haunted by the thought of Cromwell's tests, candidate match.

"You're good to go," the man says, snapping me back to the present. "Third floor, Suite fifteen."

I'm grateful the elevator isn't see-through like the one at the Vortex stem cell harvesting center. I enter, and hit the button with a three on it. My nerves bounce and my stomach seems to jiggle as I walk down the hall to Suite Fifteen. Upon entry I'm greeted by another government employee.

"Right this way, Vienna," she says. "Kelley's ready for you."

I follow her into an office so grand I instantly feel underdressed.

Floor-to-ceiling windows allow the entire room to be filled with natural light. In between the windows are bookshelves just as tall. They're made of wood I've never seen before except in the antique store. I walk up to one and rub my fingers along the grain.

"Please be seated," the government employee says, pointing to a chair.

I take a seat and wait. I thought Kelley was ready to meet. Where is she? Even her desk is made of wood. How different. I place my hand on the top to feel the texture.

"It's marvelous, isn't it?" a voice behind me says.

I turn around and see the senator. I didn't even hear her enter. "Yes, it really is."

She extends her hand as she approaches me. I shake it just as I did with Viscerous and Al, firmly and strongly. Her grip matches mine. It makes this meeting feel familiar and a bit more comfortable immediately.

"What brings you here today, Vienna?" She moves to the other side of the desk and takes a seat in a leather chair that looks old and new at the same time.

"I've learned some disturbing news that I thought you could help with," I say.

"Oh?" Is how she responds. That could be a true question or just a dissembling exclamation.

"Did you know babies are being taken from wombs to be raised in non-bio wombs even when the parents are fit?"

She doesn't answer right away but instead ponders the question for a bit. I came on too strongly. I always do. I don't have the grace or social knowhow. Maybe I should have asked someone else to do this. She's staring at me and it makes my skin crawl.

"What makes you think this?" is all she asks.

"My source has asked to remain anonymous, but we have gathered proof," I say.

Her eyebrows arch ever so slightly and she fidgets in her seat a little. What if she has a call button under her desk? I bet there's a secret latch in one of the books that will open the shelf and reveal a secret dungeon for prisoners. I take a deep breath to remind myself that she's not Cromwell.

"That's very impressive, Vienna," she says. "It is unfortunately true. But what you and your source failed to find out, I'm sure, is just how much worse the alternative is."

"What alternative?"

"Unfortunately, it's classified information," she says. "That will be all now."

All of a sudden the employee who had brought me in is beside me ushering me out. I try to object but it's no use. I leave feeling like a failure. I'm relieved to see Al when I enter my apartment. He's back when I need him most.

19

PLANET SCEPTER

Sierra

"What are they hiding from me, Yesha?"

"I wish I could offer you a seat, but of course, one hasn't been provided."

"Tell me!"

"Okay."

"Al didn't want Vienna to die. He didn't want her to sacrifice herself on Vortex. You know Cromwell doesn't even think we need beds."

"Um, but I did sacrifice myself." I point to the non-bio my memory and conscience are implanted in and look back at her. "Why are you speaking about me as if I'm not in the room? Why do you keep saying Vienna? I've been going by Sierra for some time now."

Yesha sighs. "You're a clone, Sierra."

"Excuse me?"

"Al made a clone."

150

My feet and hands tingle, and I'm unable to think clearly. I'm a clone! Black spots fill my vision and I'm out. It's just too much.

"Sierra, wake up. Are you okay?"

Yesha's quarters come slowly back into view. She's kneeling over me, taking my pulse. Then she lifts my eyelids, checking iris dilation.

"I'm fine, Yesha."

I sit up, but blood rushes to my head, so I decide not to stand.

"No, you're not. We need to continually administer stem cells in order for the non-bio not to reject your memory and conscience."

"That shouldn't be too difficult. My stem cells were harvested at the stem cell factory line on Vortex."

"Yes, but that wasn't exactly you. We need stem cells from the cloned body."

"But it's a clone. It should be identical."

"That's what I thought, too, but your symptoms seem to prove that wrong."

Vex beeps and then says, "Yes, I can confirm that the stem cells that were harvested will not be sufficient."

Well, I guess I have been experiencing some unusual symptoms.

"So what do we do?" I ask.

"We go get what you need, pipsqueak," Yesha says.

I'm actually able to smile, and Yesha smiles back. It's okay. I feel normal for a second.

"Was my body even preserved though?"

"Your mom saw to that. She was sure to save the body. It's in a cryogenic freezer. I just need to make one stop on our way."

"And we need to get Marrit and the crew too."

"Yeah, yeah, but first we need to rest. You owe me a

hammock."

When she mentions rest I feel the events of the day weighing me down and am about to collapse. I use the jackets and other things from the dresser to construct Yesha's bed. I don't worry about preserving any clothes. We're on a mission that won't require them. Then I take the dresser drawers and place them upside down and use the remaining items to make myself a bed atop them. Pretty soon Yesha's out. I fall asleep faster than I ever have before.

———

"Good morning, sunshine," Yesha says. "It's time to go get those stem cells."

She looks fully ready to go. I borrow her toothbrush and prepare for more tunnel venturing, though I'm not entirely sure it's safe.

"I'm ready." Or as ready as I'll ever be.

"Great, come on."

And so we're back in the tunnels, surrounded by the smell of watermelon.

I recognize the route we're taking together to the cryogenic freezer room. It's different from the one I used to get to Yesha but should pass by the hub. I can get information I need there to end the facility and, hopefully, pinpoint Marrit's location.

Nearing the vent above the hub, Yesha and I hear conversation that brings me back to the beginning of all this, when we were applying to the Vortex facility. Wait, though—that wasn't even me. I don't know how to wrap my brain around it. I'm too cogging upset to think clearly.

"Take a look at this application," one admin says to another. He's drinking coffee and scrolling through what looks like hundreds of forms on his holograph screen.

I place a hand on Yesha's shoulder. When she looks at me,

I roll my eyes and then give her a look, letting her know my agitation with this place is boiling over. She holds up a hand and then her index finger, asking me to give her a second.

"That's hilarious. Do they really think they can get in here?"

The first admin then glances at the time.

"Let's go get some breakfast. I'm starving."

And with that, we have the hub to ourselves.

"How did you know?" I ask Yesha.

"Remember Cromwell and schedules?" she asks. "That hasn't changed. It never will...until he's dead."

She says the last part under her breath, but I don't miss it. Then she pulls out a handheld holograph from her pocket and proceeds to hack into the hub.

"What are you looking for? We can divvy up the tasks."

"Yeah, sure. I'm downloading security access so we can lock and unlock doors at any time," she shares.

"Can you send a warning to all applicants and alarm the authorities about the facility?"

And just like before we ever met IRL, we're working together, throwing sarcastic remarks back and forth the entire time.

A sudden depression overwhelms me when I realize the memories aren't mine. I'm only a clone. Clone or not, I still can't let more people become victims of Cromwell's crimes, so I send the warnings and sound the alarm. But in the back of my mind, I realize I wouldn't exist if it weren't for Cromwell's practices.

"Okay, I'm done," Yesha says. "How are you doing?"

I want to reply with a remark that will continue our usual banter, but can't seem to find the motivation.

"I'm done too," is all I manage.

We reenter the tunnels and head to the freezer room. My movements feel mechanical as we go. The temperature drops when we near the room and keeps on dropping as we squeeze through the vent.

"It can't still be breakfast, can it?" I ask Yesha.

"I downloaded the schedules too," she says. "It's class time."

"Eew, don't remind me…" I cut myself short. It wasn't me with Yesha in the classroom.

"Let's see," she says as she walks by the floor-to-ceiling cabinets of cryogenic freezer beds, reading each label. Only Cromwell's family were given the glass-faced beds at the center of the room.

We're interrupted by voices coming from the other side of the entrance. Yesha grabs my forearm, tugging me to a hiding spot. Luckily, it has a good view. I want to see who's entering.

"It will be good for you to view them," my mom says to Cromwell.

"I don't think I can look at their lifeless forms another time," he answers back.

They walk to the beds at the center of the room.

"They would want to be themselves. We could make a non-bio body that looks exactly as Sorna did before the vulture attack."

"Non-bios have flaws too."

"Your first option didn't take."

"We could use aging programs to create as close to a teenage version of Damien as possible."

"I still blame the clone for that not working. If I'd had the biological original instead of a replicate, it would have worked."

"Can't say I'm upset about that."

"Yes, now you have a backup in place in case something happens to your daughter."

My heart sinks to my stomach. Replica, backup, is that all I am?

Before I can wallow in my sorrow a moment longer, I notice Yesha creep forward with a flame-throwing club in hand. Where did that come from?

"What are you doing?" I whisper.

"I'm finally going to kill that madman," she says.

"No, Yesha," I say. "It's too dangerous."

"He killed my brother," Yesha's voice raises and I place my hand on her shoulder gently to try to calm her. I can see the anger and hate in her eyes when she looks at me. A part of me understands her pain, but I can't let her put herself in danger. She needs to move on.

"Wouldn't that be too quick a death?" I ask, pointing to the flame-throwing club.

I see it register and she scoots back into our hiding spot. When I look back up, Cromwell's holding my mom's hands and they're looking at each other in a way they shouldn't be. My hand reaches for the club but it's not there.

"Oh, no you don't," Yesha whispers.

My mom and Cromwell exit and Yesha and I get back to searching the cabinets. I head one direction and she goes the other way. Looking at the names, I try to make sense of the order. They're not alphabetical, so I start looking at the numbers instead. They're in chronological order by birthdate. As a clone, I'm probably the youngest, but when I reach the front, my name's not there. It must be my other birth date. I see it a few feet away.

"Can you roll the apheresis machine over here?" I ask Yesha.

"Sure," she replies while standing next to the beds at the center of the room.

"How are we going to run this for days without anyone noticing?" I ask.

"That depends," she replies.

"On what?"

"Do you want to preserve the cryogenically frozen body, or can we rapidly increase extraction?" she asks. "You can always reproduce from the removed cells and freeze those in a much more portable fashion."

That's a difficult decision. Technically speaking, a quick vacuum of the stem cells out of the body is best. If it ruins the body, though, I'll never be the person I remember. But does that matter? Al's probably with Vienna. While my mom, if I can even consider her that, saved the body, she didn't exactly push to bring "me" back. The body is just an alternate for her true daughter. I press the button for full speed.

As soon as it's complete alarms ring and the room is engulfed in red light. A hiss sounds as smoke rises from the beds at the center of the room.

"If I can't have my family back, why should he?" Yesha asks.

20

PLANET EARTH

Al

"Yes, it's me," I say into Vienna's hair as our hug continues.

She pulls away and then slaps me right across the face. Cog, that hurt, but I know I deserve it. I massage my jaw and plead for forgiveness with my eyes.

"How could you just leave like that?" she asks.

I can see my pleading had no effect. "I wanted to help."

"And where is my brother, you Universe Soldier in a shining suit come to rescue the day?"

She's more pissed than I'd imagined she'd be. Good, maybe anger can help keep sadness at bay.

"Vienna, I need to tell you something," I say.

"What?" she asks. "Now you want to talk?"

"You might want to take a seat."

"Fine."

I reach to put my hands on her forearms to comfort her,

but she pulls them away and crosses her arms in front of her chest.

"How long have all of you guys been cooped up in here?" I ask.

"Long enough to have everyone's daily habits memorized," she responds, and then lets out an exasperated breath. "What is it, Al?"

"It's about your dad," I say. "I think he's more closely tied to Cromwell than we thought."

Milcah, the one whose mom is on the academy board, walks in partway through my statement. "Is that what you were able to learn on your little venture?" she asks me.

I look at Milcah and then at Vienna. They're not surprised. "You noticed him missing too," I say.

"Yeah, that, and Vienna finally figured out that Septimus and my mom have had a thing for years," Milcah says.

I seem to have missed a lot while I was gone.

"Wait, but why are you telling me about my dad?" Vienna asks. "Weren't you with my brother?"

"Your brother's in on it too," I say.

Vienna stands back up, probably to pace, just as Colsam and Harper enter the room. This isn't going to be pretty.

"Vienna, I just spoke with Yesha," Colsam says.

"Oh, good," Vienna says. "She's okay, right? Did she have any luck getting to my mom and clone?"

"She's hanging in there," Colsam says. "But Yesha saw your mom…"

"Yes," Vienna approaches Colsam. "And?"

Colsam looks nervous. I almost tell her so he doesn't have to, but he pipes up before I do.

"Yesha saw your mom and Cromwell embracing," he says.

"Like embracing, embracing?" Milcah asks.

Vienna smiles. "Oh, Colsam, you know Sorna's memory and consciousness are in my mom's body, right?"

Colsam sits, encouraging Vienna to do the same. "Remember, that didn't take. Cromwell put her memory and conscience back into her body."

I rise and stand next to Vienna since she didn't sit.

"Shoot, you're right," Vienna says, and Colsam nods his head, unable to speak. "What's wrong with my parents?"

"I'm sure there's more to it," I say. "Maybe your parents are just trying to find a way to get to Cromwell and end the new facility."

"You didn't get the memo, did you?" Milcah asks me. "All parental figures suck."

"Really, Milcah," Vienna interjects. "You say that to the one person here who's lost both parents!"

Harper goes to Milcah and holds her hand. Vienna storms out of the room and I follow, but when we get to her bedroom, she closes the door behind her, blocking me. "I just need a moment alone," she says. "Okay?"

"Okay," I say. "Are you going to meditate?"

"Yeah, sure."

"Well, let me know when you're done. It would be good for you to get out of here."

As I retreat to the living room, I notice Danver, Milcah's ex, moving about in ways that are totally illogical. As I get closer, I see the contacts, earpiece, and extremity sensors and realize he's in chip virtual reality.

"What you playing?" I ask.

"Voltball," he says. "Want to join?"

"Sure." I look around and locate another player box.

We're on opposite teams. I can tell Danver's a voltball player. His team's plays are by the book. What he doesn't know is that I've played this virtual reality game before. A guard snuck it into the facility last year. It feels like ages ago now. I sneak in a Hail Mary touchdown for the win.

"Man, how'd you do that?" he asks while putting away the equipment and sitting on the couch.

I join him. "That was fun," I say. "We should do that more often. I bet everyone here could use a little pick-me-up."

"Hey, I think it's cool that you stood up for Vienna's parents back there."

"Thanks."

"Don't let Milcah get to you. The whole parent topic is a touchy one with her."

There's a brief pause before he continues.

"Plus, I think you're actually onto something," he says.

"Oh, yeah?"

"Yeah, but I don't think they're going after Cromwell."

I tilt my head to encourage him to go on.

"Cromwell's a decoy, man," Danver says. "Just like they've set me up to be."

"I don't know. Cromwell's pretty damaging."

"I think there's worse."

"Worse than this?" I nod toward my arms and legs.

Colsam and Theopat join us in the living room.

"I think he's on to something, Al," Colsam says.

"Okay, I'm listening," I say.

"Think about it. We know Cromwell not only had connections with the Vortex government but the World Government too."

"Yeah, and Milcah's mom is part of the World Government," I say.

"But she's the president of the academy board," he says. "Could she really have pull with enforcement authorities?"

"She's connected to the draft," I say.

"Yeah, that's a piece, but come on…Septimus & Marie Perierat. Do they seem threatening to you?"

"Careful how you judge," Theopat interjects.

"Theopat, Septimus saved lives over and over again on

Vortex," Colsam says. "Marie paid a hefty price in order to try to save Vienna. These are not threatening people."

"But Septimus with Milcah's mom and Marie with Cromwell!" Theopat exclaims.

"That could be a cover for their covert activity," I say.

"Exactly, there's got to be something else," Danver adds.

"What did I hear about covert activity?" Albina asks as she and Viscerous enter the room.

"The covert activity we're going to participate in as soon as we blow this joint," I say as Viscerous gives me a high five.

Everyone begins whooping and hollering with excitement at the prospect of going out.

"What's all the racket?" Vienna asks, coming down the hallway. "How do you expect someone to meditate with this ruckus?"

"You'll have to save the meditation for later," I say. "We're going out."

"Oh, I have the perfect outfit," Theopat squeals as she runs to change. I notice Vienna smile at her out of the corner of my eye—good.

Maybe Vienna will open up to me while we're out because not only do I feel like more is going on with Cromwell and the government, there's also more going on with her.

"How in the world are we going to be able to find a place to fit all ten of us?" Vienna asks.

Milcah and Harper have joined us. They're signing so fast I don't know how either of them are understanding anything.

"We can go to Harper's parent's arcade," Milcah says, and a blush blooms on Harper's cheeks.

Walking the streets with our group is completely different from when I first arrived on Earth and traveled everywhere by myself. Back then, I had mostly noticed the lack of vegetation and cold feel of the city. Now, with more people on the streets, there's a buzz as if a charge passes from one person to the next, an electric current filling us all with energy.

I notice the artwork on the buildings. Vienna explains how new pieces are commissioned continually to make up for the lack of natural color, but I'm unable to soak in more than that. One of the pieces has brought me to a complete stop. The artwork is something I've seen before. The artist is…my mother.

"Al, what is it?" Vienna asks. "Are you okay?"

I don't respond because I can't. It's like there's a fist in my chest gripping my heart.

"Go ahead. We'll meet up with you later," Vienna tells the group.

I think I nod. I think Albina gives me a hug.

Vienna grabs my hand and pulls me into the café we're in front of. She orders a couple of drinks and sets us on the barstools at the window, not interrupting my gaze. Moments later, she can no longer remain silent.

"Hey, snap out of it," she says. "You're really beginning to worry me."

"I thought all of her work had been destroyed," I manage.

"Whose work?" she asks.

"My mom's."

Vienna looks at my eyes and then turns to the artwork. We're both silent for a few more minutes, soaking in the details and colors made with every brush stroke.

Vienna puts her arm around my shoulders. "It's beautiful. She was extremely talented."

"Yeah, but I don't understand how it got here."

"There are art collectors all over the universe," she says. "I'm sure if one ran across this they'd do whatever was needed to acquire it."

"You don't understand," I say. "After the enforcers killed my parents, I snuck back to our home before running away."

"That took courage." Vienna rubs my shoulder with her hand.

"It was probably stupid, but I got away."

"What did you see when you snuck back?"

"I didn't have to get very close," I say. "Well, I couldn't."

"Why, Al?" she asks. "You can tell me."

"Because our house and everything inside of it, I assumed, was burning to the ground."

"Oh," she says. "I'm sorry, Al."

"So you see, the only way that artwork is on the building is because they must have taken it."

She turns back to the painting. We both do. Our drinks remain untouched.

21

TIME JUMP

Vienna

THE NEXT APPOINTMENT INFOSEC SETS UP WITH SENATOR Kelley Cinema isn't for me. We learned better last time. Since Kelley and Milcah's mom have had a healthy rivalry over the years, we thought it would be more successful if Milcah met with her. It won't be difficult for her to play the role of scorned child. Infosec walks us through it, putting a secret cam and microphone on Milcah. We also design an almost invisible earpiece with Harper's help so we can communicate to her if need be.

Her experience with the senator begins like mine, but changes at the point where I hadn't played it cool and said too much too soon. She doesn't seem to be as impressed with the office as I had been either. Anxiety still creeps in when I notice Harper nervously chewing her nails as we sit and all watch Milcah full of anticipation.

"It's a pity that you and your mom aren't getting along," Kelley says to Milcah.

"Well, you know all too well how difficult she can be," Milcah responds, and Kelley nods in agreement. Milcah must smirk because Kelley does the same—it looks like a mirrored response. "What was it that caused you two to bicker so much?" Milcah asks Kelley.

"Well, now that's a long story and most of it is classified."

I think I hear Milcah sniffle as if she were about to cry. I've got to hand it to her. She's a much better actress than I ever could be.

"Hey, no need to get worked up," Kelley says.

"I wish I knew why my mom is so difficult."

"Well, you know, I think you could follow in her footsteps professionally," Kelley says. "It might bring you two closer."

"Yeah, right," Milcah says. "I think she'd fight more with me than she does with you!"

Kelley stands and approaches Milcah. "But you have thought about going into the field."

"How did you know?" Milcah accidentally blocks the camera when she rubs her nose while talking. We lose sight of Kelley for a second, but when we see her again, she has a look of sympathy and her hand is on Milcah's shoulder.

Harper stands up and fists her hands.

"You have a better than perfect GPA," Kelley says. "And a knack for being cunning. Two of the most vital necessities."

"Really?"

Now Harper lets out an exasperated huff. I'm in shock. I'd never pegged Milcah as the scholarly type.

"You think I could help improve Earth?"

"No, Milcah, you could save the universe."

And so, Kelley tells Milcah what it is that they've really been up to, why taking fetuses and raising them in the lab where they can be altered is necessary. She goes on to talk about how the universe has been expanding since the big bang, but one day will reach its max. She says at that point the universe will implode on itself. Without intervention, everything we know will cease to exist—humankind, alien kind, animals, robots, everything gone. So while, yes, it's heartbreaking for the family that loses a child, it's necessary to save us all. Before she can explain more about this and how they intend to stop it, our feed cuts out.

What happened? Harper asks.

"Something's interrupting the connection," Infosec says.

Harper paces back and forth.

What's wrong? I ask.

The senator is recruiting Milcah.

She's right. That's why she was so open to sharing information. I'd been more focused on questioning the validity of her story than her motive to share it with Milcah.

But, Harper, the implosion of the universe shouldn't happen for a billion years.

Duh!

Exactly what is she recruiting Milcah into then?

The feed returns as Milcah's exiting the office. "You'll think about my offer?" Kelley says to her as she goes.

I need to go for a walk, Harper says.

Want me to come with you?

No, I'm good.

I'm glad she declines my offer. I want time to clear my head and meditate. Maybe then I can figure out what's really going on.

"Thanks, Infosec."

She signs off and I head to my room to be alone. Once there, I sit in the butterfly position. The vision appears quickly, but instead of the past, it looks like the future. Al's older...and...I'm pregnant. There's a moment of elation, but then enforcers are approaching me with surgical devices, attempting to get a digital protoplasm-bladed scalpel near my belly. Maybe this is a daymare instead of a vision. I open my eyes, ending the meditation. That was not an ideal way to relax. Who am I kidding? I don't have time to relax. I need to figure out what the senator is really up to, or at least why it requires taking children from parents. If the government had a better alternative, surely we could get them to stop.

"Why do you look so deflated?" Albina asks as I enter the living room. I tell her about everything the senator said and we compare notes.

"I find it odd," Albina says. "All of you, Milcah, Al, you, even Damien, are or supposedly were only children."

"Oh, I guess I hadn't thought about that."

"Could your families all have been targeted?"

"No, at least I don't think so," I say. "I think Milcah's parents divorced, so that might be why they have only one child."

"Okay, we'll table that for now," Albina says. "But she is possibly being recruited now."

"True," I agree. "And Al's parents were killed before they could have more kids."

"About that," Albina says. "I found out, but it's hard for me to say without tearing up—Al's mom was pregnant when they killed her."

"That's awful," I say, thinking about how much the enforcers had stolen from Al's family. "Do you know what the enforcers had been looking for?"

"All I've been able to gather is that Al's parents knew something they shouldn't," Albina says.

"Hmm, okay," I say. "And Damien and Sorna were attacked by vultures so I think that rules them out."

"But that's the thing," Albina says. "Before the vulture attack, it had been different. I mean, Cromwell didn't build the facility in a corrupt way. In the beginning, it had actually not been bad."

"Really?"

"Yeah, and that's what's had me wondering," Albina continues. "With Cromwell knowing all of your parents I wonder if he had been trying to help them. I think someone made the vultures attack his family."

"Oh!" *Could that possibly be true, I wonder?*

"Why else would your dad stick around to help him?" Albina asks. "He felt guilty and so did your mom."

I don't even know what to say.

"If Cromwell helped them save their second child at the cost of his only kid, I bet they'd feel indebted to him for life."

The room around me begins to spin and I have to take a deep breath. All of the scents of my family home take on a tinge of decay. Albina says something but her voice is unclear as if she's talking through a tunnel that muffles sound. My mouth becomes dry but then I feel a warm embrace. Albina's hugging me.

"Everything okay in here, ladies?" Viscerous asks as he and Colsam enter the room.

"We're good," Albina says. "She's just a little concerned about our latest revelation."

"Oh," Colsam says. "I wonder if it's the same one we've had."

"What is it?" I ask.

"Are you sure you're ready?" Viscerous asks.

"Get on with it already," I say.

"Okay, well we've been thinking about how easy it was for Al to get into the academy."

"He's pretty stealthy," I say. "Maybe you're not giving him enough credit."

Viscerous clears his throat. "There's no one who believes in Al more than we do," he says, pointing to Albina and himself.

"But even I can appreciate that things lined up a little too easily on this trip."

"Okay…" I say hesitantly.

"I had Theopat take a vial of blood during his nap," Colsam says.

"You what?"

"We found traces of poison," Viscerous says in an uncomfortable voice.

"No!" Albina's voice is raised and desperation clings to her words.

It hasn't fully hit me. I can't let it. "Who?" I seethe.

"Um," Colsam chokes on his words.

"Sheesh, let it out, for goodness' sake," I say, and Colsam looks hurt.

"Your brother," Viscerous says with agony in his voice.

That's it. Maybe siblings are the greatest rivals. My nostrils expand as I fume.

"What can we do?" Albina asks through tears.

"We're running labs now to determine if there's an antidote."

I force myself to keep it together as I consider our options. Then I hear a fracas as someone enters the apartment.

You will not go back there, Harper signs to Milcah. *You said she's full of it yourself.*

You don't get to tell me what to do, Milcah signs back.

I approach and sign, *What are you two talking about?*

The senator's only after power, Harper signs. *The implosion is a hoax. They're taking babies for power and power alone.*

So send the footage from the meeting to the media, Milcah signs and shrugs her shoulders.

Harper's eyes widen and she looks at Milcah. Then she gives Milcah a hug. It really is a great idea. I wish I had thought of it. Perhaps I let my aversion to the media get in the way of seeing it as a possibility. It's hard to think you can rely on something that's dragged your family through hell time and time again.

Milcah's quite innovative as she and Harper work to expose the corruption by reaching out to contacts at different media outlets. So many politicians gained prestige and power with the unethical practices while honest, hardworking government servants were pummeled. But they were the ones to discover that the machines keeping Earth's atmosphere from collapsing after the asteroid will only last so long. Society had looked down on their ideas because they had been perceived as lower caliber. But, maybe with the media sharing the corruption, things will turn around. Barriers of entry often happen to be biased. Perhaps it's for protection…keeping information in a tight-knit circle because only the babies taken and altered will be able to travel to the world that replaces Earth.

Yesha gets word to us about the new facility not happening but that my mom will help Cromwell with moving his family to non-bios the way it should be. We are all so relieved to know that we don't have to worry about another facility. Hopefully, the nightmares of what experiments Cromwell would come up with will stop now. I'm glad he's moved to non-bios. I just wish he had done it so much sooner.

I meditate to try to find an antidote for Al because we have been anything but successful on that.

Finally perfected telepathy, Sis. Leon communicates to me the way Mom has.

What do you want? I ask.

Stop interfering with the embryo work, he says.

Why would you of all people want that to continue? I ask.

If you keep interfering, I'll be forced to administer the full dose of poison, he says.

Were you the one who did that to Al? I ask.

You should pick smarter boyfriends, Sis, he says.

I could crawl right out of my skin. I wish there were a way

I could hurt him through telepathy but I can't and that could endanger Al.

Is Dad in agreement with you?, I ask, hoping the answer's no.

Who do you think first came up with the embryo idea? he asks. *Consider the science behind it.*

Tears of frustration squeeze through my eyelids. An image begins to stream through my meditative state so I breathe calmly and focus. I see Leon. I see my brother for the first time. He has a smirk on his face, but I pay no attention to that. I focus further to the image beyond calling me.

Al's mother's artwork bleeds through, first as just a background, but then moving forward in front of Leon. It's as if she's sending me a message from the afterlife. Or maybe this poison has been used by our enemies for a long time. What I hadn't noticed before was the beautiful Purple Cicada Tree from Planet Funen in the background. The fruits from this tree can cause coma and seizures and, if too much is ingested, even cause death. The only cure is an extract from the tree's flowers. Looks like we really will be going to Funen. Thank you, Al's mom.

Wake up, Sis, Leon says. *We don't live in a fairy tale.*

Fine, I'll back off for now, I say.

Good.

I close the meditation, which ends the telepathic communication.

22
TIME WARP

Sierra

"Cog it all, Yesha!" I say. "Do you really think this is what your brother would have wanted?"

"Cromwell can't just get away with what he's done."

We don't have enough time. Sure, we could lock the doors to buy us the minutes we need and bring back the lives she's just released. Or we could use this distraction to save Marrit and the others. Then we could escape before the authorities arrive and hopefully send Cromwell to jail.

I choose the selfish option. Yesha and I are in the tunnels before the doors explode open. I have to pry Yesha away from the vent as she's sucked into watching Cromwell drop to his knees and sob. I dread the thought of when it will all come back to her, when the realization of what she's done fully sets in. I fear it will drown her in an anguish her brother would never want.

"Follow me," Vex whispers, while also projecting a captioned text. "The others are this way."

I can't stop wondering and worrying. What did Sorna ever do? What did Damien ever do? Wouldn't having them back hopefully bring an end to Cromwell's obsession?

`Mom, can you hear me?`

There's a pause and I begin to worry, but we should be beyond the blocker and able to communicate now. Then I hear her.

`Sierra, I'm here. We're a little busy right now. Is there something you need?`

`Were you able to save Sorna and Damien?`

`That was you?`

`Well, not exactly, but are they going to be okay?`

There's a pause.

`Yes, we got to them just in the nick of time.`

Maybe it's weird, but I'm extremely relieved that they're okay. I might hate Cromwell, but the thought of Sorna being alive and loving Damien left a lasting impression on me. I remember the guard in the desert saying how the facility had been a different place when they were around. Could it have been tolerable at one point, even better than that possibly?

`Good. I think non-bios are the way to go.`

`I agree, but what did you do with your old body, Sierra?`

`I need the stem cells to ward off the symptoms I've been experiencing.`

`But you ruined the body.`

`It's just an alternate, Mom.`

`My daughter would never do that.`

Silence follows, and deep down I know that's the last conversation I'll have with Dr. Perierat. Her final words to me burn deep. Vienna probably would have sacrificed herself and not damaged the body. But she also would leave her clone hanging out to dry as if I have no soul at all. Wasn't I the one worried about Sorna and Damien?

"Sierra, are you ready?" Yesha asks.

"We're above the cell holding your friends," Vex says, projecting an infrared picture of the room below us. The clopil continues to amaze me.

I'm happy to see them alive and hope that they haven't been damaged.

Yesha and Vex work together, as there's a lock on this vent that we haven't encountered before. My heart pounds as they work, wondering how far behind Cromwell will be. I picture them crammed in the tiny cell and cringe. Marrit seems to be the kind of person who likes open spaces and freedom. But I guess there are far worse things one could experience in one of Cromwell's facilities than claustrophobia.

When the vent is removed, all of their faces peer up at us and I'm flooded with relief. Royce lifts Jordan on his shoulders. How she's able to balance standing there, I'll never know. Yesha and I help her into the tunnel. Then Royce lifts Marrit and we pull her in too. I'm able to breathe a sigh of relief. Royce goes to grab Barren.

"I got it, man. How about I give you a boost?" Barren asks.

"Are you sure?"

Barren nods, yes, and with that he's providing a step up for Royce. Then Barren shows acrobatic skills I didn't know he possessed. He leaps and uses one leg to push off the opposite wall, landing with his hands on the vent edge.

As he pulls himself up, the door to the cell opens and we're quickly pulling him the rest of the way into the tunnel. But the guard who enters jumps and snags Barren's shoe.

"The newcomer below is registered as the brother to Theopat of Vortex," Vex says.

"Come with us," I say as I lean my head over the vent opening.

He tosses Barren's shoe up. "Take care of Theopat."

"But?"

"Go!"

Yesha and Vex do not delay putting the vent back in place.

Everyone crawls away as quickly and quietly as they can. I take one more look below.

"What did you find?" I hear Cromwell ask over a communication device.

"Nothing, sir," Theopat's brother says. "They're long gone."

As we crawl, worry resurfaces when I remember we won't have Yesha as a distraction to get from the roof to outside the perimeter. But the feeling of fresh air once we exit that same glass door on the roof relieves me, nonetheless.

"They're still here," Barren exclaims when we see the hovers.

Everyone runs to them, but we're distracted by the sound of wings flapping in the distance. Sure enough, every guard has turned in the direction of the parrots, too. I don't think I've seen anything quite so beautifully colored. And that's when I spot Nobilia leading the group.

My heart lurches to my throat, seeing every guard turned Nobilia's way. With a nod, Nobilia communicates to me and I sign, *Thank you*. Red dots form on some of the birds, but they dip, avoiding the shots. I have to focus on what we're doing to override my fear of the guards.

"Come on," Marrit says. "The distraction won't last forever."

While the hover departs, I turn my head around to be sure Nobilia is making it to safety. The parrot never judged me, other than for my lack of fashion sense. I never felt like a clone in the shop. In fact, I never felt like a clone anywhere in the Capital.

Then I see a red dot on Marrit's back.

"Dip, Marrit," I scream and move my body to block the red dot. She dips and I'm glad to not feel anything hit my back. I yell to the others so they know to make air combat maneuvers too but feel a little relief when I don't see red dots on them.

As soon as we're safely beyond the perimeter, the birds fly away to safety too.

I've witnessed so much selfless sacrifice, despite being surrounded by abuse and heartache. The now safe hover trip to the shuttle gives me a couple minutes to reflect on it all. I am Sierra. I have a non-bio body and will require stem cells for the rest of my life. I don't really have a home and many of the relationships I thought I had don't actually exist because I'm a clone.

Marrit must sense my anxiety because she grabs my hand. We hold each other in a reach around hug of sorts the rest of the way. I realize that her holding me feels like home. Not the apartment belonging to Vienna, her parents, and missing brother. Not with Al or anyone from the Vortex facility, but here with Marrit. Before we land, I look to see if there are any alligators or beetles, but I don't spot any.

"Vex, scan for danger," I say, and then wonder who Vex would choose, me or Vienna.

"The coast is clear for a quarter mile diameter," he says. "Nobilia made sure of that."

My debt to the bird continues to grow. "Thanks, Vex."

We land near the shuttle. Royce and Jordan begin preparing their packs, filling them with fruits and leaves from the jungle.

"What will you do now?" I ask.

"Since your friend informed the authorities about the facility, we're heading back to the Capital," Jordan says, pointing to

Yesha. "Don't worry. We'll make sure it's brought to an end one way or another."

"You'll need to meet with the others, Sierra," Yesha says. "They need our help to clear names and I owe Al an apology."

"Can't I just go to the Capital?" I ask. "I won't be much help to you there."

"You wouldn't want to leave any loose ends," Marrit says, and that's when I realize she doesn't know I'm a clone. What will she think when she finds out? Will she look at me differently? Will she push me out, not by saying goodbye but by slowly ceasing to respond at all, as if I didn't matter a bit?

"They're not really my loose ends," I say.

"Come on, now," she says. "Everyone has loose ends."

"I don't," I spout out of my control as the emotions bubble over. "I'm a clone. I'm not even a year old."

With that, Barren stops working on Vex' harness. Jordan and Royce look at me. Even Yesha rolls her eyes and puts a hand on her forehead as if I'm clueless.

Marrit takes a deep breath. "So you think you have no responsibilities just because you're new here?"

"Well," I fumble for more words, but none come.

"You have feelings from your original that you need to address before you can move on," Marrit says.

"Again, not mine."

"Then how were you able to know the amount I cared for my brother?" Yesha chimes in.

"Why do you care so much for this little guy?" Barren asks, pointing to Vex.

"Yeah, why'd you care about ending this facility?" Royce asks.

They're right. I do have deeply embedded feelings and pasts that need to be addressed.

"I feel so lost," I say.

"I'll be with you every step of the way," Marrit says, and I look at her. No doubt clouds her face—she's glowing.

"You're really going to Funen?" Yesha asks.

"Why Funen and not Earth?" I ask, remembering Al's home.

"There's been a change of plans, right, Vex?" Yesha says.

"I can confirm, Sierra," he answers.

"Funen, Earth, what do I care?" Marrit asks. "I'm with you either way." This time, the tingles I feel are not a medical symptom.

"I'm coming too," Barren says. This I had not expected, and I thought Barren unable to hide a thing. He puts his arm around Yesha's shoulders, shakes Royce and Jordan's hands, and then both he and Yesha board the shuttle.

Vex rolls in behind them. Marrit tells Royce and Jordan "Bye." Before we get on the shuttle, I hear more flapping of wings. Nobilia lands beside us.

"You bring those two back to the Capital when you're done," Nobilia says. "And then you come visit the shop."

I smile a big smile despite my dislike of fashion and give Nobilia a hug. For a second it's awkward, but then I feel the warmth of a wing on my back. Before I want to, I pull away.

"Are you sure I'd be welcome at the Capital?" I ask, doubting myself. "Would you have a place for me?"

"Why I have the perfect place for you," Marrit says as she puts her arms around me and peck-kisses my cheek.

"Oh, get out, you two, before I cry," says Nobilia.

23

TIME LOOP

Al

"It's really beautiful, Al," Vienna says.

"I know." Staring at my mom's artwork, something I never thought I'd see again, it's hard to find more words than that.

"But what does it mean?" she asks. "How...why is it here?"

"It must mean the enforcers are here or at least they were on Earth at some point."

"How can you tell if someone's an enforcer?" Vienna asks. "Maybe I've seen them before."

"They don't have a specific look, more like a feel," I say. "They remind me of the government representatives that used to meet with Cromwell on Vortex."

"But they were different?" she asks.

Where is she coming from? What is she getting at?

"Yes, they were different."

"Did they dress in the relic wear so popular on Funen by any chance?"

"Vienna, what are you getting at?" I ask, desperate to know.

"I'm not sure yet," she says. "Are there enforcers still on Funen?"

"Well, yeah, but…" I say.

"Let's go."

I take another glance at my mom's artwork as Vienna stands. She pulls out her rollable tablet. I can see her scrolling out of the corner of my eye.

"Here." She hands me the tablet.

I force my eyes away from the display on the building and I'm stoked to see another copy of the painting.

"There's a site of all the building artwork," Vienna says. "You can save it and take it everywhere you go."

I look up and smile at her, and then she gives me the warmest embrace ever.

———

Vienna had some difficulty convincing me to go to Funen, but in the end I agreed. I think because of the pain I experienced there and after all the years I spent on Vortex, I'd built a wall of protection. If I went back, I was afraid that wall might fall. Talking to Vienna about it, she'd shared how she had a similar feeling when she first spoke with Septimus on Vortex. His disinterest in leaving the facility had been like missing the hunter behind a camouflage veil to her. It had crept up and caught her by surprise. It is nice having her with me, though. Maybe Funen can again feel like the home it once was.

"So this will be the third planet we've been on together," Vienna says to me. "Funny, but at one point I thought I'd never leave Earth."

"Perhaps we should go planet-hopping after this." I smile

at her. I have my arm around her shoulders so she uses the opportunity to play-jab me in the side.

"Tell me about Funen," she says.

We're on a public gliding transit pod ride to the station so we've got some time.

"Well, the planet full of green water and beautiful nature was created on the stranded coil of a nebula," I say. Vienna butts in before I can continue.

"No, not the history," she says. "I want to know about the people and culture."

"A lot of my time on Funen was spent in homes. I had felt secure and safe until ..."

She rests her chin on my shoulder. I clear my throat.

"Maybe I'll show you my treehouse," I tell her and she grins. "It survived the fire. I've also kept in touch with an old neighbor, Mike, over the years before Vortex. But we'll do that after we figure out whether the enforcers are still an active threat or not."

She pouts.

Going through the line to the vans once we arrive at the station is much less of a pain than landing on Earth had been. At least they were able to get me on the elevator. I still can't believe Vienna and the others made the near-space sky dive. There's no way I would have jumped. We'll be on a scheduled flight to Funen that includes a cogging landing.

———

Vortex has its red-sand glow, and it's where I met some pretty freaking awesome people. Earth has technology like I've never seen, and it brought me closer to Vienna. But Funen, with its lush trees and natural colors, is perfection. There's a magical teal shimmer where land meets water. The rainbow colored swirling clouds are the final touch. As we land, Vienna stares out the window. I remember the first time I saw her long, dark, copper, wavy hair, and button nose. Her lower lip's a little tense, like she's deep in concentration now, just as it had been then.

Once we land she's able to really take in the beautiful sights. Touching live vegetation that's spread overabundantly on this planet. It's incredible watching Vienna look at a flower in amazement.

"Do you need to program your neighbor's home settings?" She extends her rollable tablet my way. "I'm so glad Mike's letting us use his house while he's on vacation."

"I'm not going to need that," I say. "It wouldn't work, anyway."

"What do you mean?" she asks. "How are solar bots going to deliver the food we need?"

"We don't have bots here," I say. "Remember, place of relics."

"So how do you get essential items?" she asks. "How will we prepare for everyone's arrival?"

Since the group has made so much headway on their tasks, they no longer need to be on Earth. When Viscerous and Albina found out we were traveling here, they insisted on joining us. Maybe Funen really can feel like home again. Even Colsam, the gomer, will be here soon. And the Scepter crew is scheduled to arrive shortly after. Mike's going to beat the tar out of me when he discovers how many people I've invited to his house. But what can I say? After all we've accomplished, we deserve a celebration.

"We go to the food distribution center, that's how," I answer Vienna, who has been surprisingly patient waiting, almost as if she's distracted. "I'll take you to one of our famous juice bars first, though." I nudge her in the side.

"Oh, yeah, that would be great, Al," she says with her head still somewhere else.

As we walk, a breeze brushes by us, causing the leaves in the trees to move. Vienna stares in awe. This planet holds so many wonders for her. She walks up to a tulip and places her nose an inch above the flower.

"Thank you for bringing me here, Al."

"Not a problem," I say and then kiss her forehead as she rises. "We're almost to the juice bar."

She locks her fingers with mine as we walk. I can smell fresh fruit before we enter, that's how blasting great the joint is. There's a steady drum of conversation from the customers chatting at tables and booths. Vienna and I walk to a couple of unoccupied stools at the bar and take a seat.

"What'll it be?" the juice bartender asks.

"What are the specials today?" I ask.

"That would be the peach mango fresca and the orange carrot zest," he answers.

"The peach mango fresca sounds good to me," Vienna says.

"And I'll have the orange carrot zest."

It's fascinating watching her try something new. I think this is technically our first date. We discuss everything on our minds and eventually get to the enforcers and how timely the display of my mother's artwork was. Vienna compares it to the timely arrival of the mural at the Vortex facility. That's when I recollect that there should have been enforcers at the landing port. We shouldn't have been able to land and explore Funen without enforcers checking us into the database. There weren't any enforcers monitoring the sidewalks either.

"Hey, man," I say to the bartender. "I'm returning to Funen after a long time away. Where are the enforcers?"

"Welcome back," he says while wiping down the bar. "I'm surprised you haven't heard. The enforcers went underground."

"What?" I ask.

"Yeah, they got fed up with being tasked with all the nasty work so they went into hiding. But between you and me, I

STEPHANIE HANSEN

think they're slowly coming back. Probably recruiting the vulnerable."

"You don't cogging say," is what I manage.

"So they just up and disappeared?" Vienna asks.

"Yeah, it was really unexpected. I'd thought we were for sure going to have a revolution on Funen. But it was like someone swooped in and talked them all into standing down," the bartender says.

"Must have been one smooth talker," I say.

"Yeah, like a time traveler came from the future to let them know how the Funen citizens were going to lick the pants off of them," the bartender says with a laugh.

Vienna snorts juice out her nose.

"You know the drink's meant to go down your throat, not out your nose, right?" I kid her.

She wipes her face with a napkin. "Don't we need to get going?"

"Thanks for the drinks," I tell the bartender.

Vienna's pretty pleased with the food distribution center but not as excited as when we'd been on the sidewalk—there's a hint of gloom about her. It has me wondering what she's up to and hoping I don't have to clone her again. Speaking of clones, Sierra's at the house when we arrive.

———

"I need to have a word with you," Sierra says as we're putting away the food.

"Okay," Vienna answers.

"Not you. Him," Sierra points to me. "Do you have any idea what you've done?"

"Easy," the red-haired woman named Marrit says. She arrived with Sierra. They've been inseparable.

184

"Do you know what it's like to realize all of your memories aren't yours but someone else's?" she asks me.

"I do know a thing or two about loss," I say as I look down at my bionic limbs.

"He thought it was necessary to save my life," Vienna interjects.

"Oh, so it all would have been fine if I'd died instead of you!"

Marrit places her hands on Sierra's shoulders to calm her.

"I've been doubting myself as a human ever since I found out I was a clone," Sierra says after taking a minute to compose herself. "But you've been the ones lacking humanity."

Then, in a mix of pain and confusion, she throws potato salad in my face. I reach for the macaroni salad to answer back in the food fight, but Vienna intercepts my hand. Marrit mouths she's sorry as she walks Sierra out of the kitchen. I go to the bathroom to wash my face.

As I'm washing, I feel a tiny bump on my neck. I look at it closer in the mirror and see the faintest hint of a scab. I don't remember getting that.

"Hey, Vienna?" I say, a bit of hysteria growing in me.

"Yeah?" she says as she enters the bathroom. Her eyes go directly to my hand on my neck. "It's okay, Al. It's all going to be okay now."

Her lips touch my neck and my panic dissipates. The feeling of fireflies in my belly returns and spreads throughout my body. We kiss as our arms wrap around each other and I swear fireworks explode from our skin. My nerve endings are buzzing. We're pulling each other closer, even though the space between us is almost nonexistent. My hands navigate to under her shirt and she pulls her mouth away from mine with a sharp intake of air. Her pupils are dilated. Then she puts her hands up my shirt and runs her fingers down my back.

We're interrupted with a knock, "Give it a rest will ya,

loverboy?" Milcah says. Looks like the rest of our crew has arrived.

"I love you," I say to Vienna with our lips still touching.

"I love you too," she says. "We have plenty of time to continue this later."

She's right and, despite all the omitted pieces in the story of our lives, I'm sure we'll fill our hearts with memories.

24

PLANET FUNEN

Vienna

AL AND I EXIT THE BATHROOM, HOLDING EACH OTHER'S hands. That had been so close. He felt the insertion point of the antidote. I guess I could tell him about how my brother poisoned him. Well, he actually had inserted a switch in Al's neck that could dispense poison at any time. I cringe at the thought, and Al kisses my cheek. It's why the cut on the back of his neck left some raised skin. The injection of the serum also caused swelling, but that should be gone by tomorrow. I don't want to tell him it was my brother because my dad finally got him into a place that hopefully will help him. I remember finally being able to communicate with Septimus.

"I'm so sorry, Vienna," he'd said. "For everything."

"Why did Leon poison Al, Dad?" I had asked.

"Oh, honey, it's taken us so long to make things right. It will take Leon years to heal after what he's been through his whole life."

As we approach the table, Sierra says, "I'm sorry, Al."

"It's okay," Al says. "Can you find it in your heart to forgive me?"

"And me," I add.

Marrit, Sierra's girlfriend, squeezes her shoulder.

"Yes," Sierra finally says.

"Did you say that you were able to speak to Mom telepathically before leaving Scepter?" I ask Sierra.

"Yes," Sierra quips. "Surprisingly, some traits survived both cloning and transplantation." She raises an eyebrow and smirks.

"You guys so have to teach us how to do that," Danver says.

Speaking of telepathy makes me wonder if I should tell Sierra about Leon being able to communicate that way, too. But I decide against it. I'll tell her after he's healed. There's no need to interrupt this fabulous meal.

"Avocado would pair nicely with that," Kitchen says through a projected holograph for the entire table to see. I know she must very much wish to be here, or rather, for us to be there. One day we'll figure out how to enable her to travel planets with us.

"Is that non-permeable clothes?" Closet asks Barren, Yesha's boyfriend, and we all laugh.

"It sure is," Barren says. "I think we need to bring Closet to Nobilia's place."

Yesha, Barren, Sierra, and Marrit all tell us about the latest developments on Scepter. The facility has been turned into a legitimate hospital free of unethical experiments. The doctors can focus on saving lives now. Cromwell was arrested but his family can now visit him since the non-bio bodies took. It's wonderful to hear about the planet's beauties. I'm so glad Yesha and all of them escaped the natural and unnatural dangers there. Watching them all sit here talking makes me realize they've become like a family. I so look forward to visiting them at the Capital, whether that's on Scepter or not. I'll visit my parents and brother one day too, when I'm ready, that is.

Viscerous and Albina sit next to one another, beaming at Al like proud parents. Viscerous nods at me. I'm so glad we were able to work together to save Al from the poison. I think they may rebuild Al's old house. They plan to try to save all of his mom's artwork, so they may be traveling the universe before they settle down.

Colsam and Theopat will go back to Vortex and see their families. Apparently, there's some big voltball game they plan to go to. They also want to rebuild Vortex to what it was before the facility and better. The future of their home is very important to them, especially now. No one else knows it but me and Colsam—Theopat's pregnant...with twins! She feels my gaze on her and looks up. She smiles and blushes at the same time. Colsam looks at me and winks. I'm glad we were able to work together to expose the corruption, so fetuses are safe now. Non-bio wombs are only used consensually the way they'd been intended to be used.

Milcah and Harper are engaged in deep conversation on the other side of the table. They look extremely happy and at peace. I'm so grateful when I look around and consider all the blessings. We've been through so much. Some of us have grown closer and some more distant. But I'm pleased with my family sitting around the table with me. I wouldn't give it up for the world.

My reverie is interrupted by more visions. This one is with a woman who looks and feels like a grandmother, or my grandmother. She is in front of me just like before. Again, the smell of freshly baked cookies overwhelms my senses. Then I feel a warm hand holding mine, a hand I'd recognize anywhere, Al's.

`What are you doing here, Al?` I ask.

`I got curious about all of your medita-tion,` he says.

`You read my mom's books, didn't you?` I say.

He smiles.

`But we're not only communicating tele-pathically,` I say. `I see and feel you.`

`Guess we have an extra-strong connection.` He shrugs his shoulders.

I want to kiss him so badly, but we need to figure out what's going on.

The grandmotherly woman speaks: `You're not done yet.`

All of a sudden the house in the vision disintegrates and now we're on a beach.

"The senator was partially speaking the truth," the old woman continues, speaking normally within the vision now.

She shows us scenes from long ago. People snatching others and taking them from an old Earth-type world to one like Funen. Instead of traveling via a shuttle, it's as if they just materialize there.

Then scenes from even a century before that appear. They remind me of the photo I saw at the antique store. But again, in this scene people are being taken.

"What does it all mean?" I ask her.

"There have always had to be protectors," she says. "And you two are protectors now."

Al and I look at each other. We both mouth "Us?" She must sense our questioning.

"Look at what you've been able to do so far," she says.

A reel of our memories appears. The first one is mine. It's from when Yesha and I were researching Vortex. We were looking at the footage, particularly the shot of Al making eye contact with the camera. Then we hear my voice say, "He's cute!" Al looks at me and smiles. I blush and burst out laughing. But then remember we have an important message to hear.

The next scene is the one of me running across the sand in my underwear on Vortex. Al looks at me and smiles again.

"Hey, I had to do that to remain unseen," I say, able to speak to Al now without telepathy. "I was trying to save Viscerous."

Al's smile fades.

The next scene is Al and Albina in a lab discussing the best way to clone me, which then moves to us getting as many people off Vortex as we could. The scenes begin speeding up. We see Sierra going through horrific brain surgery...awake. Then we see a flame-throwing guard singe the side of Al's face, which has now healed.

"What if we don't want to be protectors?" I ask. "What if we want to live normal lives?"

She smiles and moves to more images of the past. This scene is in an old, rundown building with an organ playing music and stairs winding up. There's a couple at the top exchanging vows. They look a lot like Al and I. Whoa, that got real fast. But they're not us exactly.

Then the scene morphs to a century before that and once again there's a couple somewhat resembling us. They're dancing. What is this?

"You've always been protectors," she says. "Reincarnation's never stopped that."

My jaw drops. "What?" I ask.

Al squeezes my hand.

"Don't worry, you'll have shields," she says.

Then faces materialize beside hers. They all have to zoom out to be visible. Some I recognize and some I don't. My parents from the past, Viscerous and Albina too. Rigled's even one of the faces that appear.

"Will we have to begin right away?" Al asks.

"Not at all," she says. "You decide your own schedule."

All of the faces, including hers, fade away.

Before we're back in reality, Al shows a scene from his memory to me. It's from my first time in the Vortex cafeteria when I saw Visterous and stumbled over my own feet. Al catches me before I hit the ground. This time I'm able to see what he saw. To know he could get lost staring into my eyes just as I'd gotten lost staring into his is amazing. No matter what planet we're on or place in history we share, I'm at home with him.

We hear him say, "I don't usually issue warnings to be careful while walking, but for you I'll make an exception." We both smile at the memory. The scene slowly fades away and we see the table with everyone around it again.

Albina nods at me knowingly when I look her direction. She's one of my shields, makes sense.

Listening to everyone chatter around the table is wonderful. Part of me wants to keep them all here forever, but I know that's impossible. This isn't even our house, only Al's old neighbor's.

"Vienna, there's something I want to show you outside," Al says. To which everyone oohs and aah's. I smile and then stick my tongue out at them all. Al grabs my hand and we walk toward the door.

"Would you like an escort?" Vex rolls up and asks.

"Are there any dangers along our path?" I ask.

After a few beeps and clicks, he says, "I do not register any danger."

"Great," Al says, and we walk out the door, through the yard to the next one.

"I was going to show you my old treehouse, remember?" he says.

We climb in. "It's good, Al."

"No, you are."

I put my hand on the back of his neck and say, "No, you." The feeling of butterflies becoming angels returns. His lips touch mine. The particles of my skin feel like they explode with every touch.

He pulls me onto his lap and I wrap my legs around his torso as our kiss continues. He runs his fingers down my back and my skin feels alive. He pulls me closer as my breathing becomes ragged. When his body touches mine, it's like an ocean wave crashing into me, sending my body into a drop, twist, and then rise with the ferociousness of a hurricane.

"I love you, Vienna."

"I love you too, Al."

"I could do this with you forever," he says between heavy breaths.

"For a hundred years and a hundred years after that," I say, and we both smile, lips still touching.

25

PLANET SCEPTER

Sierra

An uneasiness settles over me like a ghost stepping into my body. We're not safe. Something's not right.

There, there. No need to worry.

Cromwell? I ask, but that can't be.

Why, yes. You didn't think you'd heard the last of me, did you?

But you're in jail. How did you figure out telepathic communication?

Really, after all of my experiments, you didn't think I'd figure it out.

Whatever, what do you want?

In fact, dear Marie helped me a lot with telepathy. Escaping the hell hole of a prison was much more difficult than picking up a new kind of communication.

You, what?

Poor little clone. Your brain synapses must be slow. Do you really think the Capital is going to accept you…even with your improved fashion?

What do you want? Leave Nobilia alone.

Oh, nothing, just having a little fun with your Capital friends now.

What?

See you soon, Sierra.

What in the world was that? He can't possibly have escaped jail already. Brute force wouldn't work for him and his personality definitely wouldn't win over any guards. He'd have to hold something over their heads. Or there's always bribery. Perhaps that's how he got free. I know Dr. Perierat has been with him a lot and transferred his family to non-bios, but why would she teach him telepathy? He must still be up to his old tricks. But what worries me most, how does he know about my experience with Capital fashion?

Marrit places her hand on mine to stop me from nervously drumming my fingers on the table any longer. She looks at me with concern in her eyes. That's when it hits me. Did I just put the bird in danger? Well, despite the bird's overall stylish presence, there's only one way he could know for sure. He really is on Scepter at the Capital…or perhaps he has footage of my experience there…otherwise he's tortured information out of the bird.

"We need to get back to Scepter now," I whisper to Marrit.

Why are we all sitting around celebrating our victories when this thing is far from over? It had felt like a holiday for one brief and spectacular moment, but our job is not quite done.

Barren clears his throat and looks at us then raises his eyebrows as if to ask what's going on.

"Do you have a message, Vex?" I ask and he rolls over

immediately. I whisper to him as soon as he's next to me. "Do you have the coordinates of Dr. Cromwell?"

"I'm unable to confirm that at the moment," he whispers back.

I stand, scooting my chair back with my legs and lift my glass for a toast. "It's been wonderful spending time with you all." Everyone lifts their glasses and joins in.

"But?" Yesha says, picking up on Barren's intuition.

"Marrit and I need to get back to the Capital. We've just received word that the citizens have scheduled a meeting and our attendance is mandatory."

Vex beeps, but I wave my hand for him to hush.

"Mandatory doesn't sound free," Albina says. I roll my eyes at her, not appreciating her detective like behavior. It's the worst time for it.

"We'll go with you," Barren says. I hold back my initial reaction to say no, realizing that Barren and Yesha would be a lot of help.

"My projection can assist in the meeting," Vex says. I guess he's picking me over Vienna. I can't stop myself from smirking at that.

Speaking of Vienna, we need to let her know that we're leaving. She and Al snuck off, but Vex was able to locate them in a treehouse next door.

"Knock, knock," I say as I approach the treehouse.

"We're kind of in the middle of something," Vienna responds after a moment.

"I just wanted to say goodbye before we head back to Scepter."

"Leaving already?"

"Yeah, but you can come visit in a few weeks, you planet hoppers."

"Okay, see you."

I'm glad that went over smoothly. Navigating through

Funen territory to get to the shuttle takeoff is enough work in and of itself. There's a reason why relics are relics. They should stay in the past where they belong. The fumes alone from the vehicle that transports us is enough for me to not want to return.

———

Technically, this is my third time to travel in space, though I don't remember the first. Plus, I have memories of the flight to Vortex being a clone and all. But it still doesn't feel like a comfortable form of transportation. Perhaps that's because of the anxiety I have, wondering what Cromwell's done since he made contact. I am able to relax a little once Vex has communicated to Royce and Jordan and established a rendezvous point. They weren't able to talk long…seemed very preoccupied. Now we can all pay back the favor. Nobilia's the one who saved our hides so we could escape the facility. I'm glad to have a team to work with. Their willingness to help solidifies the feeling of belonging I have with them, making it all that much more important to save Nobilia, keep the Capital intact, and protect the citizens.

The wind is knocked out of me as we approach Scepter, though.

"It cannot be," Barren says, looking out a window.

Marrit looks out a window too. Before I take my turn to look, I notice tears in her eyes. The only way I can imagine how to explain what that look does to my heart is—cardiopulmonary resuscitation bot paddles. That moment when the electric shock bursts through a heart must feel like what mine does now.

When I look out the window, I see the expected vibrant, jungle green. But it's interrupted by the soft, yellow Capital tower that used to be suspended in the air. It's now tethered to the ground by chains. It's as if out of spite Cromwell took the one place of acceptance I have and jailed it. I want to scream. I hug Marrit tightly to my chest and make a silent vow of vengeance. Yesha's going to have to stop me because now I'm the one planning a solo mission of rampage.

Upon landing, we make our way to the rendezvous point as quickly as possible. I had grabbed a specimen jar on the way out of the shuttle. I separate from the group along the trek to relieve myself. Once I'm out of eyesight, I find the longest bamboo stick I can. Then I use the provided machete to turn my pants into shorts. The leftover material will be used to create a net at the end of the stick. Once assembled, I walk farther looking for rainbow shimmer, glad Jordan was able to upload how to capture Scepter beetles to Vex. That should be a nice surprise for Cromwell...if I can get the thing into the jar where I'll be safe from blackouts.

I'm taken aback when I return to the group because someone else has joined. She seems kind with smile crinkles around her eyes. It juxtaposes the feeling of premonition I experience with the sight of her. I put the jar in my satchel and approach.

"What's this?" I ask, interrupting the group's conversation. Why are they so openly talking to someone they don't know?

"Well hello, Sierra. We were just getting to know one another." She definitely seems familiar but I can't quite place my finger on where I know this woman from.

"Who are you?" I ask.

"Oh dear, I'd thought you already recognized my non-bio. I'm the new Sorna. It's a pleasure to finally meet you."

"I can confirm what she says is true," Vex interjects.

I remember her now from the cryogenic freezer at the Scepter facility and multidimensional prism photos in Cromwell's office at the Vortex facility though I only really took passing glances. Her non-bio appears identical.

"Sorna was just telling us how things used to be on Vortex. She even remembers my brother," Yesha says with dazzling excitement reflected from her eyes.

Then someone I never expected to see strolls up and stands side by side with Sorna. It's Dr. Perierat. Not only did I never expect to see her, but I also didn't think she'd ever talk to me again.

"That's right. We're here to help with the hospital. So things can be the way they should have been before Cromwell lost his way," my not mom says.

"Yes, true innovation can still be had. Dr. Henry Cromwell believes we can save people from the pain of losing loved ones, of not being able to have one's wishes, and we'll ensure it remains ethical."

"Where is Cromwell?" I ask.

Marrit stands beside me in support. "Where's Nobilia too? He better have not harmed a feather."

"Yeah, and why do you need to imprison our Capital to do this?" Royce asks.

"The imprisonment was simply to be collateral in case you disagreed with us," Sorna says. "But you agree with us, right?"

This is who's going to keep Cromwell in check...cog it all!

"Why don't you free the Capital in good faith and then we'll do the best we can to help you so long as it stays ethical," I say.

"Of course," my mom interjects before Sorna can say more. She approaches Vex and I don't know why, but I cringe at the sight. "Hey, ol' buddy, can you download the instructions and share with your new friends?"

"That follows protocol, Dr. Perierat," Vex says. "I'd be happy to."

Yesha steps between Vex and Dr. Perierat. "Wait a second. Let me see that." She grabs a prism chip away from Mom and inspects it. "How do we know you don't have a transcending virus downloaded on this?"

"Vex is more important to me than he ever could be to you," Mom says with a huff.

"Can you please free our Capital already?" Jordan says.

Yesha nods, handing the prism chip back and Mom proceeds to inject it into Vex. Then he projects the coordinates of each chain lock and their respective instructions for the intuitive action keys.

"It will take all day to get to the keys," Royce complains.

"Not if we work as a team." Hearing Nobilia's voice is beyond relieving. I run up and hug the bird.

"Yeah, and I brought hovers." Yesha's grin brings a smile to my face. Never did I imagine that I would have both Vex and Yesha's support on Scepter. I thought my being a clone would automatically cause them to go with Vienna or on their own. I guess Al and Vienna will be able to travel the Universe better just the two of them. And I think Barren had a lot to do with Yesha's decision.

"Wonderful," my mom says. "Well, we best be off to the hospital."

She and Sorna turn to walk away but before leaving Sorna says, "Yes, best we get back to more of Henry's brilliant work."

My mom looks at Sorna. "Only the ethical work, remember."

"Of course, unethical work only made up one percent of his practice." Sorna shrugs her shoulders.

"You really have no clue." Mom shakes her head from shoulder to shoulder, a canyon of emotion with everlasting echoes.

"I beg your pardon." Sorna's look reminds me of when Milcah's eyes blazed in anger like a mad shooting star.

"It wasn't just the experiments to save you and Damien." Mom's voice rises.

"I know, I know, he's somehow involved with the embryo research." Sorna sounds deflated.

"Oh no, Henry always has to take it a step further."

"How?" Sorna asks.

"You don't remember your miscarriage, do you?" Mom's eyebrows furrow and Sorna's seem to do the same, too.

"What in the hell are you blabbering on about?"

"He stripped those memories from you."

Sorna fails to find words.

"My embryo that was taken away from me wasn't one," Mom yells. "They were twins."

"That can't be." Sorna opens her mouth to say more and then closes it to contemplate.

"Yes, and the twin was implanted in you by dear sweet Henry."

"No." Now Sorna's the one shaking her head from side to side.

"Why else do you think Septimus did everything he could to stay on Vortex? He had to protect his son."

"That's a lie." Sorna begins pacing.

I'm in utter shock remembering the poor excuse he had to stay on Vortex. I compare the multidimensional prism photo I've now seen of Leon with the one I saw of Damien remembering the identical crooked eyebrows. Then I think of Dad's investigating eyes and it all clicks. What Mom's saying is true.

It must hit Sorna at the same time. She stops pacing and seethes at Mom. Then, before I even know what's happening, she flies at Mom. She's ripping at hair and scratching with her nails. Unlike calculated Cromwell with chain whips and flame throwing clubs, Sorna's attacking out of rage full of passionate insanity.

PLANET FUNEN

Al

IT WAS FREAKING CROMWELL. I DON'T KNOW HOW THIS can be, but there's only one reason for Sierra's sudden change in mood and immediate departure. Then, I hear it for myself and I'm absolutely positive my guess is correct.

You! I say in shock. Guess anyone can learn how to telepathically communicate. The visualization of Cromwell smiling is disturbing.

That's right, he says. You didn't think you were the only one outside the Perierat family who could talk this way, did you?

Well, I was definitely hoping I would never hear your voice in my head.

I told you only the battle had been won. I will win this war.

The evidence proves otherwise.

That would be true if the enforcers

weren't gathering in order to reinstate
their power right now.

My rage boils over, even though I know that's exactly what
Cromwell wants.

You're full of it.

Are you sure? He projects an image to me. Under the
rainbow, swirling clouds and beyond the city, I see a wall
similar to the one around the perimeter of the Vortex facility.
Inside the wall is a dirt oval. Tire tracks run along it. Movement attracts my eye, and I look to see Cromwell standing
below a checkered flag. Then I see dust billowing out behind
him as enforcers march in my direction.

Why?

Ready for another battle? He smirks and the
image fades.

"What's wrong, Al?" Vienna must sense my tension.

"Sierra sure left in a hurry."

"You're right. She did. We should check on everyone else."
She crawls out of the treehouse. "You coming?"

I pause, looking around my childhood play spot another
time. "It was really nice being back here. Thank you for
coming with me." My palms sweat a little climbing down the
ladder. It resurfaces memories I'd rather forget.

Vienna looks back at me and we both pause.

"Hey, I need to check in with Mike."

She gives me an odd look but proceeds into the house
while I make a beeline to the garage.

———

Revving up the engine to Mike's speed byte vehicle feels pretty
damn good. It purrs like a kitten. I remember seeing Dad help
Mike in the garage. Looks like his teachings paid off. Mike's
speed byte is in mint condition, despite its age.

I'm a little rusty with the control screen gear shift. It's been awhile since I've driven a relic car, but the Funen roads are branded in my brain. I make it in record time to the racetrack. This had been a favorite spot of Dad's so I'm familiar with the route.

As I approach, I notice that the enforcers who had been marching in Cromwell's vision all appear now to be the spectators buying tickets and walking to their stadium-like seats. While I had once craved to come to this place with Dad, now I find it reminds me of the Vortex arena.

I drive through a separate entrance specifically for cars and their racers. Sounds of engines and smells of fumes surround me, but it's all for show. Funen relics have been updated to not damage the environment. I recognize some of the racers I drive by making it feel like I've entered a legitimate race. Once I'm to the pit I've been assigned, I look out, trying to find him. But Cromwell's nowhere to be seen. Instead, I spot Leon and, of all people, Damien now standing under the checkered flag. Super! Why are they together? Where did Cromwell go and why has Leon decided to side with them? Is Septimus here too?

Leon and Damien step out into the sun and the crowd rises to their feet and applauds the two. That's when it hits me. They're after power. Each racer is announced and more applause occurs, though not as loudly as it had been with Leon and Damien. When I'm announced there are boos instead of applause. I can't wait to beat them all on the track.

I put on my helmet, and wham, Leon's voice is in my head. It's not via telepathy but relic wireless communication.

"Why am I always the one getting stuck with giving you vehicle instructions?"

"Who said I needed instructions?" I ask. "I'm pretty sure I'm more familiar with this planet than you."

"This isn't your usual race, pal."

"Pal? You barely said a word to me at the academy and

now I'm 'pal'?"

"Touchy, touchy! Do you want to hear about the new track obstacles or what?"

"What do you mean, obstacles?"

As if on cue, fire erupts partway through the track. Super, just cogging super.

"This isn't your normal race. It might even be your last. That's why I felt the need of extending the courtesy to call you Pal."

"Why are you siding with them?"

"I like being on the winning side."

"And you've brought the enforcers out of hiding."

"Isn't it glorious?"

"You better not get on their bad side."

"Look, I'm sorry about your parents, Al. For that, I really am. It was unfortunate they had to become collateral damage."

"They didn't deserve to die. The enforcers went corrupt."

"And you have proof of their corruption?"

That's when it hits me. I realize what Mom had. The thing they killed my parents for…evidence. All of her artwork flashes in my mind. Each piece has documentation showing their guilt. An investigation log with a warrant time stamp dated after the forced entry search. A doctor whose scalpel looks more like the blade of a sword. Subtle details with incriminating pointed fingers.

"Why don't you prove how much of a winner you are by beating me on the racetrack?" I taunt Leon.

"You wouldn't stand a chance against me.

"Blah, blah, blah, all words and no action."

"That's it." I hear clatters as if Leon's shoved someone out of the way. This is followed by indistinct noises.

Within minutes, a Red Feathering slowly drives by my pit. I don't need to see his face to know who it is.

"Why aren't you at the starting line yet?" He revs the

engine, but before I can respond, a Black Salver goes by twice as fast as regulation allows in Pit Alley.

Then Damien's voice enters our helmets.

"Let me show you two how it's done."

I hop in Mike's speed byte vehicle while Leon drives after Damien. They both are at the starting line when I get there. I try to analyze the track to come up with a plan, but it has been quite some time since I was last here.

We're given the windshield heads-up display signal and all three cars begin the dance around the track. It comes back as if no time has passed. I remember riding with Dad, the car hugging every turn and squeezing each second it can. It truly is like a synchronized dance the way you can feel another car's movement. Each lap you learn more about the other driver's habits, their car's quirks, and the smoothest versus roughest parts of the track. I'm within inches of Leon's car as we round a curve, but a vision flashes through my mind leaving me confused. Sorna is attacking Vienna's mom with a tackle and punches.

I hear Damien's car because it's next to mine. He fakes ramming my side. I should know that he wouldn't actually do it. At this speed, it would take us both out. But I react anyway. I slow quick enough that if he had not been faking, I would have avoided impact. Unfortunately, that move is enough to give both Leon and Damien the lead ahead of me.

I begin gaining back on them during the next lap, but notice spikes rising on the path. Luckily, the relic system lifts them in a domino-like effect, one after the next, giving me time to avoid. Boulders rumble down the gill on the other half, shaking the ground so hard I can feel it in the seat. But the next lap is free of traps and I catch back up. Of course, this causes a sense of relief which can't be right.

Watching the two drive together, it feels almost rehearsed. They turn and change pace in tandem. It should make getting by them simpler. I tuck in between the two and just as they both lean in, I "gas" up and shoot in front of them. They wind up taking each other out. As I watch it all occur in the review mirror, a vision takes over my sight again but it feels like it's just before Sorna tackled Marie. I hear their exchange too.

"My embryo that was taken away from me wasn't one," Marie yells at Sorna. "They were twins."

I'm able to look at the scene behind me while continuing to hear the two women.

"That can't be." Sorna's voice rattles in shock.

"Yes, and the twin was implanted in you by dear, sweet Henry."

I now have to look to the opposite section of the track. As Damien helps Leon out of his car, it clicks. They really are twins. But if Dr. Cromwell has Sierra with Sorna and Marie fighting on Scepter, why'd he draw me here to the track with the twins on Funen? Was the race a distraction so I wouldn't stop their fight? And, if they are twins, why didn't Cromwell go after Leon to replace Damien to begin with? Why even go after Vienna?

Could it be possible that Cromwell didn't even know about Leon? Had he truly been hidden the entire time? I imagine Septimus spying on every conversation on Vortex in order to protect his son. And perhaps Marie's closeness had been a form of shield, as well. Thinking of every intricate detail, I realize just how far the Perierat family has gone.

I walk up to the two I just raced. Marching with the pound of my heart. I think about how ungrateful Leon's been, even calling Vienna a decoy, and seeming generally annoyed with his family. I would give anything for one more moment with my parents and he's taking his for granted. As I approach, they heckle me, claiming I cheated to win the race. I strongly lean in with my right foot once I'm within reach and punch Leon square in the jaw.

27

SPACE

Vienna

THEY CAME WITH BRUTALITY, WITH AN EXCLUSIVE PAIN for me. Visions of everyone I care for being tortured flashed through my mind. It catapulted me into another state as if I were in a coma.

When both Sierra and Al disappeared, one after the other, I knew something was up. When will it stop? When can we get off this merry-go-round of unfortunate events? I know they didn't tell me in order to protect me, but didn't they learn from my attempts that alone is not the way to go? Not telling those you care for, keeping secrets never leads to any good. Cog it all. I've decided to put an end to the pain and loss. I'm aboard a shuttle to find the culprit behind everything. But the visions have paralyzed me. They've numbed me to the core. If they're true I do not want to go on another second.

```
Well, hello again, Vienna.
Aren't you tired yet?
```

My mission is almost complete.

What? Run out of ideas of how to cause damage?

Oh no, those have just begun.

A vision takes over me. I see Mom surrounded by lush, green jungle trees. She's fighting with someone who looks a lot like Sorna. I've never seen my mom in a physical altercation before. Mom kicks Sorna in the side, causing Cromwell's wife to fall over. Sorna regains her footing and flies at Mom, pulling her hair and scratching her skin. They topple over, with Mom landing on top of Sorna. Mom grips Sorna's neck and squeezes and then squeezes more. Sorna's extremities seize and shake, but Mom doesn't release her. Sorna's face turns a darker shade of red and then her arms stop reaching and her legs stop kicking.

The vision jumps in time to Mom being handcuffed and taken away by individuals in uniform. It jumps again to her court hearing. The punishment is life sentence aboard a shuttle with a black hole destination. Tears stream down my face.

The next visual assault is of Yesha on an ops mission. Barren, Marrit, and Sierra accompany her, silently moving in an organized approach like a military tactical team.

Next, I'm able to see Yesha's thoughts. She's imagining moving Cromwell's veins and arteries to be outside the epidermis like Viscerous. She's dreaming of removing his pigment like Albina and extremities like Al. If they make it to Cromwell, Yesha plans to perform every experiment he ever did on others on him. Then she'll kill him like he killed her brother.

The vision shakes and vibrates like a particle plexus with a bad connection. Shots ring out in the air, followed by bullets ripping through Marrit and Barren's chests. After that, Sierra's head flies back and bits of it float away. The shock of what I'm seeing makes things play out in slow motion. Al created Sierra, my clone, to save me. She had to endure brain surgery while awake and now I'm watching her experience another blow to the head. The next bullet flies through Yesha's chest, ripping a hole in mine. My best friend who helped me to cross the universe, annihilated, gone.

Cromwell's figure enters the vision with a sneer on his face. Just as I have an ill thought forming, Eucarpo flies at him. She bites him with her sharp front teeth. Her jaw is strong enough to draw blood. Seeing the koala brings back memories of school before I knew about corrupt facilities and experiments. Then feathers enter the vision. Nobilia and Aviator are pecking the villain with their beaks. It seems everyone I've ever cared for is entering into the fray.

The image flashes back to the lush green of Scepter. Up in many trees are stationed guards. The Capital isn't floating like Sierra said it would be, but instead is on the ground. Individuals like Jordan, Royce, and other Capital citizens also appear on the ground.

A distinct smell joins the vision, making it feel real. It's the smell I experienced during my first venture in the Vortex tunnels, burning. Orange, red, and blue colors soak into my peripheral sight. Looking around, I notice each guard is equipped with flame-throwing clubs. They're aiming down and firing. While the jungle isn't dry, the hot flickering seems to spread faster than bacteria. The fire engulfs everything the eye can see just as multiple helicopters drop ropes to rescue the guards, fleeing a planet going up in smoke.

Before the devastating loss of the fire can be calculated, the scene bumps back to Funen. I see Leon, Damien, and Al in race cars on a track. My skin warms at the mere sight of Al. The first lap Leon taunts Al, appearing to be attempting a relic bumper car situation. The next lap, Damien suddenly decreases his speed, causing Al's car to lose balance as it avoids collision.

Anger flashes through me, engulfing my skin in hotness. Al attempts to pass both Leon and Damien. I cringe in anticipation of how they'll attempt to sabotage his efforts. They hit him from separate sides, one in the front and one in the back, causing him to flip and crash into the wall! The coma state I'm in turns to one of tortuous pain. It's as if I swallowed one of the chain whips and it's ripping me apart from the inside out. Witnessing Al die is something I'll never be able to forget, no matter how hard I try.

Before I know it multiple individuals with a governmental feel swarm the area. Their uniforms and movements match, as if they march in complete tandem. Then civilians approach from the opposite side of the track. Both groups near the other at a sprinting pace. All chaos ensues as hand-to-hand combat begins. Blood flies and bodies hit the ground. Fighters are falling left and right on both sides. My heart feels as if it constricts witnessing such brutal force and gut-wrenching loss. Looking forward, a governmental fighter removes her helmet and bashes it into a civilian's face. I turn around in the vision to look away, but there I see a civilian flip a government fighter onto his back. The civilian tackles the downed fighter and then strangles them. I psychologically close my eyes, not wanting to see anymore destruction.

Then a serene image of Albina and Viscerous coming in to tend to the wounded appears. Viscerous and Albina tear up in a heart sickened way at the sight of Al's car, but they quickly move on to healing the fallen. Even after all the damage, perhaps things can be patched. They can be beautiful once more.

As if on cue, Cromwell's image appears. He smiles with vindictive triumph and an eerie feeling settles over me. Next, I smell a gas enter the area. This isn't one of anesthesia. This is one with a death penalty. One by one, those exercising care fall. It hits Albina first. She drops to the ground. Someone next to her places their fingers on her neck, but as they nod "no" they drop too. Viscerous sees this and runs to another helper, pushing them to safety, but he's too late. The gas has its targets and chases with unrelenting swiftness. When both Viscerous and Albina drop, it's as if imaginary fingers wrap around my heart and squeeze, suffocating it.

Next, instead of Cromwell's face, I see him outside of the scene. The rainbow swirling clouds have been replaced by sand. He's back on Vortex with the city landscape as a backdrop behind him. He hops on a hoverbike and zooms toward the city. People give him odd looks as he drives through the streets, but no one stops him. He parks just outside a small house and walks to the front door. He doesn't knock or ring the prism bell, but kicks it down instead. As he enters, I see Colsam reaching for a chain whip, but Cromwell sends the killer gas in Colsam's direction before he can make any advancement.

Colsam drops to the ground and I squeeze my hands into fists. Cromwell steps forward, grabbing the chain whip out of Colsam's hands. He then walks through the hallway to a bedroom. There, Theopat's holding a baby. She sees Cromwell and what he's holding. Theopat places her baby in a 3-D printed crib and steps away. As she holds her hands out pleading, Cromwell murders her. When he picks up the baby, I psychologically scream my guts out. When will these visions end?

The image shifts but doesn't go away. I see Harper, Milcah, and Danver locked in cells side by side. Both Milcah and Danver are buckled over in pain. A high-pitched noise is being used as torture against them. Harper sneers at a hidden perpetrator and then looks at Milcah with visible anguish. The high pitch matches the tinnitus Harper has and, therefore, the torture doesn't mess with her. She should pretend it does to give her an advantage for possible escape.

The next image whirls in fast. I'm upset to my stomach by their pace and disturbing scenes. This one places me back in the apartment where I should feel warm and at home, but I feel anything other than that. Parts fly out of the kitchen and my bedroom as both Closet and Kitchen are being torn apart. Memories scrape through me as I hear the computerized cries of my dearest caregivers. They morph to short-circuited sounds and eventually fade to silence. The hallways are so cluttered with debris I feel trapped by heart wrenching events. I want to give up. I'm tired. It feels like I've been through this for centuries.

But I wade through the removed parts to see if the orders I'd heard came from the voice I recognize. I introspectively crumple to the floor when I see my dad's face. Why is he doing this?

The image moves to a new one. Cromwell's performing another brain swap. He looks younger, as if this view is from the past. I'd say it's from a decade ago. The body on the gurney is Dad. I sob and I cry until my face is so blotchy I can't feel it. Cromwell's finally succeeded. If these images are true, he's broken me into a thousand of microscopic pieces. I no longer exist. I'm less than nothing. Good job, Cromwell! You win! I forfeit!

28

PLANET SCEPTER

Sierra

BEFORE I'M ABLE TO GET TO MOM, RED DOTS APPEAR everywhere and I hear the approach of guards. The rustle of jungle leaves and rushing river rapids are interrupted by the pounding of boots. My mind races, trying to put together an escape plan while fear trickles in. Flashes of my not past stream through my head. Images of Lucretia and Quintus assault me. At least the red dots aren't flames and whips. And we're not in a facility. We have trees to shield us but every plan I devise in my head leads to someone left behind. We can't all fly on Nobilia, plus I fear that would put the bird in harm's way. Armor clinks as they near us. And then they emerge from the green.

"One way screen image up," I say to Vex. The image will only last a few minutes but it might be enough to allow us to prepare.

Royce and Jordan make signs to each other, crouching, and moving to the best points of attack.

They both pull sling shots from their belts by the time the image has stopped working and scoop mud from the ground. The red dots slowly become fewer and fewer. Then metal clinks against wood as guns fling from soldier hands and bang into trees. As the first round of guards pick their weapons back up, a second group comes in and red dots reappear. When did Cromwell have time to recruit so many? Pictures of Sorna and Damien spreading false charges and sending manufactured calls to duty enter my mind. It's time to end Cromwell at last. Where is he?

Royce and Jordan have another round of mud sling shotting and the red dots are gone again. But just as quickly as they go, more show up. It feels like when Cromwell's crane lowered my dad's gurney into the tank of water.

Just as Septimus held his breath then I hold mine now. Next, as if on cue, I hear the magnificent sound of flapping wings. Parrots are all over the sky dropping nets made of vine with rocks tied to the perimeter. As one falls on a guard, I see the rope is tied in such a fashion that it causes the net to twist upon contact, trapping the poor soul it fell on. Once again, the red dots go away one by one. I smile at the birds grateful for their grace.

"Sierra, take cover," Yesha yells.

I look down and find three red dots on my chest. I jump and then roll behind a tree, but more dots appear. I have to keep moving to avoid being a hit target. How are we going to survive this?

"Vex, call in the squad." Yesha rolls to him.

"What?" I ask, but before she can answer, a spectacular ship appears in the air. It's as long as a school, in the shape of an arrowhead, and has multiple windows to the loading dock. Next, all-planet vehicles (APVs) drop from the sky with parachutes. They maneuver through the trees and drop beside us. When they fire at our enemies, I'm in shock. Part of me is happy that the red dots have been diverted. But another part of me feels like we've taken the role of antagonist.

"Infosec and Mantis called in some favors," Yesha says.

The APVs travel over terrain without any problems. They not only have four tires underneath but two on each side, including the front and back and four above, allowing them to roll any direction needed. Strings of blue light come from the machines and hit the guards, knocking them down.

I'm not exactly sure how to telepathically project the images in front of me, but I concentrate as hard as I can. I take a deep breath in and a deep breath out while envisioning meditation circles. With the expansion of the final circle, I picture what I just witnessed. Once I see it, I push it forward.

Is this what you wanted?

So, I was able to lure you to Scepter. Cromwell answers.

And you can see how doing that is leading to the demise of your guards.

I can always get more guards.

A loud commotion pulls me out of the trance and our conversation comes to an end. Something's interfering with the APV blue lights that had been firing at the guards. Looking around, I find our crew littered with red dots a-freak-ing-gain.

A shot rings out, followed by a gasp and a groan. When I look in the direction of the sound, I see Marrit on the ground with a hand clutched to her upper chest toward her shoulder. No! I drop to my knees beside her. Fear wells up inside me while all chaos unleashes around us.

"Are you okay?" I ask, which is stupid. Of course she's not okay. She was just shot in the chest.

Marrit sucks in a gulp of air and grimaces. The look on her face churns my emotions.

"Just hang on," I clumsily say while running through ideas in my head. With turbo speed robotic stem-cell treatment we could fuse back Marrit's injured parts. I look around to see Barren and Yesha flying on hovers to each APV. Right after they stop at each the machine is able to shoot the blue rays again.

Maybe I could use one of the hovers to take Marrit to the hospital. I look up, searching for long, brunette hair. It takes a bit, but I recognize her the second I locate her. She's holding a gun I never knew she could handle and dispelling one of the laser dots I fear. Did she shoot Marrit? No time, I do not have time to consider that.

"Mom!" I stand, putting myself in danger.

"Get down," she yells as she runs my way. Something about the mere act of protection causes a subtle ache deep in my bones.

"I need your help." I point to Marrit, who looks like she's holding in a yell. "Can you get us to the hospital pronto?"

"I don't think there's time for that." Vex rolls over and begins scanning Marrit.

"What's the prognosis?"

"The bullet must be removed." Two metal pieces eject out of Vex' body, one with a scalpel at the end and the other with tweezers.

"Did it hit anything vital, Vex? What about infection? We're in the middle of a battle here." I internally wish and hope for good answers. Mom has her back to us, keeping lookout.

Another shot rings out and I cover Marrit's body to protect her. Are Yesha and Barren okay? Now Infosec and Mantis are in danger with us. What about Royce, Jordan, and Nobilia? I hear the thud of a body dropping to the ground and look up.

"Mom," I gasp.

She looks at me in the eyes and so many unspoken words are communicated. Leaves rustle behind me and then her arm's above me, shooting a gun at something past me.

I turn to look at what it was. Sorna's lifeless body lies on the ground. Her arm's extended my way, a gun below her hand on the ground.

"I love both sets of my twins." Mom places her wrist on my shoulder. She drops the gun she'd been holding and passes out.

"Vex, can you help them both?"

"I will do everything I can, Sierra. What about the third injury…Sorna?"

"I think it's too late for that one."

Vex moves the scan to Sorna for a second. "You are correct." Then Vex returns to treating Mom and my girlfriend. While my heart feels like it could crumple to a million pieces, I look back at Sorna's corpse and project an image again. It's easier to make contact with Cromwell this time.

`And this is what you get.`
`Silly clone, I'm prepared for that now.`
`What?`
`Why I've cloned the non-bios.`
`How could that…`
`I cloned them one hundred times.`

"Sierra, I could use your assistance," Vex's communication pulls me out of the meditative state and back in the jungle.

"What is it, Vex?"

"Could you please secure the perimeter?"

I look around to find red dots on APVs, parrots, and even Yesha. They're everywhere, but mixed in with them are the streaks of blue, causing everything to turn an almost purple. When I look down to see how Vex is doing, I even see a purplish glow on Marrit. That's when I remember the specimen jar. I pull it out and remove the lid. Instantaneously, the purplish light explodes, followed by darkness, and I fall.

———

I'm unsure how long everyone has been out when I awake, but I don't see any laser beams so that's got to be a good sign. Guards approach in peace to gather Sorna's body. Yesha gives Infosec and Mantis high fives before they reboard their APVs. Somehow, the ship sucks the machines and passengers back on board after that.

Vex continues to work on the two I care about so much, but the amount of blood pooled on the jungle floor around me is worrisome.

What was all the fighting for if they were just going to stop because of something as simple as beetle induced paralysis / amnesia? Did the guards decide it wasn't worth it? Speaking of guards, I see them all marching away with Sorna's lifeless body in their grips reminding me of Rigled. I guess we'll have to figure out the way another time.

Nobilia and the other parrots disperse in order to release all the locks and free the Capital.

"Be sure the chains don't drag. We want to avoid any further damage."

Other parrots nod their heads and set off to the task at hand. Then Nobilia approaches me. "How are they doing?"

"We need hospital equipment to properly treat Dr. Perier-at," Vex interjects, and I'm on my feet at once.

"Yesha?" I yell. "Vex, will Marrit be okay?"

Marrit stirs at the sound of her name.

"I'll be fine," she says with a groggy smile. "Feels like a mosquito bite."

As soon as Yesha arrives, we plan how to get mom to the hospital. Yesha will fly one hover with Mom behind her and me behind Mom. Vex will be on my back. Barren will fly with Marrit and keep hold of her the entire time. Royce and Jordan need the other hover to prepare the Capital for movement.

Hearing them discuss security makes me wonder what planet is safe from Cromwell. None, until he's gone. Why did he lure me here if he's somewhere else? If we somehow survive all of this, where will my home be? What planet could be better than Scepter for Capital water collection? Hanging on to Mom, I wonder if she'll join me on the floating Capital where we can meditate and fly on beautiful parrots all day long.

"Vex, you doing okay, buddy?"

"I've told you before, having more than three on board is against hover safety manual policies."

"I know. Hang on for just a bit longer."

In the distance, I see the same perimeter but thankfully no guards. Plus, we won't have to enter from the roof or crawl through tunnels this time. Will we receive any friction when the staff finds out what's happened to Sorna? Speaking of staff, how did so many arrive? Our team had been doing everything possible to keep that from happening. Then I think of Sorna and Damien's non-bios and the number of clones Cromwell mentioned. Is that how they're fully staffed? Is that how there were so many guards?

As we land. Mom's head falls off my shoulder. She's complete dead weight.

"Vex, can you still help Mom?"

"We must hurry, Sierra."

I watch as staff members roll the not mom who saved my life away.

29

PLANET FUNEN

Al

LEON STUMBLES BACK, BUT DAMIEN CATCHES HIM BEFORE he falls. The crowd goes silent, no more cheering. Enforcers begin to stand in the crowd, causing my muscles to tense and a tingle to go up my spine. Then someone I'd rather never see again walks up behind Damien. It's Marcus the brave. The fighter who killed Rigled on Vortex. Bile rises up my esophagus when Damien sneers at me. As he raises his arm to point in my direction, I smell dirt stir in the air behind me. Another vehicle has approached. Viscerous and Albina exit. As they walk in my direction, I see they're not holding weapons like I wish they were.

"Kill all three of them," Damien barks at Marcus. The enforcers who stood in the audience now descend the stairs approaching the track. All I can think is that we're about to be slaughtered. Viscerous and Albina, my second parents. I refuse to watch them die.

"Get back in the car and leave this place." I gently but firmly nudge them both in that direction.

Albina grabs my bionic forearm. "Not without you."

A second vehicle approaches and parks next to the one Viscerous and Albina arrived in.

"You didn't think we'd show up without back up?" Viscerous pats my back.

The passenger door slides open and my heart breaks when I see who it is. Another person who gave solace and comfort on Vortex. Cora steps out onto the track and joins us. The resolved look on her face encapsulates the years of pain she's experienced since Cromwell took her daughter's life. My fear for her decreases and I kind of feel bad for Damien and Leon instead. The enforcers pause their approach with looks of confliction. Marcus switches sides, approaches, and hugs Cora!

"It's okay," she says to him. "You don't have to fight if you don't want to."

Then another door on the vehicle slides open and Mike steps out. I thought he was on vacation. What's he doing here?

A memory flashes through my mind of when Dad had once been helping Mike in his garage. Their voices had risen, but I can't remember what they said. I do remember looking back and watching Mike's eyes follow Dad walking away. I felt as if the phone call Mike made while staring at my dad seemed very sly.

"I got an alert when you took the car," Mike says to me as he approaches. "Then I found these two in my garage and they filled me in on what they believed you to be up to."

"I thought you were on vacation." I shrug my shoulders. "Had to take the car…it was an emergency." I nod my head in the direction of Damien and Leon.

Then I look in the brothers' direction. Damien has a sneer on his face. Guess he doesn't like that I have back up. But Leon shakes his head, looks down, and then smiles up at Mike. "Took you long enough."

As Mike steps forward to their side, anger fills me. I clench my jaw as it all clicks into place. "You're the one who sent the enforcers to kill my parents." I lunge forward, but Viscerous holds me back.

"Wait, we're not ready to engage in battle," he says under his breath. "They still have all the enforcers on their side."

"Your parents deserved it." Mike looks down at me. "Your mom thought she could get away with sharing classified information."

"Do you mean classified or incriminating?" I struggle against Viscerous' hold.

We're interrupted as someone else exits the vehicle and joins us. It's the juice bartender that Vienna and I spoke with before the gathering at Mike's. What's he doing here? Viscerous gives him a handshake and then returns.

The bartender approaches Cora and hands her a prism chip, which she inserts into a collapsible tablet. I catch him whispering to her...something about enforcer backgrounds. Then he speaks aloud. "I brought reinforcements. We're tired of the enforcers pushing Funen citizens around. People enter through the racer entrance. There are dozens and then dozens more. "These are the revolutionists."

As they approach, I notice that they're armed with relic compact assault rifles. While it's nice to feel protected, I can't help but think we're crossing a line with this. First, it was the gas and now massive assault weapons. Where does one draw the line in battle between good and evil, between fighting for those you love and becoming corrupt?

Then Damien punches Viscerous in the jaw. Before I can go help him, Leon's throwing a punch my way. As all four of us engage in a fist fight, the enforcers and revolutionists begin battle around us. Mike and the bartender appear to be leading the opposing forces. The bartender signals and bullets fly from the revolutionist rifles, but the enforcers have engaged shields that deflect the bullets. Mike gives an order and the enforcers charge the revolutionists. An all-out fistfight erupts around the entire track. It probably looks like a vibrating ant pile from the sky. Fighting swallows up the place as Viscerous and I deflect punches from the brothers. I notice Albina and Cora head to the announcer's booth. I also notice many of the revolutionists fall when enforcers pull out laser Karambits and stab them in the sides.

I don't see more because Damien and Leon flip in the air, circling each other, and swapping places. Viscerous and I continue blocking their strikes, but we're beginning to tire and they're not. It's like they've been altered to hold more energy than natural. Viscerous and I have sweat dripping from our brows but the brothers' skin is dry. Their breathing doesn't reflect an ounce of labor, either. What did Cromwell do now? How did he change them? Viscerous gets a punch in but seconds after Leon's lip cracks and bleeds it's self-healing. Okay, that changes things. Damien gets a punch in and instantly my vision begins to blur. Luckily, fighting pauses as announcements boom out. I hear Cora and Albina's voices reaching all and notice they've caught most of the enforcers' attention.

"Is this really what you want?" Albina yells even though she doesn't need to with the intercom system.

"We have your files," Cora says next. "They all have something in common—emotional abuse. Your leaders knew this and used that knowledge to fuel your anxiety in order to mislead you."

"This is how they've manipulated you to fight on their behalf," Albina says.

The sounds of tapping a tablet interrupt the talk. I look around and while the fighting has stopped, revolutionists still carry rifles at the ready and Karambits remain in strong enforcer fists.

A rifle rings off. I'm not sure if it was on accident or purpose but fighting resumes all over. Blood flies left and right. More shots blaze out and weapons swing through the air.

I notice Viscerous give a thumbs up in the direction of the announcement stand. Next a loud, high-pitched sound rings out through the track. Everyone stops what they're doing so they can put their hands over their ears. Then Viscerous holds both thumbs up. Albina or Cora flip a switch I was previously unaware of and all weapons fly. As they hit the speakers up out of anyone's reach I smile in relief. But then I'm punched again and I stumble to the ground.

"Is there a C.J. McKenna on the premises?" Cora says.

I hear someone yell, "That's me."

"Your file indicates that you had a rough upbringing," Albina says.

"So, what's it to you?" C.J. responds. "Things were rough when my mom passed. We did what we could."

"And you protected your little sister during all that time," Cora says.

"How'd you…"

"They've used your worry for her to convince you to fight," Albina's voice rises in anger.

"Who else has a sibling they're protecting?" Cora asks.

Cora and Albina list more enforcers. More and more people in the crowd make connections. Before too long revolutionists and enforcers are no longer fighting at all. I hear chattering and even see some people from one side shaking hands of those on the opposing side. Viscerous helps me back to my feet.

Looking around I see that I'm not the only one who'd been knocked to the ground. People are moving around approaching the injured to help. Some just need to brush it off. Others are injured and may need hospitalization. But some bodies don't move. I see a revolutionist bend on their knees next to a body, place their fingers on the neck, shake their head side to side, slump their shoulders, and leave dejected. When I look to see where Damien and Leon are, I find them next to another unmoving body.

It's Mike. Serves him right for causing my parents' death. Some of the enforcers crowd around him. I wish I could have been the one to kill him. It would avenge for my parents. I take a step in that direction hoping there's still a pulse. A group of revolutionists push by me, one even knocking me with their shoulder. Where are they going in such a hurry? They approach another body and, against my will, my feet head in the same direction. I recognize the juice bartender twenty feet away. Shit! Why did he have to die? He was a good guy to Vienna and me. He organized the revolutionists to help us in our fight. Why?

I telepathically project an image to Cromwell of all the enforcers getting along with revolutionists, of all the fighting that's not happening. An image that shows a group of people huddled around the vehicles talking about what's under the hood. I project the group huddled in a circle playing some kind of game. Then I focus in on the terribly upset Leon and Damien kneeling next to Mike.

`Is this what you expected?`

Silence. There's no response.

`Hello, Earth to Cromwell.`

`What do you want?` he asks.

I send the images again.

`Is this what you call winning a war?`

I can see Cromwell's sneer turn into a wicked smile as if he were in front of me.

`Silly, silly! That's just another battle, just another decoy!`

30

SPACE

Vienna

My face still feels blotchy upon waking up. The shuttle's walls in front of me are smooth enough that anything thrown against them would bounce or roll right off. They're hard too, which is what I need to be if I'm going to continue. The images of everyone I care for suffering and ending have left me completely shook. But, without giving me recovery time, another vision appears. The grandmother, along with the smell of freshly baked cookies, are in front of me now.

`Your loved ones are okay,` she says.

`But the images,` I say. `They were so vivid. They felt very real.`

`I know,` she says. `I'm deeply sorry you had to endure that.`

`Where were my shields?` I can't help remembering the vision of Albina and Viscerous falling from lethal gas as I say this. It brings tears to my eyes.

STEPHANIE HANSEN

`The shields will do the best they can, but they have flaws and weaknesses too.`

Suddenly memories surface. One of the displays at the antique store had been a joker card, next to a pipe and mirror. I also remember these same objects in a dream on a planet like Funen, but fantastical with empathetic objects. A house that felt like home had these same objects on a hexagonal side table.

`Your reading is doing well,` the grandmother says. `Soon you'll have it. Concentrate.`

That's when me from the past speaks in my head. I really need to study reincarnation. `It's him,` she says. `It's always been him.`

The joker is Cromwell, and the visions were his smoke and mirrors. I need to get to the bottom of this. What better way than to go to the root cause.

`Cromwell!` I telepathically yell, my heart still aching with the pain of grief, but anger's trying to take its place.

`Vienna, good of you to finally communicate back.` I want to wipe the sneer off his face. `Did you enjoy all the suffering?`

How he thinks such vile things are entertaining is beyond me. `What do you want? You have your family back. Why all of the destruction?`

He moves his shoulder blades, adjusting his medical coat. `You know we're actually quite alike,` he says without answering my question.

`No, we aren't,` I snip back fully knowing this is what he wants. I just can't help it.

`We both are willing to go to the ends of the universe to save those we love.`

Truth, what he says is true, but we're still different.

`Even though they betray us,` he continues without waiting for my response.

I was a kid and my parents couldn't tell me everything they were doing. That's different.

So you're saying it was right to have you believing that your father had just disappeared for a decade.

Again, that was for my protection.

My, what baloney you've been fed. You can't even tell it apart from the real thing anymore, can you?

I blow hot air out my nose. You still haven't told me what you want. I know that you're saying this for a reason. I'm not as naïve as you claim.

See I told you that we're alike. I prefer getting to the point sooner rather than later, too.

I roll my eyes. Any day now.

While you've always viewed my actions to be evil, at least I was honest with you from the get-go. I never tried to pretend to appear to be good.

I think of the manipulation it took to get me to Vortex. How he'd wanted me there so much sooner so he could swap brains at an even more juvenile stage. He's really lost it if he thinks he's been transparent and honest.

Perhaps this will help you understand. My dad's face emerges next to Cromwell's. No! A lump rises in my throat. I feel helpless, tired of the fight. My initial motive for ever leaving Earth is double-crossing me. Would you like to continue our discussion about honesty?

No, I'd rather not, I spit back. Will you tell me what it is that you want already, Cromwell?

Listen to me, child. I hear the grandmother's voice, but neither Cromwell nor Dad respond. They don't flinch or anything. It's as if they didn't hear her at all. **There are many worlds, but they all have something in common.**

What is it? I ask and again neither Cromwell nor Dad act as though a sound were made. I'm able to hold side telepathic visions and conversations, I guess.

They all either have someone in power, attempting to gain power, or, if it's a peaceful world, break the system to force power.

But they all have something else too, don't they? I can feel her warm smile in response to what I've said.

Why, yes. They all have hope, hope that good will win, hope that love will rise above, and hope even in evil turning a new leaf.

Then, why? I ask. Why can't we all just get along? Why have we had to reincarnate century after century to fight this, not just us, but our shields too?

They lost their way, child. The fear and heartache of losing a loved one causes them to cross boundaries they shouldn't.

Suddenly, visions of a happy Cromwell and Sorna enter my mind. They're young and entirely content just to be together, strolling through a park and holding each other's hands.

But then I remember all the horrible things he's done and the vision changes.

I can't forgive him.

I think back to Quintus and Lucretia being burned and

torn to shreds. All they had wanted to do was stop the experiments done without consent from the patient. Two innocents that love one another abused just because they wanted to help other innocents like Viscerous, Albina, and Al. He doesn't only cause wreckage of anything in the way to save his loved ones. He manipulates and grooms his victims to live in a constant state of fear. Cromwell even plants seeds of anxiety within involuntary guards. I shudder thinking of Marcus' ax taking purchase into Rigled's neck. The blood had flowed like a waterfall as Rigled dropped to his knees and plummeted like a timbered tree. Cromwell even convinced me, though I had believed I'd been the one finagling to earn his trust and get the upper hand, to perform an experiment on his behalf. The flashback of dangling arms submerged in an icy bath like virtual reality algae in a wave causes my body to shake as if the shuttle were in liftoff instead of floating in outer space.

But you know what I want, what I've always wanted. I cringe at the sound of Cromwell's telepathic voice. I want Sorna and Damien back. I want my family to be whole again.

Don't you have that, though?

Cromwell's telesthesic face looks stoic.

Wait, did something happen to his family again? I've been so preoccupied with visions and communication, I've lost track of where everyone is and how they're doing.

Dad's image is still beside Cromwell's. I recollect Viscerous talking about how Septimus saved his life during Cromwell's procedure. Dad also saved Al during his. He can't be working with Cromwell. There has to be another explanation. I notice Dad looks stoic as well. Is Mom okay? We've had doubt about her position too. But she's the one who went through a brain transplantation. She can't be behind this but pulled in due to necessity. It's like me from the past said. It's Cromwell. It's always been Cromwell. The Grandma said everyone's okay, that the visions were just that. I sincerely hope that's true. It is finally time to give Cromwell a dose of his own. I'm going to send images of suffering and failure telepathically to him. An eye for an eye!

He would expect me to send images of Sorna and Damien falling so I opt for something else. The connection between us allows me to transform it. The new nexus will focus on collapse of his empire. Anger flares through me, bringing my heartbeat to a rapid pace.

The first image flashes to what Al's shared about how the Vortex revolution looked. This is when Cromwell had escaped as his loyal guards fought. In the vision, I change things. His guards instead double-cross him. They help in his capture in lieu of fighting the rebels. The image of his loyal guards holding their right fists over the left side of their chests brings a smile to my face. I actually laugh out loud when they strap him into an upright gurney like Dad had been held in when he was taken to replace Viscerous' punishment.

Next, the vision morphs into his gurney being rolled to the lab where the arm transplants took place. After that, Yesha removes Cromwell's arms. His telepathic face is no longer stoic. A look of horror is creeping in now. Yesha connects Cromwell's new arms.

The image glides along and Cromwell goes through a bone marrow biopsy, pigment extraction, and so much more. His face becoming paler and paler with every new image. Finally, he's rolled into the room where Damien and Sorna's brain transplantations took place.

You're going to be the third live subject to receive four foreign brain components, I mimic what he once said to my clone. You'll never make scientific history.

In the vision my scalpel enters Cromwell's skin as his had once done with Sierra's. Even though it's not the sound of my bone crushing, I still wince with the sound of the drill hitting his skull. Different surgical bots help during the process even though it's only a vision. His nerves must be on the verge of malfunction, thinking about how making the wrong cut or too deep drill would cause the brain matter to be useless. Everyone will be so happy for your reign to come to an end, I mimic his words again.

His image holds no expression. In fact, it looks like he's asleep.

Cromwell?

No answer. He should be yelling at me or taking over the images, shoving more images of abuse back.

Cromwell?

He's not going to answer, Vienna, my dad's sad voice communicates to me.

Why? Where is he?

No longer here.

Is he in a coma?

My dad hesitates. His image now even looks dismal.

He's dead, Vienna. He just died of a heart attack.

No?

There's silence for a minute.

You can save him, right?

His head shakes from side to side. I'm afraid it's too late for that.

Cromwell had a heart attack because he couldn't handle the images I sent him. Of course, he didn't hesitate to put my mom and clone through the same process, well actual instead of telepathic. Maybe telepathic is stronger. Either way, I'm a murderer. I killed Cromwell.

31
PLANET SCEPTER

Sierra

"SHE'S SUFFERED QUITE A BIT OF BLOOD LOSS," THE doctor I just met says.

"Is she going to be all right?" I ask, standing from the uncomfortable waiting room chair.

The doctor nods and relief floods every pore in my body.

"Can I see them yet?" I take a step forward.

She places a hand on my arm. "They need to stay calm and heal. They do not need to be riled up." She lifts her eyebrows at me.

"I understand. Please, can I see them?"

She lowers her hand. Vex rolls beside me as I walk down the hallway to my mom's room.

"Sierra." Mom reaches her arms out to me for an embrace. I walk forward and lean down. When her arms wrap around me, I smile. I have to lower my head into her shoulder for a minute to keep from crying.

"I'm so glad you're okay." I take a step back so I can look into her eyes.

"I'm pretty tough." She smiles. "Sierra, I noticed you meditating during the chaos back there. While I'm glad you were meditating, that wasn't exactly the safest time to do so.

I hesitate, looking down, and running the toe of my shoe along the floor. "I wasn't just meditating. I was communicating."

"You communicate telepathically with someone other than me? Who was it?"

I know she'll be upset with my answer, but I can't lie.

"Sierra, your heartrate is rising," Vex interjects.

"Cromwell, it was Cromwell," I blurt out.

"Sierra, that's not healthy. He's still deeply corrupted in manipulation."

"I know, but I couldn't ignore his threats…and I wanted revenge."

"You should block his telepathic communication." She sits up in her hospital bed. "I can teach you how."

I urge her to lie back down. "Wouldn't it be better to know his plans?"

"You're saying he told you about his plans with honesty?"

Before I can answer Mom, Marrit enters the room. She's bandaged and her arm's in a sling, but she appears healthy otherwise.

"Glad you pulled through," she says to my mom.

"Same to you."

"Sierra, I just got word that the Capital is safely in the air again."

"Oh, good." I gently hug her. "Do we know what planet the Capital will go to next?"

"Not quite yet." She looks at Mom and then back to me. "Want to come take a look at your new place while that's decided?" Her smile is genuine, full of dimples and light.

I look at Mom for approval. She's nodding and shooing all of us (Vex, Marrit, and me) with her hands, encouraging me to go with Marrit. "Go, I'll be fine."

"Will you be joining us once you're fully recovered?"

"That would be amazing, but no. There's still so much to be done. But you don't need to worry about it. I've got it under control."

Reluctantly, I leave with Marrit and Vex knowing there's no way I can talk Dr. Perierat out of continuing her work and doubting she'd ever choose to go with me and realizing that I'm okay with that. She saved my life. We can love each other from a distance.

———

Barren hovers us back and once again I'm mesmerized by the Capital floating in the air. Yesha sends the hovers with Infosec and Mantis' ship before it departs. Parrots give us rides to the Capital.

We check in on citizens once we're at the Capital to be sure no one was harmed during the imprisonment. After a bit, I notice Marrit moving slower than the rest of us. She even grimaces when she thinks no one's looking.

"Can we go see my new place now?" I put my hands together to mock plead with Marrit.

"We can come with you to help in case any stuff was disturbed. Plus, I'd like to show Yesha the place." Barren grins at the friend that chose me.

"Are you guys roommates? Are we all going to be roommates?" I can't hold back my excitement.

"You're going to wish for alone time before you know it." Marrit raises her eyebrows at me.

"Oh, really?" I hold her hand.

Walking along the pathway, I remember when I first set

foot on the Capital, passing the school, and entering Nobilia's place. Just as the gate for Nobilia's opened automatically for me, the one we finally approach does, too.

"Welcome home, Sierra." Marrit moves her hand in a half circle in front of her, introducing the place.

There aren't the curling leaves of Scepter, but instead, multiple hammock-like chairs litter the yard hung from beautiful, living trees. There's even a garden in the front yard.

We all sit and relax for the first time since we left Funen. "Guys, has anyone spoken to Vienna and the others?"

"Yesha asked me to connect, but I wasn't able to," Vex says.

I'm glad Yesha was thinking about them. I've been so consumed with the injuries we've faced, I dropped the ball.

"Let me attempt something." I try to focus on them as I meditate. First, I see Al. He looks nervous and is inside a relic race car of all things. What in the world? Here I'd felt guilty, and he's playing.

"Al's in a race car." I half laugh.

"That doesn't sound like Al. At least he didn't like when I had the vultures race on Vortex." Yesha shrugs her shoulders.

Then what's he doing? I concentrate again and this time I see a group with an air of authority surrounding the track. An uneasiness begins settling over me again. I try to search for Cromwell but don't find him anywhere. I do see who I believe to be Leon and Damien. Next, the feel of the vision rapidly changes as if a summer wind blew in. I see Cora with an angelic light behind her.

"I can't fully explain why, but I get a strong sense that Al's going to be okay."

They all nod.

"What about Vienna?" Yesha rubs her fingers against her pants in a nervous tick. She's worried.

I refocus, this time targeting Vienna. She's meditating, but it's like she's convulsing while doing so. It's almost as if the visions she's seeing affected her so much that she's physically shaking. And then it's like a beam of light shoots out of her, which may be okay, but I hear Cromwell's laughter in the background. I fist my hands together in anger.

"We can go help them." Marrit's voice pulls me out of the trance.

"What?" I ask her. As I open my eyes, I see that she's out of the hammock chair and I remember the grimace she made earlier. "There's no need, but thank you. It means a lot to me."

"Are you sure?" Now Barren's standing.

"Yes, they fought and won just like us."

"Oh, that's spectacular," Marrit says.

"Was anyone injured?" Barren asks.

"Not fatally. Maybe Vex will be able to reach them once we've settled in."

As Barren and Marrit turn to lead us inside, Yesha backhand slaps my arm and winks. Then she leans in and whispers, "Don't worry, I'll go after Cromwell. I'm going to perform every experiment he ever did on others to him."

"But won't that kill him?" I whisper back.

"That's the point, but slowly." She winks at me again.

"What's all the whispering about?" Barren asks.

"We've planned dinner," Yesha says. "I'm just going to gather a few things from the garden. I'll meet up with you in a bit."

I stare at her as she goes realizing she's still on her solo mission. Silently, I send love and strength with her. Then I ponder how many questions I can ask during the tour to keep Barren and Marrit preoccupied.

"Go with her," I whisper to Vex. "Take care of her, old friend."

I step inside, closing the door behind me. The ambiance I felt outside follows us in. It's like we're in a massively advanced treehouse with walls made from real wood and vines hanging all over. It reminds me of Scepter, which is nice. It's like I'll be able to take a piece of the first planet I considered home with me.

"You're going to love this." Marrit grabs my hand and pulls me toward a room where Barren holds the vines blocking the doorway to the side. As I step in, I see shelves from floor to ceiling with relic books. It's amazing!

"This is my favorite one." Marrit hands me a book. The cover's texture rubs against my hands. I open it and touch my nose to a page, smelling it.

"Wow," is all I can muster.

"You have to see the kitchen." Barren exits the library and I reluctantly hand the book back to Marrit.

I notice tree stump stools surrounding a long wooden table as we walk. But what stops me in my tracks is who is sitting at the table. Nobilia stands and walks my way. We hug as if we were lifelong friends, which considering my actual length of life is about true.

"You didn't think you could hide from me, did you?" Nobilia puts her wing around me as we speak. I smile.

"You're just in time, Nobilia." Barren walks behind the island and pulls a box out of the refrigerator. "I have your favorite for desert. Yesha and Sierra are planning the meal but I say we have desert as appetizer after all that we've been through."

"You do know how to win a bird's heart." Nobilia joins Barren in the kitchen as they discuss this evening's activities.

"There's one more room I'd like to show you." Marrit grabs my hand, pulling me toward the stairs. Then she turns back to me and says, "Ours."

The bed has a natural silk charmeuse blanket on it. When I squeeze it in my fingers it feels like the softest thing I've ever touched.

Then I feel fingers on my chin as Marrit turns my face to

hers. I notice the gold flecks in her eyes and smile. She tilts her chin and our lips touch. It's like a thousand tiny explosions on my skin. Our kiss becomes more passionate and I try to pull her body as close to mine as I can. She pulls away for a second. "See, we can make plenty of new memories, real memories."

I pull her back in for another kiss and then take a breath of air. "A thousand new memories." I smile, happier than I've ever been before.

32

PLANET FUNEN

Al

SOMETHING STINGING PULLS THROUGH MY HEART LIKE A vine full of thorns dragged through my arteries. If this was just a battle or decoy as my enemies keep labelling things, the war is happening in the mind with condescending thoughts as ammo. The thing closest to my brain is the organ pumping warmth to it. My heart belongs to Vienna. Where is she?

I try to telepathically reach her, but I'm overwhelmed with visions from space. Star after star, as far as the eye can see, lay before me. Our universe is an infinite sea of spots. I feel like an ant on the ground, considering the size of space. It's like being a cell inside of an ant. Our universe is one of too many to count. That's why time even collapses in on itself, the infinite cycle of cycles. Cromwell's fighting Vienna in her mind.

A slideshow of heartbreaking images suddenly flash through my mind. Vienna on a shuttle falling to the floor and holding her head. I home in to try to view what she's seeing. A gavel hitting a wooden lectern as Marie's convicted for Sorna's murder. She's sentenced to death. Vienna's vultures joining in a space fight with her against Cromwell and dying in the process.

Vienna cries in convulsions on the shuttle floor. I wish I could be there to comfort her. She's not paying attention to the physical attack approaching her because she's too focused on the emotional one. I need to get to her. We need to help. She'd finally learned not to try to take on Cromwell by herself, and we left her alone and exposed.

Viscerous and Albina join me as I walk across the track. I lock my jaw in frustration but release it before approaching the annoying boy from the academy and his brother, whom we just battled. Not sure why, but I know I'd regret not giving a try at least.

"Leon," I say. "Damien."

"What do you want?" Leon stands scowling.

Albina grabs my arm. "Are you sure?"

"Yeah, are you sure?" Damien mocks.

"We were just fighting these creeps," Viscerous says. "What do you want with them?"

"Look around," I say. "The battle's over."

"So, what are you doing here?" Leon makes a 'well duh' face.

"No one here will fight for you anymore." I take a step closer to him.

Albina grabs my arm, holding me back. Then she speaks to Leon and Damien. "Plus, I think there's something you two should see instead of thinking about fighting."

I open my mouth to argue, but Viscerous grabs me and gives me a noogie.

"Back off." I shove his hand away.

"Listen." He points to the announcer booth.

"Do you know what you could have had?" Cora asks. "What you still can have."

A visual broadcast projects from the booth onto the ground in front of us where Damien and Leon can see.

"We home bots keep more than an inventory of clothes," it's Closet's voice coming over the intercom now. "We keep memories too."

The broadcast shows a holograph video of Marie and Septimus smiling at a multidimensional prism photo. There are two fetuses. Septimus has his arm around Marie. Her smile is brighter than any of her smiles in the photos around their apartment.

Next is a holograph video of Marie reading a story to Vienna. It's sprinkled with information she can use throughout life. After that, we witness Septimus running through an experiment with his daughter.

"You can finally be a family together and safe," Albina says to Damien and Leon.

"I already have a family." Damien's voice is raised.

My prominentia laryngea rubs against my esophagus as I gulp.

"Well, I didn't get to grow up with mine," Leon says. "I'm ready for a civilian life."

"Traitor." Damien looks at Leon with disgust.

"Really?" Leon says. "You want to keep up this life of torture?"

The two huddle and speak in hushed tones. Then Damien addresses us. "We want freedom. To choose family time or go our own way no matter what we pick."

"So long as it's not harming others, I think that's all right," Viscerous says.

"And," I interject. "You help me save your sister."

"Whoa, now," Leon responds. "No one said anything about going against our dads."

"Wait," Albina gasps. "Plural, as in, Cromwell AND Septimus?"

"How else did you think all of this was accomplished?" Damien asks.

Uh, I don't want to feel anything anymore. Having parents, not having parents, love, pain, betrayal, I want it all gone. But then I wouldn't feel my love for Vienna, who is in trouble right now.

"It doesn't matter," I say. "We can't do nothing. Vienna needs our help."

"But why would Septimus side with Cromwell?" Viscerous asks.

"Mom—Marie and Dad—Septimus needed to work something out so they wouldn't lose their twins—us," Leon says. "They developed deals so the government wouldn't take us." Leon points to Damien and himself.

"So, that's why Septimus came to Vortex," I say. "It also explains other connections."

"You catch on so quick," Leon says snidely.

"Whatever. Can we go help your sister already?" I walk to the closest race car. "They're currently fighting in space." I point up.

"But Septimus wouldn't hurt his daughter," Albina says before I'm out of earshot and her words bring me to a halt.

"Not to point out the obvious, but Cromwell has a way of manipulating people into things they would otherwise never do," Cora says. She's left the announcer booth and joined us.

"It doesn't matter what Septimus is doing," I almost yell. "I know Vienna's in trouble."

"We'll come with you," Viscerous says.

"I'm not sure that our joining you will help," Damien says.

"What now?" I ask. "We need to get going."

"If we help and Cromwell goes after us," Leon begins. He pauses and then lets out an exasperated breath.

"Go on," I urge.

"He'll save us over her," Damien finishes on Leon's behalf.

"What, why? And none of this decoy crap. I've had enough."

"Because we're his sons. We can carry on the legacy."

"You two are shits," I say. "Stay here. You're perfect for each other."

What in the actual archaic hell? Are they trying to cover something up? I can smell bull crap all over their story. We don't have time to figure it out. Vienna needs us. She definitely does not need them. They could use major therapy. I mean Damien's had his entire world rocked with being dead for years and recently resuscitated. And Leon's been stuck at the academy, left behind for years. Sprinkle in the fact that all of their guidance has come from corrupt adults and voila.

"You ready for a space fight?" Viscerous asks as he, Albina, Cora, and I get in the car.

"I'd rather race in a shuttle than on a vulture, that's for sure."

I notice a few cars driving alongside us as we go.

"Um, I think we have a tail," I say.

"No, no dear," Cora says. "I recruited some of the revolutionists. Actually, follow that one."

"Okay."

"They work for the Funen shuttle takeoff site," Cora lifts her chin. "We already have clearance for liftoff lined up." She smiles.

Good, I'm glad we won't have to wait. I'm ready for a fight. I'm ready to finally give Cromwell what he deserves. I might not have been able to be the one to kill Mike, but I will be the one to kill Cromwell.

33

SPACE

Vienna

It's okay, Daughter, Septimus tries to console me. Then I hear something over the communication system. Not any more telepathic voices or images, but a real, live one and it's like all telepathic connections cease. It's Al! I don't know if I'm ready to see him, though, for him to find out what I've done. I remember the looks of disbelief I received when trying to get closer to Cromwell on Vortex. When I think about the look Al will give me when he finds out that I'm a murderer, it feels as if my heart drops to my stomach.

"Prepare airlock for arrival," I hear him say to the shuttle bots over the comms system. Different clicks and bot announcements let me know of his progress. And then finally I see his face. We're in an embrace the second he's out of the space suit and to the main cabin, before we even exchange any words. I bury my face into his chest as tears stream down.

Before I'm ready, he places his hand gently under my chin and lifts my head to look into my eyes.

"What's wrong?"

I hesitate, not wanting him to ever look at me differently than he does now. But, knowing I could never ever keep this a secret from him. I tell him, "I killed Cromwell."

His jaw clenches before he pulls me back into an embrace. I feel his back muscles flex as he holds me. Instead of the beautiful butterfly feeling, it's mixed with nervousness, like cocoons hanging from a mesh habitat carried clumsily by preschoolers. Is Al upset with me? Part of me thought he'd be happy. "It's going to be okay."

"But I'm a murderer."

"If you didn't do it, somebody was going to…you're more like an executioner than a murderer. You saved many."

"Oh yeah, like who?"

His cheek moves against the side of my head as he says, "Me" and smiles.

I smile too. "I can live with being an executioner."

"Ready to travel the world?" he asks, knowing that a change of subject would do me good. That's what partners do. They know what you need without you having to ask. They support you just as fiercely as you would them.

"I can't think of anything else I'd rather do than travel in this shuttle with you."

He smiles his bright smile at me. "Initiating sequences."

"Where to?" I ask. "Shall we see the Capital?"

"One day," he says. "I think Sierra and Marrit as well as Barren and Yesha are a little preoccupied.

It warms me through, knowing they'll be together and happy. And no longer in danger of freaking Cromwell.

"Should we go to Earth?" I ask. The images of Kitchen and Closet being ripped apart haunt me. I would really like to see that they're okay. I have mixed feelings about my parents and brothers. So many lines have been blurred I don't exactly know where they stand. To think that all I wanted when I first set off to Vortex was to see my parents back together again. It's as if that painting in my head has melted off the canvas, leaving it blank for a new picture to be made.

"One day, but first, I'd like to take you to a place you've never been," Al says and holds my hand.

"Everyone's okay on Earth, right?"

"Well, I guess there are many different levels of okay."

"Al? What about Kitchen and Closet?"

"They're fine. Why wouldn't they be?"

I realize I haven't told him about the horrible visions Cromwell sent me. Once I do that, I'll have to tell him how I killed Cromwell too. I'm not ready for that. "Just wondered."

"Your brothers are in therapy."

"That's good." I can tell he's wondering if I'll ask about my parents, whether they've reunited or not. That would be a dream come true for him, to have his parents alive again and for them to be together. But, after everything, my sense of my parents is cloudy.

"Your parents are in therapy, too. They all have to guard what they say though."

"The laws they've broken?"

He nods in agreement.

Maybe one day I'll go back. Perhaps we can have a family gathering. It will definitely feel different no longer being an only child.

"What about everyone else?" I ask him.

He rubs his bionic thumb over my hand before responding. "Milcah's mom has been arrested."

Despite the loathing I've had of Milcah throughout school, I feel a bit of despair for her now.

"Danver, Milcah, and Harper got a place together."

"Really?"

"Yeah, they even have koalas as pets. One's named Eucarpo."

Ah, good. The koalas have a home. It's relieving to hear confirmation after confirmation that Cromwell's visions were not true. Without the love and care from animals along the way, I wouldn't have survived. First, Aviator helped me on Vortex and then Nobilia on Scepter. I put my arm around Al's shoulders and take a deep inhalation.

"You don't want to go back to Funen?" I ask.

"No, Viscerous and Albina aren't ready for us."

"Ready?"

"Yeah, they're restoring my parents' house," he says and then pauses. His cheeks turn a shade pink.

"What is it?"

"They're renovating my old room into a guest room. And adding a nursery."

"Like a green room? I do love the Funen vegetation."

"No—like one with a crib."

"Are they expecting?" I ask in shock, but Al looks down.

"No," he says while still looking down. "It's for us. When we're ready."

Excitement hits me first, but then it's replaced with fear and a bit of anger. Would they want Al to reproduce with a murderer? Do I want to bring a child into this world? I change the subject fast.

"That will be perfect for when Colsam and Theopat visit. How are they?"

"Things on Vortex have vastly improved. Colsam and Theopat have found the best nanny."

"Who?"

"Cora."

She would be perfect. I can envision it now. I know it will take Vortex years to recover, but I'm glad to hear it's happening.

"So we're not going to Earth, Funen, or Vortex. Where are we going?

We're finally free to do as we wish. No more overhead announcements of doom. No more mysteries to solve. We can go exploring. We're safe—at least in this life. The thought of reincarnation reminds me of the grandma and shields. Of times in the past. A century and a half ago, protecting others from harm.

Of course there's a bit of worry, for the future but I just want to be in the current moment, to really soak it in.

Al pulls up a holographic map. "Close your eyes."

I comply and laugh. "Okay."

"Now point anywhere in front of you."

I do as he says.

"Open your eyes."

My finger has landed on Planet Forset. Al and I look at each other and smile. Forset is a land of mostly animals and non-human inhabitants. Bugs look like the fairies of old tales. The animals are free of lab generated genetic mutation and yet many speak. While some animals may be considered danger-ous, stories of Forset all mention a friendliness bestowed on human visitors. What's best is Al and I can finally be alone. We can pass the days in peaceful, unharming studies and pass the nights in each other's arms.

He softly brushes his hand up my arm and the particles of my skin explode with every touch. My peach fuzz arm hairs rise to follow where his hand leads. As he continues, my breathing finally slows down. It's as if I'm crashing from it all. Every muscle he touches tightens at first, but eventually calms. Remarkably, for the first time since before this whole thing began, I can relax easily, free of visions.

———

Don't miss your next favorite book!

Join the Fire & Ice mailing list
www.fireandiceya.com/mail.html

THANK YOU FOR READING

Did you enjoy this book?

We invite you to leave a review at the website of your choice, such as Goodreads, Amazon, Barnes & Noble, etc.

DID YOU KNOW THAT LEAVING A REVIEW...

- Helps other readers find books they may enjoy.
- Gives you a chance to let your voice be heard.
- Gives authors recognition for their hard work.
- Doesn't have to be long. A sentence or two about why you liked the book will do.

ABOUT THE AUTHOR

Stephanie Hansen's short story, *Break Time*, and poetry has been featured in *Mind's Eye* literary magazine. The Kansas Writers Association published her short story, *Existing Forces*, appointing her as a noted author. She has held a deep passion for writing since early childhood, but a brush with death caused her to allow it to grow. She's part of an SCBWI critique group in Lawrence, KS and two local book clubs. She attends many writers' conferences including the New York Pitch, Penned Con, New Letters, All Write Now, Show Me Writers Master Class, BEA, and Nebraska Writers Guild conference as well as Book Fairs and Comic-Cons. She's a member of the deaf and hard of hearing community.

www.authorstephaniehansen.com
www.authorstephaniehansen.com/blog

facebook.com/writer.stephaniehansen

twitter.com/hansenwriter

instagram.com/stephaniehansenauthor

pinterest.com/writershansen

goodreads.com/writerstephaniehansen